UNIVERSALITER ACCEPTOS

BOOK 1

JEFF BERTOLUCCI

outskirts press

Universaliter Acceptos
Book 1

v1.0

Outskirts Press, Inc.
http://www.outskirtspress.com

ISBN: 978-1-4787-9355-7

PRINTED IN THE UNITED STATES OF AMERICA

One

McCracken watched the highway through a night-vision monocular and said as little as possible, as usual.

Buscado's bowels were grumbling—a result of nerves and the chicken tenders he had eaten two hours earlier. The wool mask made his runny nose itch.

Perlman, a GPS jammer in one hand and a cell phone in the other, crouched in the sagebrush and shivered.

"Now?" he asked.

"Not just yet," replied McCracken.

"Maybe we're too far out," Buscado said.

They hiked closer to the road. Headlights came into view, then the outline of a freight truck.

"Now!" shouted McCracken.

Perlman activated the jammer. The truck continued at the speed limit.

"Shit!" said Perlman, checking the jammer again.

The truck began to slow. It passed them and came to a full stop fifty yards to the west.

"Yessss," hissed Perlman. "On lockdown. Cameras activated. Phoning home … or trying to."

McCracken rose to his feet. "Fifteen minutes," he said.

"Twenty, if we're lucky."

"Let's go," said McCracken, hoisting a shoulder-fired grenade launcher on his shoulder.

Perlman scoffed. "Seriously?" he asked. "You'll tear the trailer to bits."

"Not if I aim right."

They reached the road, keeping an eye out for approaching headlights.

"This thing's itchy," said Buscado, pulling up his wool mask.

"Leave it on!" Perlman snapped.

The autonomous truck idled quietly, blocking the westbound lane. The rig's seats had been removed; a rack of blinking electronics occupied the passenger side.

"Star Motorworks S3000," said Buscado. "Used to drive one of these for Silvertone."

McCracken listened for unusual noises.

"Smash the cameras?" asked Buscado, pointing at the circular lenses ringing the truck's rooftop.

McCracken shook his head. The cameras wouldn't matter if they moved fast. The trailer had a carbon fiber frame that was lighter and more durable than aluminum, yet stronger than steel. Its rear doors could only be unlocked via satellite or a wireless transceiver at the truck's destination.

McCracken checked his grenade launcher.

"Gimme a few minutes," said Perlman. "I can crack the doors."

"No."

McCracken walked around the trailer, thumping its metal walls with the palm of his hand. "Hear anything?" he asked.

"Just you hitting the truck," said Perlman.

"Inside, listen," said McCracken, thumping and stopping for a few seconds. "Anything?"

"What are we listening for?"

The truck's destination was Mt. Charleston—a 45-minute drive from Vegas at this hour. According to Howser, the rig was hauling $150,000 in rare whiskies to the new Charleston Peak Casino & Spa.

Lights approached from the east.

They scrambled off the road and slid into a ditch.

"Shit, my face itches," said Buscado, removing his mask when the others weren't looking.

A semi slowed to a stop 100 yards east of the stalled rig. Four men in dark windbreakers jumped out of the back of the truck and hurried to the rig. One man, much taller than the others, was wearing a lighted helmet.

They opened the trailer's rear doors and began unloading large wooden crates, carrying them back to their truck.

"Put your mask back on!" Perlman whispered.

"In a sec."

McCracken grabbed his monocular for a closer look. The men worked swiftly without talking. Their clothes had no emblems or other identification. The crates were huge, but the men didn't appear to be straining.

McCracken looked back at the truck. There it was—the boomerang symbol.

He heard a buzzing noise overhead.

The drone resembled a gigantic insect with glowing eyes. It swooped over a hill and buzzed their heads, momentarily blinding Buscado, who stared at its cameras for only a second.

"Goddammit!" shouted Perlman, trying to cover Buscado's face with his hands.

The drone went behind a hill, then turned

back toward them. McCracken aimed the grenade launcher at it and fired.

The impact was deafening as metal and plastic fragments rained across the desert floor.

Shots rang out in the distance.

They sprinted to a Ford truck parked on a fire trail, tossing their gear in the truck bed.

McCracken drove east with the lights off.

Two

They climbed a short hill, giving McCracken a clear view of Highway 95 a mile ahead. Nothing out of the ordinary: big rigs, a charter bus, and a few cars.

"I overreacted," said McCracken.

"Oh, *that's* what you call it?" Perlman snapped.

"Howser won't be happy," added Buscado.

"Maybe because you got your photo taken by a fucking drone," said Perlman, tossing his ski mask on the floor. "Shit, you guys are amateurs."

They drove in silence for a minute, bumping along the fire trail before turning onto Highway 95.

Perlman felt he deserved better than this. He had been kicked out of some of the finest universities in the nation—Caltech, MIT, University of Michigan—as well as a few community colleges. At Caltech he got caught stealing professors' passwords and, for a reasonable fee, changing grades from Fs to As. At MIT he was expelled for masturbating under his jacket during an Advanced Calculus for Engineers lecture. Details of the U of M incident were sealed by court order.

"Let's get breakfast," he said. "I haven't eaten in 18.5 hours."

"I'm hungry too," Buscado seconded.

McCracken had his concerns but needed food as well.

They agreed to eat at Gold Town Casino, which was on the way to Pahrump.

Perlman wouldn't shut up about Gold Town's cinnamon rolls. "Man, the way the icing drips off the sticky buns, they're super gooey," he said. "Who knows what that pastry chef is doing back there, know what I mean?"

McCracken made a mental note: avoid the cinnamon rolls.

The drive through Vegas was uneventful: a two-car fender bender on I-15 near The Mirage; a construction slowdown near McCarran. Nothing unusual.

Perlman wanted to lighten the mood.

"Hey, did I ever tell you guys about the time I played poker with a one-legged hooker in Bangkok?" he asked. "She ran out of cash, accused me of cheating, and called her bouncer boyfriend into the bedroom."

"Shit, what happened?" asked Buscado.

"Well, they stripped off my pants, pulled my briefs down to my ankles, and bent me over a bed-post," said Perlman. "Then they threatened to ram my ass—with the hooker's peg leg, no less—if I didn't give back her winnings."

McCracken wasn't listening to Perlman's story. "You guys didn't hear anything unusual in the trailer?" he asked.

"Thought I'd either die or be shittin' splinters for years," Perlman continued. "But I wasn't about to give those peckers any of my hard-earned money."

"So what'd you do?" asked Buscado.

"Compromised. Showed 'em my fake ATM shutter module, the one I'd rigged specifically to rob cash machines."

McCracken was upset. He should have shot at the men, not the drone.

"It's a beautiful thing, really," Perlman went on. "See, the fake shutter attaches to the front of the ATM's dispenser slot. I use Scotch tape. Then you stake out the ATM and watch people try to withdraw their money. They put the card in, tap in the amount they want, and see the message telling them to remove their cash. But the *fake* shutter doesn't open! So then they figure the ATM is broken. Some throw a shit fit, but eventually they all just walk away. But the cash is there. After they leave, I remove the fake shutter and grab the money."

"That's not cool," said Buscado.

"Who cares, it's the bank's money," said Perlman. "Anyway, we cleared 45,000 baht—about fifteen grand American back then—but the boyfriend pistol-whipped me and took the loot. Story of my life."

Buscado laughed.

They reached Gold Town at 4:30 a.m., right when the breakfast buffet was opening. McCracken wanted an unobstructed view of the room, so they sat in a corner booth in the back.

Buscado's hand shook as he poured himself a cup of coffee. "My little boy, Trevor, he loves pancakes," he said, trying to smile. "Man, he just pours on honey; not syrup—honey!"

A bald man wearing sunglasses sat alone at the counter. McCracken wondered why the man was wearing shades at five a.m. The man turned twice and appeared to be looking at them.

"Who is that guy?" McCracken whispered.

"What guy?"

"Over there, the counter."

"If you're thinking cop, it's way too early," said Perlman. "Those government guys are lazy. Besides, nobody died when you shot that drone."

The man turned again, making McCracken uneasy.

"He's staring at us."

"Chill out," said Perlman. "We're done here, right? Pay the bill and let's cruise out to Pahrump."

McCracken was determined to extract information from the mysterious man. But when he glanced at the counter again, the man was gone.

The sun was rising as they headed west on Highway 160.

McCracken navigated the AM dial, finding mostly sports and religious talk. Buscado closed his eyes but couldn't sleep.

Perlman was bored and wanted to talk more. "When the feds busted me, they jacked my Curaçao account," he said. "Two mil stashed away there, man, set for life. Had a 15-year-old beauty waiting for me in Mauritius. Cottage by the sea. Everything."

"Fifteen?" asked Buscado.

"Yeah, her dad was cool with it."

They drove for a minute in silence.

"How come you're not in prison?" asked Buscado.

Perlman chuckled.

McCracken found a news station and turned up the volume.

"This dude I knew in college, huge WoW fan, asked me to set up a darknet," said Perlman, raising his voice over the radio. "So I went on Craigslist, paid $300 cash to some grandma in Henderson for her shitty Dell laptop, installed Linux with a transparent Tor proxy, and looked the other way."

"What's that mean?" asked Buscado.

"It means exactly what I said."

"Just a bunch of tech crap."

"Do I need to spell it out, dumbass? They were pic collectors, and not the kind of pics you're supposed to be collecting. I'm not in jail because I spilled the beans on them. Not my thing, so I did the world a favor."

No one spoke for two minutes.

"But you set it up in the first place," said Buscado.

"No, I set up a peer-to-peer file-sharing network, a very secure one. And that's all I did, so fuck off."

McCracken cranked up the volume for the top-of-the-hour news:

Lee Canyon Road between Highway 95 and Deer Creek Road has reopened after a truck fire and explosion early this morning closed the road for several hours. The Nevada Highway Patrol says a faulty fuel line on a westbound big rig caused the mishap. No injuries were reported.

"That's not what happened!" said Buscado.

"No shit," said Perlman. "McCracken, what do you think?"

McCracken remained silent.

Three

The hideaway was a three-bedroom, two-bath stucco ranch with a faded lime green exterior. Blinds covered the front windows, each protected by a wrought-iron grill.

There was no lawn. The front yard was filled with pink and tan rocks. A healthy cactus grew from a center hill the size of a pitcher's mound. Two metal coyote sculptures stood nearby. A strip of blue turf connected the gravel driveway to the front door.

McCracken turned the Ford truck, an F-250 he had owned for years, onto the driveway and killed the engine.

"Jesus Christ, what a shithole," said Perlman. He had been here once before, but late at night when it was too dark to see much of anything.

The neighborhood consisted mostly of desolate, dried-up lots, each dusted with desert plants. The nearest house, a two-story colonial, sat on a weedy corner lot ringed by an eight-foot wire fence.

This was Buscado's first time at the hideout. He noted how quiet everything was, and how he could hear things he normally wouldn't catch.

McCracken knocked on the front door four times, pausing briefly between each knock.

A middle-aged white man opened the door. He was lean and angular with grey around the temples. Despite being an inch taller than the six-foot-five McCracken, he was a good fifty pounds lighter.

"You weren't followed?" the man asked.

McCracken shook his head.

The man was David Howser, a former Caltech professor and motivational speaker. His Wikipedia page said he was an expert in robotics and artificial intelligence.

They entered a darkened living room.

"Nothing like stale carpet freshener," said Perlman.

As their eyes adjusted, they detected three more people—one standing, two sitting on the sofa.

"Something to drink or eat?" Howser asked.

"We ate already," said McCracken.

"That was unwise," said another male voice.

A black man, mid-fifties, with a bald head and salt-and-pepper beard rose from the sofa. He was Dr. Charles Baldwin, a DNA analyst from the University of Florida Genetics Institute. He reminded Buscado of his high school biology teacher.

"You could've been spotted," Baldwin said. "Did you change vehicles? Apparently not, judging by that monstrous truck outside."

"Chill, Doc," said Perlman, plopping on the sofa beside a brown-skinned woman in her early thirties. "You shoulda been there, babe," he told her. "Hot chick like you would've distracted everybody, made our job easier."

The woman, Rosa Fuentes, stood and walked over to McCracken.

Howser shook Buscado's hand.

"For those of you who haven't met our new colleague, this is Christopher Buscado," he said. "He's a former trucker with many skills that will enhance our team."

"He's also great at getting his picture taken by a drone," added Perlman.

Buscado frowned but said nothing.

"I run our website," said Fuentes, smiling at Buscado.

"What website, I've never seen a website," said Perlman.

Fuentes continued, saying her day job was dealing blackjack at Barnaby's Casino in Vegas.

Buscado tried not to stare at her as she spoke. He found her very pretty, especially her soft skin. "People always think I'm Mexican because of my complexion," he blurted. "But I'm really French, Basque, and Italian. Buscado is my stepfather's name."

"Thanks for sharing," said Perlman.

"That's enough," warned Howser.

The last person Buscado met was Cheryl, who sat on the arm of a La-Z-Boy recliner. Howser insisted that everyone be called by their last name except for Cheryl. He never explained why.

Cheryl was slim with greying brunette hair and green eyes. Buscado, who placed her age at fifty—a well-preserved fifty—found her very attractive too.

Howser tapped Fuentes on the shoulder. "May we speak privately?" he asked her.

McCracken watched them leave the room.

Baldwin fidgeted, placing his weight on one leg, then the other. He checked his watch. "I hear things didn't go exactly as planned," he said to Perlman.

"Authorities got there too fast," Perlman replied. "And then Rambo here went crazy."

"I told you discretion was paramount."

"Look, the whole idea was stupid," said Perlman.

"You sent us to rob a heavily secured auto-rig carrying a few crates of booze? Shit, you could've lifted that from a loading dock somewhere."

"We're not common criminals, we're sending a message," said Baldwin.

Howser and Fuentes reentered the room. He whispered something in her ear. "Now?" she asked. "It's gotta be now?"

"The radio news said a bad fuel line caused the truck explosion," said Buscado. "That's not what happened at all."

"We're not responsible for news media coverage," said Howser. "The report you heard was characteristically inaccurate."

Cheryl, staring at the carpet, mumbled something in a soft monotone. Buscado tried to make eye contact with her, but she wouldn't look up.

"Another thing," said Perlman. "Nobody sends a fuckin' SWAT team and drones to protect a few cases of Scotch."

"Authorities are concerned about autonomous truck hijackings, particularly on isolated stretches of open road," said Howser. "It's no surprise that early deliveries might bring along additional support."

"Support, yeah, that pretty much sums it up," said Perlman.

Buscado caught the quiet woman watching him. He smiled; Cheryl smiled back. He liked her face. She was a little older than him, but that was okay. He liked her mysteriousness and high cheekbones. She wore a long black dress, thick wool leggings, tan boots, and a bulky sweater. Pahrump was awfully hot for all that clothing.

Fuentes was hanging all over McCracken now. They kissed; Perlman was jealous.

"Yes, we're sending a message," Baldwin repeated.

"Jobs are being lost," added Howser. "The damage is incalculable."

"Well, a computer could replace just about every college professor I've ever had the displeasure of knowing," said Perlman.

"Society is on a very dangerous path," said Howser, watching Fuentes and McCracken out of the corner of his eye.

"Very significant," added Baldwin.

As Perlman launched into a diatribe against the Federal Reserve, McCracken and Fuentes disappeared down the hall.

Buscado decided to chat up Cheryl, but when he looked around the room, she was gone. He went to the front window and peeked through the blinds at the street. No people, no cars.

A loud crash shook the walls, followed by a man's wail. They raced down the hall as a white chair flew out of the master bedroom and broken into pieces against the wall. Fuentes screamed.

Perlman entered the room first and saw McCracken, naked, sitting on the edge of a twin bed, his back to them. Holding his head in his hands. Weeping.

Fuentes, wearing only panties, cowered in a corner and covered her breasts with her arms.

"Would everybody please leave!" she shouted.

The walls were bare, save for an Ikea print of a three-masted 17th-century merchant ship sailing the high seas. Buscado's eyes went right to the condom on the bedside table.

"Would you like to talk about it?" Howser asked.

"Just go!" said Fuentes. "He'll be okay in a few minutes."

"Outbursts bring unwanted attention," said Baldwin.

"I got this. He's fine," Fuentes replied.

"No, *you're* fine, babe," said Perlman.

"Fuck off, asshole!"

Buscado grabbed Perlman by the collar and flung him into the hall. He slammed the door shut, muffling Perlman's swearing.

McCracken, taking deep breaths, sniffled and stared at the print of the Dutch ship. Howser grabbed a shirt off the floor and draped it over McCracken's shoulders.

Baldwin handed Fuentes her blouse and—insisting Buscado do the same—turned away to give her some privacy.

"I need to make it right …," McCracken whispered.

"We're going to change things for everyone," said Howser.

"That's not what he's talking about!" snapped Fuentes.

"I know quite well what he's talking about," Howser replied.

"I just want …"

"We'll help you, just like we promised," said Howser.

"But promise us you'll behave," added Baldwin.

McCracken asked for a tissue. Nobody had one, so he grabbed his sock and blew his nose into it.

Four

McCracken spent his early years in Modesto, California, where he lived with his mother in the Oakwood Estates Mobile Home Park. A head taller than the other boys, he could run faster, jump higher, and throw a football farther than anyone in his neighborhood. He never met his father, but heard he was a nice man.

Rhone Ellison lived alone in a spacious double-wide in the northwest corner of Oakwood Estates. He had many hobbies for a middle-aged man, but mostly enjoyed taking photos of local boys playing in the park. The ten-year-old McCracken—athletic, blond, and blue-eyed—was his favorite. Many McCracken photos lined the walls of Ellison's home office and bedroom.

One afternoon in late October, Ellison looked out his kitchen window and noticed the other children had gone home, leaving McCracken alone on the private street. The boy was tossing a baseball in the air, then running and catching it. A couple of times the ball landed on Ellison's front steps. The man felt excited and agitated when the boy jumped onto his porch to retrieve the ball.

Everything happens for a reason, he told himself. This had to be a sign.

Sitting at his kitchen table, Ellison grabbed his SLR camera and zoomed in on McCracken, marveling at the boy's grace and agility. He scooted his chair up to the window, pushing the lens between the blinds to capture the child tossing and catching the ball, over and over again.

The ball landed in a potted plant on Ellison's porch. The boy ran over and began searching the front of the house, but couldn't find the ball.

Ellison studied the surrounding homes carefully; the sun had set, and no one else was outside.

His heart pounding, he walked to the kitchen counter, removed an 8-inch cook's knife from the bamboo block, and placed it gently on the Formica countertop.

Ellison took a deep breath and went to the front door, opening it quickly and stepping out onto the porch. The boy was on his hands and knees, looking under the house.

"Did you see my ball?" the boy asked.

The young man didn't seem intimidated by the sudden appearance of an adult—a trait that surprised and angered Ellison.

"Sure did," said Ellison, smiling.

"Really? Where?"

"I heard it roll under the house," said Ellison. "I'll help you find it."

He walked down the steps and pretended to join the search.

"Could you turn on the lights?" the boy asked. "It's kinda dark."

"How about a flashlight?" asked Ellison.

The boy didn't reply.

"Come on, I'll get you one."

The boy stared at Ellison, who considered standoffish behavior rude.

"You want to find your ball, don't you?"

"I'm not supposed to go inside someone's house when I don't know the person."

"Come on, we see each other every day. I wave at you boys, you wave back. We're neighbors."

"I've never waved."

"Well, somebody in your group does. The kid who's a little chunky."

"Tommy Morris."

"That's him. Tommy always waves."

The boy thought it over. "Okay, but don't tell my mom," he said.

Ellison smiled and walked inside the house. "It's in the kitchen, this way," he said, his heart pounding. The boy followed. It was all so easy.

Ellison had several large burlap potato sacks stashed in the guest bedroom, as well as a 300-foot spool of jute twine, just for this occasion. He finally was going to get his money's worth.

They entered the kitchen and Ellison stopped at the counter, using his body to hide the knife. He pointed at the dinette table in the corner. "Over there," he said.

A red Eveready flashlight sat beside a bowl of wax fruit. When McCracken went to retrieve the flashlight, Ellison grabbed the boy's neck from behind.

McCracken screamed and wiggled free. Ellison grabbed the knife and swiped at the boy but missed, slicing only air.

The boy ran down the hall.

The little shit, thought Ellison, feeling more aroused by the challenge. The front door was locked; there was no escape route. The boy wasn't screaming or crying, which Ellison found strange. But it didn't matter.

Ellison hurried into his bedroom, tripped, and slammed his head against the bedside table. Dazed, he felt his forehead. Warm blood.

He looked up and saw the boy standing near the door, staring at him in silence. Then he saw his 44-inch metallic gold floor vase, the one with the clean lines of an egret, lying on the carpet. The boy had used it to trip him.

Ellison was still holding the cook's knife, but was afraid. Fear made him angry. He was the predator, not the prey.

The child ran from the room.

Ellison rose to his feet and woozily gave chase. He entered the kitchen and immediately collapsed to the floor, his right kneecap exploding in pain. He grabbed his leg and saw the boy, kneeling by the dishwasher, holding Ellison's Arc de Triomphe metal paperweight. It must have weighed a good ten pounds.

The little fucker had kneecapped him.

The knife. He still had the knife.

Ellison lunged at the boy, who jumped back and smashed the paperweight on Ellison's hand, fracturing two metacarpals. The knife fell to the floor.

Ellison grabbed the boy's ankle with his good hand, pulling the troublemaker toward him. It was time to end this. He intended to strangle the boy in the cruelest manner possible.

He saw the knife coming toward him. It pierced his neck before he could react.

It wasn't supposed to end this way. He never even saw the boy pick up the knife.

Ellison slowly lost consciousness, his blood pouring onto the green linoleum. He tried desperately to clot the wound with his hands, but was too weak.

He stared at the strange boy, who studied him without fear. Expressionless.

The story made international headlines: *10-Year-Old Fights Off, Kills Attacker*. Front-page articles featured Ellison's five-year-old mug shot, detailed his lengthy rap sheet, and quoted detectives who explained how a schoolkid managed to fight off a convicted sex offender.

The coroner's report concluded the knife had pierced Ellison's carotid artery below the left ear, causing him to bleed out. A lucky strike, noted investigators, who nevertheless praised the boy's quick actions.

McCracken's relationship with the other children changed after the incident. Moms in the neighborhood were wary of a ten-year-old kid who could kill a grown man so easily. The boy's calm was unnerving too.

Everyone was happy the predator was dead, but they wondered: could the boy do the same to their kids?

It didn't matter. McCracken's mother soon got a job in Phoenix.

A year later in 6th grade, McCracken wrote a poem about the Ellison incident. His English teacher showed the poem to Principal Dake, who contacted the boy's mother. McCracken had to spend six weeks in hourly sessions with the school counselor, talking about his feelings.

Five

The tedium of modern life wore him down: bills, supermarkets, cooking, laundromats, parking fines. He hated all of it.

What McCracken loved most about his time in Special Forces was its simplicity. Often he found himself stuck in some miserable place, even under fire, but life was good. Uncomplicated. He had only one worry then: making it through the day alive. Everything else—food, clothing, transportation—was managed by someone else.

Fuentes was the only one who could guide him through his dark moods, which were happening more frequently. She believed in a higher power. He believed in retribution—a philosophy that gave him strength to get out of bed every morning, brush his teeth, eat a nutritious breakfast, and do all the things he was supposed to do.

McCracken didn't rent an apartment. His personal belongings, the few he had, were warehoused at a public storage facility in Henderson. He slept in his truck or at Fuentes' place, showered at 24 Hour Fitness on Charleston Boulevard, and ate healthy fast food whenever possible.

Perlman once called him a "nancy boy"—whatever that was—for ordering the Artisan Grilled Chicken Sandwich with a Garden Side Salad at McDonald's. McCracken didn't care. He understood the value of healthy living.

Today was important: a second chance to rob an autonomous rig. McCracken didn't want to fail again. He planned things more carefully this time, forming a close collaboration with Howser and Baldwin.

It would be a daytime heist, one McCracken hoped would showcase Perlman's hacking and Buscado's driving skills. He saw his team as a renegade Operational Detachment Alpha, or ODA—a term he'd borrowed from his Special Forces days.

They were somewhere in the Mojave Desert, a

dirt road off Highway 127 on the California side of the border. A Ryder rental was their vehicle of choice for hauling stolen cargo.

They had spent the night at Pecos Bill's—a state-line hotel and casino with 978 cheap rooms, 50 outlet stores, a topless revue, and a roller coaster.

The original plan had been to meet for breakfast, but Perlman's late arrival scuttled it. Now they were going to have to pull off the heist with less preparation than McCracken had hoped.

Perlman was unusually subdued for ten a.m. Leaning against the hood of the Ryder, a sequined silver cowboy hat covering his eyes, he groaned and sipped his Starbucks venti Americano. An hour earlier he had popped several Tylenol Extra Strength Caplets—the only painkiller available—but was still hungover.

Buscado was enjoying Perlman's misery. "So how many last night?" he asked.

"Don't fuckin' talk to me," mumbled Perlman.

McCracken was pissed.

"I told you to show up ready," he said. "A good dinner, plenty of sleep, and parking lot by eight."

"Almost made it."

"No, you show up at nine, looking like shit."

Perlman rubbed his eyes and removed the hat.

He squinted at the sun and sighed. "Thank you, Robert McNeil."

"What?"

"Tylenol kicking in."

"Whatever," said Buscado. "At least you're not coughing up any more green shit."

"Probably bile," McCracken added.

"Nope, pretty sure it's crème de menthe," said Perlman. "Drank about eight Green Hornets last night—brandy with green crème de menthe for you plebs. Pretty sure I passed out during the titty show."

"Where'd you sleep?"

"Woke up behind Pecos Bill's kitchen, folded up like a fetus near the trash dumpsters, shivering. So I walk over to the outdoor Jacuzzi, strip naked, and slide in. Security shows up a few minutes later and tells me I gotta put on shorts—no nude bathing allowed. So I stand up to grab my boxers when a wave of nausea hits me. Boom! Blow chunks right into the water."

McCracken checked his watch: thirty minutes and counting.

"Then it got interesting," Perlman continued. "Two security goons make me get dressed, right? Walk me down to some underground bunker with all the monitors, you know, where they watch for card cheats. Sit me down and start playing a video from last night."

Perlman finished his Americano and tossed the empty container in the Ryder's cab.

"Okay," said Buscado. "Then what?"

"There I am, on stage during the titty revue," said Perlman. "On all fours, shirt off, braying like a goddamn donkey. I'm daring the audience to jump onstage and slap my ass. Well, two security guards swoop in and drag me offstage. I'm calling 'em Nazi Stormtroopers and jihadist motherfuckers—all kinds of crazy shit. Then they stop the video."

"You don't remember any of that?"

"Not a goddamn thing," said Perlman.

"You gotta start taking this seriously," McCracken snapped. "You'll jeopardize our mission with that sort of bullshit."

"T minus thirty minutes," said Buscado.

"Twenty-seven, to be exact," said Perlman. "And, yeah, I'm on board, pecker. Watch me bring that rig to its knees."

This time they would slow the truck to a crawl, allowing Buscado and McCracken to jump aboard and take manual control. The key was to override the emergency system and beacons, preventing the rig from entering full sleep mode and calling home for help.

The hack was inspired by one Perlman had heard about six months earlier. Researchers from Tel Aviv University had found a way to steal decryption keys by recording radio signals from a laptop. One of Perlman's buddies in Satan's Hot Load—a coalition of phreaks who once wiped terabytes of data from NATO computers—had written an attack app to exploit the Israeli acoustic hack.

"You sure you're ready?" McCracken asked him.

"How many times you gonna ask me that?"

"As long as you're sure."

"You want me to leave *right now*? Leave the fuck right now?"

McCracken didn't answer.

"Because if I do, you and shit-for-brains over there have no way to pull this off."

McCracken stared at Perlman for a second or two, then turned and walked away.

"Where's my laptop!" shouted Perlman, shuffling toward the Ryder. He checked his phone: 96 degrees at 10:15 a.m. It felt hotter.

Six

The target was hauling medical supplies from San Bernardino to a five-star resort and clinic at Death Valley Junction.

Barely a year old, the Paragosa Hot Springs and Spa specialized in liposuction, breast implants, nose jobs, facelifts, eyelid surgery, and Botox injections. Patients convalesced with Vicodin and Chardonnay, reclining under swaying desert palms and listening to recorded audio of gurgling springs.

Baldwin knew several cosmetic surgeons who moonlighted at Paragosa, one of whom tipped him off to the shipment schedule of driverless delivery trucks packed with significant quantities of prescription opiates.

Their plan: jack the rig, steer it off-road for a mile, and transfer marketable cargo to the Ryder.

Midday traffic on State Route 127 was light. The Ryder was hidden behind a desert mound about a hundred yards east of the highway. McCracken's F-250 was parked at a campsite a few miles south.

An old billboard provided excellent cover for the trio, who sat in the shade under a rusting, 14-foot sign advertising a casino long out of business. McCracken and Buscado watched the road while Perlman analyzed a map on his laptop. A blinking blue light—the autonomous rig—moved rapidly toward their location.

"How's it coming?" McCracken asked.

"Three minutes ETA," replied Perlman, trying to breach the truck's onboard controls. "Shit, a real driver would be speeding out here."

"Shouldn't we be seeing it by now?" asked Buscado.

McCracken checked his watch. The rig was a minute behind schedule.

"It's going the speed limit. Man, computers are wimps," said Perlman. "Wait for it … yes … yes ..."

"You're in?"

"I own that bitch! Where do you want it stopped?"

"Right where we're standing," said McCracken. "Make it gradual, nothing out of the ordinary."

"A big rig stopping on the highway isn't ordinary."

"Slow it to five, we'll jump aboard."

"Don your apparel, gentlemen," Perlman said. "You're highwaymen now."

Perlman's laptop acted as a remote terminal, showing the auto-rig's actual display: an array of digital gauges—voltmeter, engine temperature, oil pressure, tachometer, odometer, speedometer—plus a cluster of smaller warning lights. By moving dials on the screen, Perlman slowed the truck to 55 mph … 45 … 30 …

"Should be visible by now," he said.

McCracken walked to the edge of the billboard and peered down the highway. A slow-moving big rig was approaching from the south.

He signaled to Buscado.

"Let's roll!"

McCracken pulled a black ski mask from his back pocket and slipped it over his head. Buscado cringed but did the same. The sensation was miserable and claustrophobic—desert heat trapped against his skin.

They waited by the side of the road. McCracken was concerned a passing vehicle might spot them, but other than the approaching truck, the highway was deserted.

"Yippee ki-yay, motherfuckers!" shouted Perlman. "Door locks off, autopilot off ..."

Buscado squinted and studied the truck closely. "Peterbilt 389, sleeper cab," he said, frowning. "I thought this was supposed to be a European rig?"

"Does it matter?"

"Doesn't make sense," Buscado replied. "Why carry a sleeper cab for no reason. I mean, all that extra weight."

"Could be a retrofit."

Buscado sighed and scratched his neck. "Shit, this mask sucks," he said.

The truck slowed to a crawl, rumbling along the road in front of them. McCracken opened the passenger door and jumped inside the cab. Buscado followed, climbing clumsily over McCracken to get to the driver's seat. He slammed his knee into McCracken's crotch.

"Goddammit!" hissed McCracken, gently cupping his balls. "Why the hell didn't you just get in the other side?"

"Really sorry, man, but you never run in front of a moving semi, no matter how slow it's going," said Buscado, doing a quick visual check of the controls.

Everything was in place: steering wheel, accelerator pedal, floor gear shift, 18-speed transmission, 10-inch color touchscreen, full gauge package. A closed door separated the cab from the sleeper compartment. This bothered McCracken, who reached back and tried unsuccessfully to open the locked door.

"Move fast," he told Buscado.

The interior was elegant—newer and fancier than most of the rigs Buscado had driven. Blackwood finish trim. Black leather seats with red stitching. He could live in a rig like this.

The touchscreen showed four video feeds from cameras mounted inside and outside the truck. One feed was a wide shot of two masked men inside the cab. Buscado waved at himself.

"Stop dickin' around."

Buscado slammed the truck into gear, deftly working the clutch and accelerator to gain speed. The rig lurched forward. The video feeds vanished, replaced by a stream of computer code.

"Man, I'm dying in this thing," said Buscado, tugging on the edges of his mask to let in a little air. "When can I take it off?"

"When I say so," McCracken replied. "Turn left in five miles, Western Motel."

Buscado pushed the rig up to 45, enjoying the

sensation of the mighty Paccar MX-13 rumbling beneath him.

The sleeper door flew open and two armed men burst out of the compartment. One was bald, the other had black hair and green eyes. They wore identical clothing: black slacks and white collared shirts.

They stood behind Buscado and McCracken, pointing guns at the back of their heads.

"Proceed slowly, pull over when we tell you," said the bald man. "And take off your masks."

McCracken removed his first, then Buscado.

"We've been monitoring you all along, your work is sloppy," the bald man said.

McCracken spotted the boomerang emblem on the man's shirt pocket. "What's that mean?" he asked, pointing at the emblem.

"Shut your mouth."

McCracken mulled his options. Both men had guns, yes, but seemed inexperienced at this sort of thing. They looked like engineers.

"The trailer, what's it carrying?" he asked.

"I told you to shut up."

The green-eyed man tapped McCracken's head with the barrel of his gun. "No more from you," he warned.

McCracken didn't like the man's green eyes, but wasn't sure why.

"You picked the wrong truck," said the bald man. "Nothing to fence here."

"What's in the trailer?" McCracken repeated.

"Are you a retard? What did we just say?"

"I'll tell you what we have back there," the other man said. "Some very creative things."

Buscado pushed the rig up to 60.

"Slower!" yelled the bald man, keeping his eyes on McCracken.

"Why won't you tell me what's back there?" asked McCracken, trying to determine which of the two was most vulnerable.

"If you say one more fucking thing, I swear—"

"Not now," the green-eyed man said.

McCracken was quiet for a few seconds, but had trouble keeping still.

"Anything living?"

The bald man chuckled and leaned closer to McCracken's ear. "You like animals?" he whispered.

McCracken noticed the man's hand was shaking.

The man tapped McCracken's head with the gun barrel. "You like them a lot, asshole?"

The green-eyed man chuckled. "You'd love what we got back there, man."

"Why is that?" asked McCracken.

"It's like a goddamn circus," he said.

"What do you mean?"

"It's a menagerie, things you've never seen before."

The bald man laughed. "Kids. You like kids?"

McCracken whipped his hand around, grabbing the bald man's gun and pulling the trigger.

A bullet pierced the floor near the green-eyed man's foot.

McCracken leaped over the back of the passenger seat and jumped on both men, jamming his fingers into their eyes. Both guns went off; one bullet pierced the bald man's kneecap, another hit the passenger door.

McCracken punched his attackers repeatedly in the groin and stomach. Each folded into a fetal position to shield against the blows.

Grabbing the guns, McCracken turned to look out the windshield. "Faster!" he shouted.

The green-eyed man pulled a knife from his pocket and jammed it into McCracken's right calf.

McCracken screamed and fell to his knees. His attacker, one eye open, lunged over the back of the driver's seat and fought Buscado for control of the wheel.

The semi veered off the highway, barreling toward an abandoned concrete structure blanketed with graffiti.

The green-eyed man bit Buscado's shoulder. McCracken grabbed the man by the hair, slamming his head into the touchscreen and cracking the glass.

The rig bounced off the highway and scraped along the structure's long back wall. The trailer uncoupled from the semi and flipped onto its side.

The semi plowed over two cacti and came to a bouncy stop in an open field.

"You hurt?" McCracken asked Buscado.

"No," said Buscado, kicking open the driver door and jumping to the ground. He sprinted to the motel parking lot, where he bent over to catch his breath.

He heard two gunshots.

McCracken, holding a revolver, hobbled off the rig and limped toward Buscado.

Sirens in the distance.

"Over there," said McCracken, pointing at the damaged trailer.

"No, we gotta go!"

A loud, thumping noise was coming from inside the trailer. Rattling and clanging.

"What's that?" asked Buscado.

McCracken checked his phone: no text from Perlman. He pointed at the trailer again. "Come on."

The noises continued. They sounded like growls to Buscado, but not from any animal he had ever heard.

The sirens grew louder. A helicopter appeared over the horizon, then another.

McCracken limped toward the trailer.

"Fuck, McCracken, let's go!"

"There's time."

Buscado ran over and grabbed McCracken, who pushed him back.

"Hey, you wanna stick around and get caught, that's your problem," said Buscado. "I'm outta here."

Buscado started sprinting toward north toward a group of cacti.

"Hold up!" shouted McCracken, skipping to catch up.

They jogged eastward toward rolling hills, traveling a quarter-mile before resting in a shady ditch behind a rock outcropping. Sagebrush provided good cover from aircraft, but they knew they were still too close to the crash site.

They had no water. Buscado's shirt was soaked with sweat, his throat dry and sticky.

"Any word from Perlman?" he asked.

McCracken checked his phone. "Resort's three miles east," he said. "I'll tell him to meet us there."

"Maybe we should wait until dark."

"Too dangerous to stick around."

McCracken lifted his pant leg to check the knife wound. The cut had stopped bleeding and wasn't as deep as he had feared.

He buried the gun under a pile of dirt.

They headed northeast. The hills allowed them to move quickly without being seen from the highway.

Helicopters were hovering above the crash site, but not exploring the nearby terrain.

They rested again at the base of a 30-foot mound covered with evergreen shrubs. McCracken crawled to the top of the mound for a better view of the crash site. Another big rig was at the scene. A dozen or so people were moving large boxes and crates from the damaged trailer to the new truck.

"How's it look?"

"Hard to tell," said McCracken, sliding down the mound. "Let's get water."

They hiked another hour before reaching Paragosa Hot Springs and Spa, which sprawled across several acres of a narrow desert valley. From a hill overlooking the resort, they fixated on a blue swimming pool shimmering between a U-shaped complex of Spanish Colonial adobe buildings. The midday temperature was well over 110 degrees. They felt lightheaded and dizzy.

"Perlman's got water?"

"Haven't reached him yet."

Buscado couldn't take his eyes off the pool. "I'm gonna jump in that," he said. "Take my clothes off and jump."

He rose to his feet; McCracken pulled him back down.

"I'll get us water."

McCracken limped down the hill toward a wing of rooms where housekeepers were cleaning. One maid parked her supply cart in front of a room and went inside. McCracken dropped to his knees, crawled to the cart, and grabbed four water bottles. He hobbled back up the hill, dropping the bottles twice.

"Take two," he said.

Buscado twisted open a bottle and gulped the liquid. He opened a second bottle and did the same. He was still thirsty.

They found shade under a 20-foot mesquite tree and remained there until sundown. McCracken texted Perlman, telling him to meet them in the parking lot.

No response.

They were thirsty and hungry now. Buscado

suggested buying takeout in the hotel cafe. McCracken called the idea stupid, saying they were too dusty, sweaty, and bloody to act like guests.

They watched the sky grow dark.

"Why'd you do that?" Buscado asked.

"What?"

"Kill those guys in the truck. We would've gotten away anyway."

McCracken mulled the question. He didn't have a satisfactory answer.

His phone pinged—Perlman.

"He's here, north end of the lot," said McCracken, tapping a reply. "Says to stay away from the south end."

Hiking northwest around the resort took extra time, but was the safest route. Buscado was dehydrated again, and the desert shapes and shadows were making him paranoid.

McCracken led the way, hugging boulders and brush and edging along the perimeter. A half-moon provided sufficient illumination.

Buscado saw something strange. He stifled a scream, but grunted loudly enough to piss off McCracken, who punched his shoulder.

"Shut up!" McCracken hissed.

"Did you see it?"

"What?"

"Coyote, I think, but its face ..."

"What?"

"Flat and white," said Buscado. "Hairless."

McCracken turned and resumed walking.

They stopped at the edge of an adobe building and peered out at a massive gravel lot. The Ryder was parked inconspicuously between an RV and a Ford Explorer.

At the southern end of the lot, the self-driving semi and mangled trailer were cordoned off by police tape. An armed guard kept watch.

The darkness provided excellent cover now, as did the resort guests heading to and from their cars. McCracken and Buscado walked nonchalantly to the Ryder.

Perlman, sitting in the driver's seat, unlocked the doors as they approached.

McCracken threw open the driver door. "Out of my seat," he snapped.

They headed south on Highway 127. No one was following, as far as they could tell.

Buscado fought to keep from crying. "I'm a murderer now," he whimpered.

Seven

Buscado was weeping in the Ryder. McCracken and Perlman did their best to ignore the sniffles and whimpers, but there was only so much they could take.

McCracken considered asking Buscado if he wanted to stop for a milkshake—ice cream always made him feel better when he was sad—but decided against it because Perlman might laugh.

Perlman was literally biting his tongue. He fantasized about all the insults he could fling at Buscado, and how much fun he'd have eviscerating the dweeb with his laser-sharp wit. But he refrained for good reason: they were in too deep and couldn't afford to have Buscado turn on them. While it was unlikely the guy would run to the cops—he was an accessory to double murder—one never knew.

"I'm done, guys," Buscado said. "Just drop me off in town somewhere."

"Can't do that," said McCracken.

"Maybe if, you know, you took a few deep breaths or something, you'd feel a lot better," Perlman said.

"Just take me to see my kids."

"No," McCracken replied. "We gotta return the truck to Pahrump."

"Just drop me off here then. I'll walk home."

"No."

"Chill, dude," said Perlman. "Deep breaths."

"I want out, guys."

McCracken wasn't sure what to do. Should he stop the truck, let Buscado out, and then do a choke hold and render him unconscious? There was rope in the cargo area. He and Perlman could tie up Buscado and bring him back to Pahrump …

No, he had a better idea—lights ahead, Burger King. "Anybody hungry?" he asked.

"I could use a Double Whopper with cheese, large onion rings, maybe some mozzarella sticks," said Perlman.

Buscado shrugged.

McCracken drove a few hundred feet past

Burger King and pulled over. He handed Perlman two twenties. "Get three of whatever you order, plus a large chocolate shake for Buscado," he said.

They ate most of the meal in silence.

McCracken's phone pinged—a text from Howser: *Don't come here tonight.*

"Pahrump's out," said McCracken.

"That asshole," said Perlman. "What's the reason?"

"Didn't say."

"Guys, if we go to prison, do you think we'll ever get out?" asked Buscado.

"Nobody's going to prison," said McCracken.

"Why?"

"If you keep your goddamn mouth shut, we won't," said Perlman. "Besides, that shooting was in self-defense … right?"

No one answered.

"Well, legally speaking, it was," said Perlman. "And what were you saying, Buscado? That weird shit you heard in the truck?"

"In the trailer," replied Buscado. "Things moving, animal sounds, sort of."

"Howser and Baldwin are fucking with us," said Perlman. "These hijackings, I don't know what's going on."

"I don't care anymore," said Buscado, chewing

his last mozzarella stick. “I just wanna see my kids.”

“There’ll be time for that,” said McCracken. “But first we gotta get my truck.”

They reached Walker Basin Campground in 35 minutes. A popular destination in winter, it was deserted now except for a lone F-250 parked under a patch of juniper trees by a dry lake bed.

McCracken parked the Ryder and left the motor running. “Perlman, take the rental back to Pahrump but don’t go to the hideout,” he said.

“Roger Wilco.”

“You’ll meet Cheryl behind the Albertson’s off 160. She’ll return the truck in the morning.”

“Okay, sure, but I gotta take a whiz first.”

Buscado was flipping through photos on his phone. Perlman signaled McCracken for a private meeting outside.

Buscado didn’t look up when they left the truck. McCracken, limping slightly, followed Perlman to a juniper and looked up at the night sky.

Perlman unzipped. “Dude’s bad news,” he said. “If he freaks and goes to the cops—”

“He won’t do that,” interrupted McCracken.

"How do you know?"

"I won't let him."

"Look, bruiser, just because you kick—"

The Ryder spun in reverse, did a flawless one-eighty, and sped off before Perlman could finish peeing.

McCracken, rummaging through his pockets for keys, hobbled toward the F-250. Perlman dribbled down his pants leg while trying to zip up.

The dirt road back to the highway was bumpy. McCracken drove fast but couldn't gain on the Ryder, which had a mile head start.

"He's haulin' ass, dude's a pro," said Perlman.

They reached Highway 127 and followed Buscado south.

"Contact Howser and fill him in," McCracken said. "Text, don't call. He never answers his phone."

"Neither do I."

"I figure Buscado's going to Henderson."

"Why?"

"Ex-wife lives there. Kids."

The Ryder was flying—85, 90, 95. Late-night traffic was light. The F-250 was a half-mile behind and closing the gap.

Buscado turned on Charles Brown Highway,

passing a Safeway truck on a narrow incline and nearly colliding with a Subaru Outback heading in the opposite direction.

"Crazy fucker!" shouted Perlman.

Perlman's phone pinged: Howser again, passing along the address of Buscado's ex-wife.

"Boyfriend lives there too, I think," said McCracken.

"Man, this could get ugly."

"Maybe."

"Whoa, look at that!"

The Ryder was attempting another risky pass, this time around a slow-moving tractor-trailer flashing its hazard lights. Buscado veered into the opposite lane, topped 100, and then swerved back to avoid an approaching minivan.

"Somebody's gonna call 911 if he keeps this up," said Perlman.

"Possibly."

"*Possibly?* Is that all you've got to say?"

Perlman shook his head. "You, Howser, Baldwin—like dealing with a three-headed sphinx."

Buscado hit a flat stretch of highway and slowed to 80, passing vehicles only when necessary. McCracken followed at a safe distance. The pursuit slowed to 65, even 55 at times, and then sped up again as they got closer to Vegas.

Perlman grew bored and played *Angry Birds* on his phone; McCracken turned on the radio and listened to *Coast to Coast AM.* A doctor was talking about alien implants.

"You buy that extraterrestrial shit?" asked Perlman.

McCracken thought it over. "People have seen weird stuff," he said.

"Yeah, *they* want you to believe that."

McCracken's leg was throbbing. He was tired and wanted to be in bed with Fuentes, who hadn't texted him all day.

They entered the outskirts of Vegas and passed a suburb under construction. The Ryder slowed and made a hard right onto a four-lane road leading to a cluster of homes, all less than five years old.

Buscado entered a gated community called Smithington West. The gate was wide open and the security station deserted. The two-story homes had ceramic rooftops and rock landscaping.

The F-250 was a block behind, tailing discreetly.

"What do we do when he stops?" asked Perlman.

"Park and wait."

"For what?"

McCracken wasn't sure. Would Buscado start a fight? Kidnap his kids? "We have to keep the peace," he said.

"You keep the peace."

The street came to an abrupt stop, ending at a desert moonscape. Buscado parked at the third house on the left and ran up the walkway, opening the front door without knocking.

McCracken parked behind the Ryder and waited. The front door was open and the lights were on inside.

"What now?" asked Perlman.

"Roll down your window and listen."

Perlman did. Silence, mostly; maybe a few crickets. It was past midnight and the neighborhood was asleep.

McCracken exited the truck, leaving his door ajar, and signaled Perlman to follow him. They moved quietly up the walk. The front door was wide open.

They paused briefly, listening and watching before entering. McCracken nodded and moved in.

Buscado was sitting cross-legged on the living-room carpet, head in his hands.

"They're gone," he said softly. "Just like she said she'd do. She and the motherfucker have taken my little ones."

"Furniture too, looks like," said Perlman.

"We gotta go," said McCracken.

"That's illegal, what she did," said Buscado,

pulling out his phone. "She won't get away with it."

Before Buscado could make a call, McCracken snatched the phone from his hands. Buscado leaped to his feet and lunged at McCracken.

"Gimme that!"

"Calm down."

"Fuck that! That bitch took my sofa, my big screen, *and* my kids. She's been talking about moving to Houston, I'll bet that's where she is."

"We gotta go."

"I told you, I'm not going anywhere!"

They heard footsteps out front. McCracken pointed toward the kitchen as a possible escape route.

Howser and Baldwin entered the house, closing the door behind them.

"What do we have here?" said Howser, studying Buscado.

"They're gone," replied Buscado. "Everything I had is gone."

Howser helped Buscado off the carpet and gave him a hug.

Perlman smirked.

"She can't do that," said Buscado, sobbing. "It's illegal."

"Yes, it is," said Howser. "There are people who

can help find your kids, but we can't call the police. The best thing to do now is leave."

McCracken went to the bathroom and shut the door.

"These people, who are they?"

"Specialists," said Howser.

"Sounds expensive," said Buscado. "I'm out of money."

"We all are," added Perlman. "Two blown missions and no money. Explain that, Howser."

"Today's effort was an abomination," said Baldwin.

"You set us up!" said Perlman. "They just happen to have two armed guards on the rig we target?"

"We most certainly did not set you up," replied Baldwin.

"There are other parties involved," Howser added.

"The truck today made noises," said Buscado.

"Excuse me?" said Baldwin.

"Weird noises."

The room fell silent. They could hear McCracken's pee splashing in the toilet.

"Listen to me, all of you," said Howser.

The toilet flushed. McCracken reentered the room, drying his hands on his jeans.

"What happened today was unfortunate, but

we must move on," said Howser. "I guarantee each and every one of you that your efforts will not go unrewarded."

"What about the dead guys?" asked Buscado.

"There are always casualties in battle," said Howser. "Be patient. In two days we're having a rally here in town. I expect you all to be there."

"And not to belabor the obvious," added Baldwin, "but don't discuss our recent activities with anyone."

Eight

Perlman couldn't figure out why he was here. There was no valid reason to spend Sunday afternoon cooped up in a shuttered Crown Books in North Las Vegas.

But here he was, surrounded by malcontents eager to hear how automation was evil, and how Howser would fix the ills science had wrought.

Yeah, right.

Howser was born with charm and charisma to convince anyone of anything.

Perlman could never persuade people to hear him speak, much less cough up cash for a bullshit cause. He was smart—genius-level, his high school physics teacher once told his parents—but charm wasn't his strong suit.

And then there was McCracken.

Perlman glanced across the aisle at that beast—a throwback with a tenth of his intellect. He seethed as McCracken cozied up to Fuentes. Did she know he had killed two men in cold blood a few days earlier? Maybe she did. Maybe she liked it.

Perlman had gotten his fair share of girls over the years, but usually there had been a transaction involved: money, gifts, weed—even his coding services—in exchange for sex. That wasn't fair. He may have been only five foot seven and average-to-ugly in the looks department, but nobody topped his intellect.

It was all too weird. Not a bleep in the news about the Paragosa truck heist or the killings. The guys McCracken had shot certainly weren't cops; otherwise the media would have been all over it.

He was tempted to bail. Thailand? No, he had a history there. There were other options, though.

First, the money.

The crew was scheduled to meet after Howser's speech. Excellent—he had a lot of gripes to share.

Baldwin took the podium, tapped the mic gently, and asked the crowd of about 80 to take their seats. Sitting in the front row, Perlman turned and watched the faithful plop their asses onto rented folding chairs.

The movement attracted a rainbow coalition of disgruntled Americans. Perlman judged them silently: old white guy wearing a vintage 1970s Teamsters cap and red Aerosmith windbreaker; Asian woman—maybe Filipino, short, early forties, gaunt, stern, rail thin—her black t-shirt showing a coiled snake above the words *Don't Tread On Me*; middle-aged black guy holding a sign that read *Automation Sucks*; two working-class white dudes, mid-twenties, bragging to an elderly black woman about kicking some programmer's ass on the Strip.

"You boys shouldn't have done that," she told them. "That's not what we're about."

"Serves him right," said one of the guys. "He's making this happen."

The woman frowned. "I don't condone violence," she said.

Baldwin cleared his throat.

"Please, everybody, take your seats," he said. "Full house today, which we're delighted to see. Not everyone may find a chair."

Perlman spotted some late arrivals standing along the back wall where the magazine racks once stood. The new attendees looked anxious. Few were smiling.

"I'd like to thank you all for coming today ..."

Baldwin droned on for a good ten

minutes—monotone platitudes about living wages, progressive tax structures, and folks paying their fair share.

Blah blah blah, Perlman thought.

Baldwin was a medical researcher—some sort of genetics whiz—but he didn't know jack about computers, programming, engineering, or transportation.

Perlman quickly reassessed his own abilities and decided he should be speaking. He'd kick ass up there, telling the plebs why the country was ripe for revolution. And, yes, cash donations would be mandatory.

He was ready to take a cigarette break when Howser came to the mic. The crowd applauded wildly.

"Welcome, everybody!" said Howser warmly.

What a dick.

"It's so wonderful to see a packed house today, although we do apologize for not bringing more chairs. We will next time or … you can replace me with a robot!"

The crowd laughed.

"Our movement is growing rapidly, and today's turnout is a great indicator of that. Similar grassroots efforts are being organized across the country—and Washington is starting to take notice."

The reaction was raucous and rowdy. The Filipino woman jumped to her feet, arched back, and gave a middle-finger salute to the ceiling.

"Automate *this*, fuckers!" she shouted.

"A.I. can kiss my ass!" yelled someone else.

Howser was clever, Perlman thought. Work this pack of jobless jackals into a proletarian frenzy, lift their hopes up high, and then move in for the monetary kill.

Brilliant.

"There's a terrible curse afflicting our great nation, a dark movement that's growing with every passing day," Howser warned. "I've felt it in my personal life. I'm sure many of you have too."

Perlman stifled a laugh.

"As many of you know, I've long been associated with Caltech in Pasadena, although I recently moved on from that post. My new title is Research Professor at the University of Eastern Nevada, which means I'm now living here in Las Vegas with my lovely wife Eileen, who couldn't make it today. Our two sons are away at school. Jake, who's 18, is a freshman at the University of Michigan, my alma mater, where he studies engineering. And Jeremy—he's 21—will graduate next spring from Georgetown University with a bachelor's degree in philosophy. We're very proud of them both."

Scattered applause.

Way to connect with the common man. Half the plebs here haven't even finished high school.

"And while it's true I haven't lost my job to automation, robotics, or artificial intelligence—not yet, anyway—I have a deep, personal connection to this issue, one I'd like to share with you today."

Wish I had a blunt right now.

"It's very painful for me to do so, but through my revelation I hope you'll gain a deeper understanding of why I've started this movement, and why my commitment to you will never waver."

A pretty blonde woman seated next to Perlman, enchanted by Howser's oratory skills, leaned forward in her chair. Perlman leaned forward too, hoping she'd notice him.

"Several years ago, I used to do quite a bit of work for the military," Howser continued. "It was important work, much of it classified, so I can't reveal everything today. I was proud to participate in actions I believed would make our great nation stronger than ever."

Perlman glanced over at McCracken, who was staring intensely at Howser.

"I was part of a team developing what we called a 'robotic dog,' a semi-autonomous, four-legged robot with multiple sensors for navigating rough terrain. By the way, what I'm telling you has been declassified—you'll find dozens of videos on YouTube of similar military robot prototypes—but keep in mind that many details of our mission ... well, I simply cannot go into detail without federal agents bursting in here and hauling me away."

The crowd chuckled.

Perlman recalled reading about cadaver-hunting robots retrieving soldiers' bodies from combat zones—places where it was too dangerous for humans to enter. The machines would work at night when enemy forces couldn't spot them and drag the cadavers back to base.

"I was designing software for a new breed of robotic creature—a crocodile-like learning machine that moved stealthily along the ground. Unlike noisier, older robots, it could sneak up on the enemy," said Howser. "It was very powerful and could unleash all sorts of mayhem. And during one of our numerous beta runs, I witnessed this mayhem firsthand."

Maybe this isn't a total waste of time.

"The story I'm about to tell was made public during congressional hearings last year, and has since been declassified. I'm redacting sections that remain classified, however," said Howser, pausing for a sip of water. "Not long ago I was on military assignment in a remote and dangerous stretch of Africa, testing a robotic prototype we named 'Niley,' which somewhat resembled a Nile crocodile, including a snout and mouth cavity with a moveable jaw, as well as three dozen sharply pointed teeth constructed from a titanium alloy. As a piece of technology it was quite remarkable—and seriously menacing to look at. It did, in fact, move and act very much like a crocodile, albeit a small one about a meter in length."

Perlman's eyes turned again toward McCracken. Fuentes had her hand on his knee. Was she rubbing his thigh?

"One night we were beta-testing Niley on the outskirts of Malakal—a war-ravaged town in the northeast of South Sudan. I was there as a consultant for the Marine Corps' Advanced Warfighting Unit, and we chose Malakal for its isolation. Technically speaking, we were there as 'consultants' for the South Sudanese army, but we weren't doing any actual consulting. Niley was highly classified at the time, and Malakal's remote location on the banks of the White Nile River made it an ideal testing ground for three key attributes: the robot's amphibious capabilities, its ability to move stealthily—a unique and critical attribute for a combat-ready robot—and its ability to function autonomously in patrol situations."

Perlman couldn't get Fuentes' wandering hand out of his mind. Even worse, the blonde was ignoring him.

"Niley's job that evening was to accompany our squad—a dozen or so Marines and me—on a training exercise. It was the rainy season, and our reconnaissance team had come upon a string of abandoned buildings near the river's edge. Malakal had largely been abandoned ... and thoroughly looted ... just weeks earlier—an unfortunate result of Sudan's bloody civil war at the time. Aside from a handful of brave Red Cross workers and the occasional industrious thief, the city was deserted. Niley had been programmed to scramble into empty buildings, identify potential threats, and use its 'bite force'—mechanical jaws ten times stronger than a pit bull's—to incapacitate an enemy combatant and drag him outside the structure."

Perlman tried to picture Howser on military patrol, maybe wearing some Banana Republic shit with the tags still on, or a token Marine field uniform too baggy for his toothpick frame.

On the plus side, the pompous dweeb sure could hold a crowd—rapt attention all around the room. Perlman himself found the story compelling.

"Niley trailed us closely, almost like a pet dog, as we moved along the river's edge, going from building to building, which in many cases were simply rusting metal shacks. Again, Niley was remarkably quiet for a robot, apart from the sloshing of its mechanical feet across the muddy banks. We would stop at each building and Niley—acting autonomously, mind you, not receiving commands from any squad member—would locate the building entrance, scurry in, and explore while we waited outside. The scene was quite surreal. Niley had two cameras embedded in its 'head,' if you will, each with a red LED that would light up when active. The effect was rather eerie, giving Niley a hound-from-hell appearance."

The crowd chuckled.

"For thirty minutes we moved quietly through the mud—no flashlights—guided only by the full moon. Niley entered three shacks, explored, and exited. At the fourth building, it raced in as usual. Seconds later we heard an animal's panicked cry, followed quickly by a series of ear-piercing shrieks coming from inside the building. Then … silence. Moments later, Niley emerged from the building, carrying a small, bloodied mongrel dog between its jaws. The animal, as you might've guessed, was dead. Torn to shreds."

The audience gasped. Perlman stifled a laugh. *Man, kill a dog and everyone goes batshit crazy.*

"Niley's thrashing of the poor animal wasn't unexpected, given the crudeness of the prototype's autonomous code. There was a lot of programming work to do, and I asked our squad leader—a young man I'll call 'Hal'—to postpone the rest of the mission, thereby allowing my team more time to correct Niley's shortcomings. Hal was understanding, perhaps because some of his men were repulsed by what they had just witnessed, but he had his orders: complete the Niley tests. His superiors, all the way up to the Pentagon, were bullish on robots in combat situations, and they wanted our effort to advance quickly. The more field time Niley got, the better."

Perlman scratched his scrotum. McCracken and Fuentes were holding hands now.

"So we continued. Niley rushed a few more shacks, found nothing in two, and drove a few terrified rats from another. It was 0200 hours and squad leader Hal decided to call it a night, so I deactivated the robot via my handheld. Two Marines lifted Niley off the ground and grunted as they carried it, as the machine was deceptively heavy. We turned away from the river and moved toward what remained of the city center. A children's hospital, once the pride of Malakal, was now in ruins. Hal pointed to the hospital. 'In there,' he said, 'one more try.' I asked why, and Hal said we needed at least one test where Niley explored a large, multi-room facility, which we hadn't found down by the river. Reluctantly, I agreed. We set Niley on the ground, rebooted, and let it roam the hospital.

"We waited by a bullet-pockmarked wall outside the hospital's reception area. The roof had been blown off, and we could hear Niley scampering across the floor. Then … silence. No sounds other than wildlife—crickets and frogs, mostly—as Niley penetrated deeper to explore other rooms."

Howser paused, pulled a handkerchief from his back pocket, and wiped his forehead. His hands were shaking.

Perlman was intrigued.

"That's when we heard the scream," said Howser, his voice cracking. "A child's shriek, then louder shouts and screams—mature voices—all coming from inside the hospital. We ran toward the entrance just as Niley bolted out, dragging a crying toddler by the leg and racing toward the river. I tried to deactivate the machine but couldn't before it bolted into the darkness and out of wireless range."

The audience fell silent. A man wailed.

"A family of seven—mother, father, five children—had been hiding in the hospital for several days, fearful of the soldiers who would rob, rape, or kill them if they stayed in their home. Why hadn't they left town like everyone else? Our interpreter never found out. The parents were screaming about the 'demon beast' that had stolen their little boy. We spent the rest of the night—all of us, Marines and family—searching the riverbank but found nothing. Around dawn, one of the Marines found Niley, batteries dead, lying in a thick jumble of weeds. A child's bloodied leg was protruding from its titanium jaws. Minutes later we found what was left of the boy's body, floating in a shallow pool nearby. He was two years old."

Howser paused here and dabbed his eyes with a handkerchief.

"What could we do but apologize? How ridiculous that sounds, I know. A family loses a child, and all we can say is, 'We're very sorry.' The Pentagon later paid the family the equivalent of a year's income—a paltry sum, of course—and considered the matter closed."

An elderly woman in the front row rose to her feet, walked up to Howser, and gave him a hug. No one said a word. Howser thanked the woman and resumed.

"A truly horrible story. But what happened afterward is something I find even equally disturbing.

I requested permission to shelve the combat robotics effort until we resolved its very significant problems, but they refused. The program was too significant to delay, they claimed, adding that 'collateral damage was always a risk' in field tests. Well, like you, I found that cavalier disregard for human life quite disturbing. It's the same attitude we see today from government and business leaders who embrace automation without a moment's hesitation, and without considering the dramatic sociological and economic impact of thinking machines replacing humans."

Perlman mulled how much Howser and Baldwin might rake in today. Many of these folks were unemployed, some retired. Passing the hat wouldn't fund a two-week Bangkok blackout. Or would it?

"It's clear that automation is causing troubles our leaders hadn't anticipated, and I'm not just referring to long unemployment lines," said Howser. "Social unrest is here. Just the other day I heard of self-driving trucks being attacked in Southern Nevada. One can only imagine the consequences of job-killing automation spreading to multiple industries across our nation and around the world. Millions of people out of work, people trying to feed their families, raise their children. And yet we glamorize technologists and CEOs determined to automate us out of existence. We cannot allow this to happen!"

The applause was deafening.

People to the left and right of Perlman jumped to their feet. Soon the entire room was giving Howser a standing ovation.

Perlman stood reluctantly and joined in. Inside he was freaked out. Why had Howser mentioned the highway hijackings? Carelessness in a moment of rhetorical exuberance, or something more sinister? The bungled heists had not been reported by the news media, which probably meant the police were keeping the details under wraps. Or maybe the police were in on it?

His heart raced. If FBI operatives were in the room—and he knew there were—then what?

Howser made his closing remarks—a few platitudes and the expected request for donations.

Perlman looked over at McCracken, who appeared to be crying. Fuentes was consoling him, whispering something in his ear. It didn't seem to be helping.

More applause. Speech over.

Howser and Baldwin stood together, shaking hands and answering people's questions. Perlman spotted that freaky Cheryl chick, the one who never said anything. Standing beside Baldwin, she was holding a hat and collecting donations. An actual fucking hat! How corny.

Thirty minutes passed before the last of the malcontents left the room. Perlman knew he'd have to stick around for Howser's mandatory insider meeting. He hoped things would move along quickly so he could get drunk and check out the Velvet Rhino.

Baldwin instructed Buscado to build a circle of seven chairs. "Let's go, people," he said in an officious tone.

McCracken, brooding and silent, sat first, followed by Fuentes, Cheryl, Buscado, Howser, and Baldwin. Perlman sat last.

"So," said Howser, "how does everyone think it went?"

McCracken bolted from his chair, grabbed Howser by the collar, and tossed him several feet across the floor. Fuentes screamed.

"Motherfucker!" McCracken yelled. "That story, how dare you take my—"

"Stop it! Stop it!" shouted Baldwin, tugging on one of McCracken's biceps. Buscado and Perlman grabbed McCracken's other arm. Together they managed to pull McCracken off Howser, who was turning blue.

"Chill out, man!" shouted Buscado.

Cheryl and Fuentes tried to help Howser, who waved them off and rose to his knees. "I'm fine," he whispered hoarsely.

"Control yourself, sir!" Baldwin scolded McCracken, who covered his eyes and sobbed.

"All things will be explained in good time," said Howser, rising to his feet and straightening his slacks. "Let's call it a night, shall we?"

Nine

Parts of the Niley story were true, only the incident hadn't occurred in Africa, nor had it involved an impoverished Sudanese family. It had, however, involved McCracken, and the real story was even stranger.

McCracken joined the U.S. Army at age nineteen. The move made sense.

He was doing little with his life other than working at Oil Monkey and having sex with his girlfriend Marissa, who he had been dating for over a year. Living in Phoenix, McCracken and his mother shared a two-bedroom rental, complete with covered parking and a kidney-shaped pool that was closed often. They split the rent 50/50.

McCracken spent a lot of time at Marissa's

apartment, mostly to avoid his mom's boyfriend, Josh, a 30-year-old guitarist who didn't have his own place. Josh was nice enough but didn't contribute to the rent, despite sleeping at least four nights a week at the McCrackens'. The walls were thin and McCracken hated hearing Josh having sex with his mom, which sometimes went on all night. They liked to do it up against the wall, too. Josh moaned the loudest, which disgusted McCracken even more.

The other nights Josh would crash on a friend's sofa, or have a late gig and go home with a girl. McCracken's mom knew Josh was cheating on her, but didn't complain.

Marissa lived alone. She worked thirty hours a week as a hostess at Wild Bronc Hotel and Indian Casino, and wanted McCracken to move in with her. He liked things the way they were, which made him feel a little guilty.

Did he love her? He wasn't sure.

One night while she was sleeping, he ate a microwave burrito and watched a Discovery Channel documentary on what happens to the brain during sex. When a woman has an orgasm, the show said, her brain releases a hormone called oxytocin, which causes her to bond with her partner.

Marissa had a lot of orgasms—more than

McCracken could count—and maybe that was why she wanted a deeper commitment. He felt sad he didn't feel the same way.

The Army might solve his problems.

When he told Marissa he was signing up, she didn't cry or make a scene. "I'm pregnant," she told him. "Maybe you should join. We'll need a steady income and medical."

McCracken asked if she'd consider getting an abortion. She got angry and kicked him out, but only for a day.

He spent the next week seeking advice from everyone he knew—the guys at work, his mom, even Josh. The consensus was clear.

McCracken proposed to Marissa. They drove to Las Vegas and got married at Chapel o' the Strip. His mom paid for their honeymoon suite—her gift to the newlyweds—but the trip lasted only two days because Marissa had to be back at work.

McCracken did basic training at Fort Jackson, South Carolina, where he impressed his drill instructors with his bravery, physical prowess, and mental toughness. During the Night Infiltration course, where recruits crawl for 150 meters as live ammunition flies over their heads, McCracken saved the life of a fellow recruit, who had a panic attack and rose to his knees halfway through the crawl. McCracken yanked the recruit to the ground and held him in a headlock until the instructors stopped the drill. A week later during a pugil stick bout, where two soldiers battle with padded sticks to mimic hand-to-hand combat with rifles, McCracken knocked his opponent unconscious with a swift blow to the head, even though both were wearing football helmets.

And McCracken was the only recruit who didn't get pneumonia or pinkeye during the ten-week camp.

On Family Day, the day before graduation, McCracken was posing for pictures with Melissa, his mom, and Josh, when the battalion commander came over and shook everyone's hand. "There's someone you should meet," he said to McCracken. "Please excuse us for a moment," he told the others before escorting McCracken across Hilton Field to meet a middle-aged black man in a grey suit.

The man, looking stiff and uncomfortable, was standing by himself, sipping orange juice.

"Private McCracken, I'd like you to meet Dr. Charles Baldwin."

"Nice to meet you, sir," said McCracken, shaking Baldwin's hand.

"My pleasure," replied Baldwin.

"Dr. Baldwin has a few things he'd like to talk with you about, Private, so I'll take my leave," said the battalion commander, who walked away before McCracken could salute.

"Well, I see they weren't lying about your physical attributes," said Baldwin, cracking a smile.

McCracken wasn't sure how to respond.

"I'll get right to the point, as I see your family is waiting," said Baldwin. "I'm leading a team of researchers working on new scientific strategies—astonishing things, really—that will help keep our country safe. Would you be interested in participating?"

McCracken was flattered. Of all the basic-training recruits, they picked him. Of course he was interested.

"What's your MOS?" asked Baldwin.

"Infantryman, sir. My goal is to lead an infantry team in combat operations."

"We'd like to run a few tests on you next week. Don't worry, nothing dangerous—endurance tests, mostly—right here on the base. I've arranged everything with your superiors, and you'll resume infantry training as soon as we're done. Should only take a few days."

McCracken was excited when he arrived Monday at the Dorn VA Medical Center for phase one of testing. He envisioned a high-tech scenario: a room filled with super-advanced diagnostic equipment and computers; a team of scientists in white lab coats, each jotting notes on a clipboard while he performed hours of grueling physical tests, maybe with electrodes strapped to his body.

But instead McCracken was directed to a dingy waiting room in the basement. The flickering fluorescent tubes in the ceiling made his eyes ache. The room had only two chairs, a coffee table, and a corner stand with a Mr. Coffee, a stack of Styrofoam cups, and packets of Coffee-Mate.

McCracken sat in a chair and examined his surroundings. He liked the smell of coffee but didn't drink it. He wished there were doughnuts too. He glanced at the coffee table and was surprised to see the magazine selection was limited to *Playboy* and *Penthouse*.

Baldwin entered the room. Wearing a lab coat over tan slacks and a dress shirt, he smiled politely at McCracken and poured himself a cup of coffee.

"Want some?" he asked. McCracken declined.

Baldwin sat in the opposite chair and set his

cup on the table. He pulled a small plastic container from his coat and handed it to McCracken.

"We need a sample from you," he said. "If you need help, try one of the magazines."

"Sample?"

"Semen sample."

McCracken took the container from Baldwin and looked at it. "So you want me to …"

"Ejaculate into the cup, yes. When you're done, bring the sample to Nurse Artena at the front desk. You probably saw her when you got off the elevator."

McCracken had taken the stairs down, but had noticed the pretty nurse at the desk. She had even smiled at him when he passed by. The thought of handing her a cup of his jizz made him cringe.

"I'm just wondering ... what is this for?

Baldwin stared into his coffee. "Well, without getting into too much detail, I'm spearheading a project designed to, for lack of a better description, expand human capabilities," he said. "By mixing and matching attributes, we can improve conditions for everyone."

"I … don't understand."

"There's a nearly infinite number of use cases, but since you're a soldier, here's a military example. A force with enhanced biological attributes could withstand the most extreme combat trauma with minimal physical and psychological damage."

McCracken looked at the sample cup again. He still didn't get it.

"We've selected you based partly on your impressive basic-training performance, and also on our investigation into your personal history."

"What history?"

"We ran an extensive background check on you, and a particular incident from your childhood did play a major factor in our decision," said Baldwin.

McCracken nodded.

Baldwin leaned closer.

"If we could isolate your most outstanding attributes—physicality, bravery, decisiveness under pressure, and extreme aggressiveness—we could share those traits via genetic therapy," he said. "Alternatively, we might encode your traits elsewhere, but that's further down the road."

McCracken caught a noxious whiff of coffee from Baldwin's breath. He leaned back in his chair.

"That's all I gotta do? I mean, into this cup?"

"For now, yes, but we'll also need blood and hair samples later. For now, focus on the cup," said Baldwin.

Once Baldwin left the room, McCracken

completed his mission. He found he didn't need the magazines, although he didn't get very aroused. There was a certain degree of patriotic pride in doing his job well—his first military assignment—and he didn't want to disappoint his superiors.

He did not disappoint. A few days later, McCracken got a phone call from Baldwin, who told him the test results were exactly what they had hoped for, although he didn't go into detail.

"Is there something I can help you with?" Baldwin asked.

McCracken said he wanted to join Army Ranger School right away. Baldwin pulled strings to make it happen.

McCracken aced the Ranger Physical Fitness Test. He did more than 120 push-ups in two minutes—80 to 100 is considered excellent—and 30 pull-ups, eight more than the second-place candidate. In the Mountain phase, where students endure 20 nights of hunger and sleep deprivation in harsh terrain, McCracken had no problem living on one or two MREs per day. He simply refused to feel hungry. He found it easy to block unpleasant feelings from his mind, although sometimes they'd rush in so fast he couldn't stop them. Too often his ability to block anger wasn't very good.

In the Florida phase, a 16-day test of candidates' leadership and patrolling skills in a jungle setting, McCracken distinguished himself by treating two soldiers with hypothermia when their boat capsized in a swamp on a foggy, cold evening.

McCracken heard from another soldier that the instructors were always talking about him, although they never praised him to his face.

Finn was born when McCracken was stationed at Hunter Army Airfield in Savannah, Georgia. The boy, healthy and curious with blue eyes and amber hair, instantly changed his father's outlook on life. McCracken had always focused on his own needs, but that vanished the moment Finn was born. His deepest hopes and fears now centered on the child. Was the boy eating enough? Were dangers lurking in the apartment—uncovered electrical outlets, sharp glass edges, a rickety crib—that might hurt Finn?

McCracken was surprised by his own parenting skills. He was only twenty-one—still a kid, really—and here he was a husband, father, and proud member of the 75th Ranger Regiment.

Marissa appeared happy in her role as wife and

mother, although she complained about trying to raise a child on a Ranger's meager salary.

When Finn was a year old, Marissa persuaded her mother Sharla to move from Phoenix to Savannah to be the boy's nanny. Sharla took the offer, which didn't pay but included free room and board. Marissa found a job right away—a noon-to-8 cashier at Best Buy—and brought in much-needed extra income. McCracken didn't like her working there. Marissa talked a lot about her cocky 28-year-old supervisor—a tall, skinny smart-ass whom she claimed to despise. But she always laughed and smiled, usually at the dinner table, when describing the things he'd do to tease her at work.

"I think you got a crush on that boy," Sharla told her daughter one evening. Marissa freaked out, told her mom to fuck off, and marched to the bedroom, slamming the door shut.

After dinner, McCracken and Sharla ate bowls of peach ice cream and watched *Dancing with the Stars*.

"You better keep an eye on those two," Sharla said quietly.

McCracken thought about going to the bedroom to console his wife, but decided she needed some personal time. It was wiser to let her cool off on her own, he thought. He enjoyed his personal time. She probably did too.

Work weighed on McCracken's mind. Though technically a Ranger, he found himself assigned to the secretive project managed by Baldwin and another scientist, Dr. Howser, from some big-name university in California. They kept him busy most days with physical endurance tests and medical exams. The data they collected on him, they said, would help them design automated systems that might someday make the world a safer place.

McCracken respected the two men and liked being a part of something so important. But he made it clear he wanted to leave the project soon and rejoin his fellow Rangers in combat training. The things Baldwin and Howser made him do were dull, repetitive, and often embarrassing. The worst part was the daily semen sample. McCracken would dutifully fill the plastic container every morning, but feared the task was hurting his marriage by dampening his sex drive, which made his wife feel ignored. No wonder she went on and on about her smartass boss.

Marissa's mother took McCracken aside one morning and warned him to step up his game in the bedroom. "Are you doing your duty, boy?" she scolded. "You doing your duty?"

At least his relationship with Finn was great. The boy's face lit up whenever his dad entered the room, and McCracken enjoyed playing with Finn after work and on weekends. He had always wondered what kind of father he would be. He knew next to nothing about his own dad, and once heard that a lot of guys weren't very good at child-rearing. But for McCracken, fatherhood was a blast. He would take the boy to the park on Saturdays and to the apartment pool when it was warm, often getting admiring glances from the young moms who congregated there.

McCracken could tell which moms were unhappily married, and figured he could have sex with them if he was so inclined. But he was fiercely loyal to the institution of marriage and family. Besides, seeing his boy every day was hugely important. If he started fooling around with the horny, unhappy moms, Marissa could take Finn and move away. The thought terrified him.

The Baldwin/Howser project ended with a whimper. The two scientists thanked McCracken for his participation, adding that his efforts would reflect positively on his military record.

"We may call on you from time to time, if that's alright with you," said Howser, grinning and shaking McCracken's hand with both of his hands, as he always did.

McCracken agreed, and asked when and why they might call. Howser deferred to Baldwin, who said, "We'll let you know."

To show their gratitude, Baldwin and Howser pulled strings to get the inexperienced Ranger admitted to a two-month leadership course. As before, McCracken's skills impressed his instructors, who watched him extra closely.

Field-training exercises kept the students busy twenty hours a day—often with only one meal—to test their ability to think clearly in harsh combat situations. Not everyone could handle the physical and mental stress.

One student, Dewey Clapper, decided to make McCracken's life miserable. Short and stocky, an American eagle tattooed across his chest, Clapper taunted McCracken often, calling him either *Lurch* or *McCrack-ass*.

"You ain't nothin'," he told McCracken at least twice a day. "I've knocked out dudes twice your size."

Early one morning after twenty-four sleepless hours, the students got a two-hour break before the next drill. McCracken curled up under a tree and fell into a deep sleep. He dreamed of being chased around the barracks by Rhone Ellison. In the dream McCracken was wearing a U.S. Army hoodie but was naked from the waist down. He tripped over a rock in a playground—one where Finn played every day—and felt a stream of warm liquid with a strong ammonia scent running down his face.

Someone was peeing on him and giggling.

McCracken woke with a start, spitting and coughing as warm urine ran down his face. Standing over him was Clapper, laughing. McCracken rolled away from the piss stream, jumped to his feet, and smacked Clapper in the jaw with his right elbow, followed by a left uppercut.

The loud *crack* startled the other soldiers. An instructor rushed over to pull McCracken back.

Clapper was flat on his back, holding his bleeding mouth and whimpering. He was sent to a nearby hospital with a broken jaw, and was expelled from Ranger School the next day for inappropriate behavior.

McCracken wasn't punished at all.

He had several deployments over the next eighteen months. Most were short-term operations lasting only a few days, but some dragged on for weeks at a time. The destinations were generally inhospitable: Saharan Africa, Philippine jungles, Afghanistan-Pakistan border, and so on.

McCracken had few close friends in his platoon but was generally well-liked. His fellow Rangers saw him as brave. Vicious when necessary.

He wasn't a big talker, but when he did chat it was mostly about his boy. He would send Finn silly videos of himself clucking like a chicken, or singing a nursery rhyme—anything to stay in touch.

Once in Afghanistan, McCracken was shooting a Finn video when a firefight broke out. The squad leader was hit in the chest and McCracken placed himself in the line of fire, dragging the man to safety.

Another time during a predawn raid in the Philippines, McCracken pulled a suspected terrorist from a hammock and flex-cuffed him. The man tried to kick McCracken, who reflexively punched the suspect in the neck, severely damaging the man's trachea. An emergency tracheotomy by the squad's medic saved the suspect's life.

Rumors swirled that McCracken might receive an award for the Afghanistan incident, but nothing happened. Other gossipers claimed McCracken's award was nixed because of Clapper, whose father was a high-ranking Pentagon official. Dad reportedly was pissed that McCracken had coldcocked his son right out of the Rangers, the story went.

Finn's fourth birthday party was held at Rigdon Park in Columbus, not far from the apartment complex where the boy lived with his parents and grandmother. McCracken rented an inflatable bounce house for Finn's preschool friends, and Marissa baked an Elmo cake that Finn said looked like the Cookie Monster.

The park, adjacent to the Chattahoochee River, was green and damp that day—the result of four days of nonstop rain. McCracken felt happy as he sat on a park bench, basking in the sunshine and sipping a Bud Light Lime. He was proud to be an Army Ranger, his relationship with Marissa was pretty good—despite her gripes about his shitty pay—and his kid was doing great.

He was twenty-five with his full life ahead of him.

McCracken wanted to lie back and nap in the sun, but Finn tugged on his pants leg, begging to go down to the river to see the fishes.

"Probably won't see any fishes today, little

man," said McCracken, his eyes closed. "Just a whole lotta water and mud."

Finn was insistent, though, and two of his friends came over and joined in, pulling on McCracken's leg and asking to see the fishes.

"Looks like you're seein' the fishes, dude," another dad joked.

McCracken reluctantly agreed. The toddlers started sprinting across the grassy field toward the riverbank, their moms shouting at them to wait for Finn's dad.

McCracken rose to his feet, resigned to the fact that his lazy afternoon was over. Holding his beer, he trotted after the kids, telling them to wait for him by the riverwalk.

The boys, all four of them, did stop and wait, much to McCracken's surprise. "Okay, guys, we're gonna walk to the riverbank," he said. "Everybody hold hands and nobody go in the water, okay?"

The kids agreed.

Walking single file, they crossed a paved bike lane and ambled down a dirt path that cut through a thicket of bushes and descended to the water. McCracken held one boy's hand—he couldn't recall the kid's name. Finn was at the end of the line.

The Chattahoochee, calm and blue-gray, reflected the midday sun. McCracken's foot sunk three inches into the muddy bank. He decided not to take the kids any further, saving him from having to deal with parents griping about their kids' sludgy shoes.

"Looks like we're at the end of the road, guys."

"Already, Dad?"

It was Finn's voice. Gentle, inquisitive, and a little disappointed.

McCracken heard a loud *whoosh* and the rapid snapping of twigs. The intensity of the sounds startled him.

The kids screamed.

He turned and counted three kids behind him ... just three ...

Finn.

His boy was gone.

Toddlers crying, shouting, babbling about a monster racing through the thicket, a monster grabbing Finn and taking off.

Parents sprinting toward the path. McCracken abandoning his post, sprinting through the bushes, frantically shouting his son's name.

Every parent joining the search. "Finn! FINN!" Stomping, trampling plants for a better view of … what exactly? A boy? A wild pig? A feral dog?

Police arriving. Marissa, crying hysterically, jumping in the river, crying out for her son.

Current carrying her into the twining branches of a partially submerged wisteria. Marissa nearly drowning, maybe wanting to drown, being pulled free by a nearby fisherman.

McCracken searching for hours. For days. Weeks.

They all did.

It didn't matter. Finn was gone.

McCracken and Marissa saw a marriage counselor a few times before splitting up. The man must have repeated the same line a dozen times: "Maybe if you tried to gain closure over Finn's death …"

Closure.

What a bullshit word. McCracken wanted to punch the asshole. The therapist had no idea what it was like to lose your son, to have him simply *disappear.*

There was no magic solution, no chanting "closure" to make the pain go away. Their little boy had vanished.

And McCracken had been only a few feet away. He could have stopped it.

Police and psychiatrist interviews with the other children revealed little useful information.

One boy said a tiny metal animal with sharp teeth had clamped on Finn's ankle, pulling the boy from the pack. Another remembered a machine with a human arm, maybe even a partial human face attached to a shiny frame.

The police suspected a feral dog was to blame but couldn't find paw prints in the mud. No animal tracks of any kind, in fact.

For months McCracken would return daily to the scene of the vanishing, retracing his steps, checking the ground for any clues the investigators might have missed. But always … nothing. On one level he was hoping for a miracle, no matter how unrealistic and far-fetched it seemed. Finn adopted by wolves, living on regurgitated squirrel and rabbit meat. Skinny, mangy, but ultimately reparable. Hugs and tears, a few days of reporters buzzing around, maybe a TV movie, and years later a crazy story Finn would retell countless times.

It was all garbage, though, and he knew it. Every night for a year he'd wake up at three a.m., screaming, wishing the boy dead. The thought of his child kidnapped and suffering …

He learned to block those thoughts.

Two months before McCracken's twenty-sixth birthday, Marissa's mother moved back to Phoenix. Then Marissa moved out, telling her husband she needed to get on with her life. McCracken didn't try to stop her. Marissa wept as she packed her clothes, asking McCracken to deal with Finn's toys and things, which she hadn't had the heart to give away. As he stood on the curb and watched her drive off, he looked at their condo and decided he didn't want to live there anymore either.

He drove immediately to TGI Fridays, sat at the end of the bar, and drank a Grey Goose Cooler. Then another. Then two more. The bar was filling up fast and he was feeling annoyed by the people around him. His bladder was full and he was a little nauseous from the swirling mixture of vodka and sugar in his stomach.

McCracken walked to the restroom and was bummed to see a line of three guys waiting outside the door. His bladder was ready to burst. He spotted a red EMERGENCY EXIT sign at the end of the hall and decided to relieve himself in the alley. As he opened the back door, he heard someone behind him yell, "Hey, asshole!" He kept walking, figuring he'd have to apologize to the manager or assistant manager or chief busboy for pissing outside. No big deal.

He found a good spot between two stinking dumpsters, unzipped, and began peeing against the wall. He sighed with relief as the warm stream left his body, shutting his eyes but quickly reopening them as his head began to spin. Hangover tomorrow, he thought. How many shots of vodka were in each Grey Goose Cooler? Maybe he had drunk eight cocktails, not four.

"Hey, I'm talking to you, asshole!"

The obnoxious screech sounded familiar, but McCracken couldn't place it. He turned and saw Clapper, the douche whose jaw he had busted back at Ranger School.

Here he was, the little shit. Fists clenched. Same ugly snarl.

"Hey," McCracken said, zipping up. He had no interest in fighting. What really sounded good right now was a brisk walk, a Lumberjack Slam at Denny's, and two cups of coffee. He'd be sober enough to drive home, where he'd pop a couple of aspirin and hopefully not throw up on the sheets.

"What the fuck are you doing out here, loser? Jerkin' off?"

McCracken found that funny, but not laugh-out-loud funny. He pushed past Clapper and walked away.

"Turn and fight, you pussy."

"Not interested."

"Whaddya afraid of?"

McCracken stopped and stared at Clapper, more confused than angry. "What's your problem?" he asked.

Clapper took a step closer. "I'll tell you what," he snarled. "Big-ass motherfucker, all that Ranger shit came so easy to you, didn't it? All athletic and shit. Guys like me had to work twice … no, three times as hard."

"Whatever," said McCracken, realizing Clapper was very, very drunk.

"And you know it, don't you!" shouted Clapper. "That's why you were disrespecting me the whole time."

"I didn't disrespect anyone."

"Maybe not to my face, fucker, but it got back to me," said Clapper. "Guys like you always badmouthing me when I wasn't looking. You knew who my dad is too, didn't you? Badmouthing me cuz I wasn't making it. Then you made sure I was out for good."

Clapper's eyes were watery. McCracken felt sorry for him.

"Never did any of that," said McCracken, walking away. "Good luck with everything."

"This isn't over between us!"

McCracken knew the little shit was following him, maybe a step or two behind.

He can follow me all the way to Denny's, he thought. *I'll buy him a Lumberjack Slam.*

"This isn't over!"

"Yes, it is."

"You're gonna pay for what you did to me."

Don't respond. Keep walking.

"Turn and fight, motherfucker."

Don't turn. Keep walking.

"What … too chickenshit?"

Just keep walking.

"Your wife gave me a blowjob once. I fucked her too!"

McCracken laughed. What a stupid thing to say.

"I'm glad your fucking kid is dead!"

McCracken's reaction was so quick, so instinctive, that he would later wonder if he had planned it in advance. He whipped around and swung upward from the waist, striking Clapper square in the neck and sending him tumbling to the pavement. McCracken knew immediately what he had done—any Ranger would have—but wasn't sure if murder had been his goal.

Clapper, holding his neck, gasping for air, thrashed around like a fish on a hook. His larynx was crushed.

A few buildings down, someone popped open

TGI Fridays' emergency door—the same one McCracken had exited. Voices flowed from the building.

Was this how it would end? Prison? Maybe a death sentence?

The punch wasn't even intentional. Or maybe it was. Clearly, he had been provoked. Yes, definitely self-defense. But who would believe him? Not Clapper's dad, not the Rangers.

He began to panic.

McCracken jogged down the alley and turned left on the next street, which was poorly lit and devoid of pedestrians. He heard someone yell, "Hey!"

He walked a mile to Denny's, figuring he'd backtrack later to pick up his truck. The cool night air gave him a chance to sober up.

His hands were shaking as he ordered the Lumberjack Slam. He hid them under the table, hoping the waitress wouldn't notice.

Two weeks later McCracken decided to quit the Army. He had lost interest in keeping the world safe. He had failed to protect his own son. His wife was gone. And there was the alley incident. He no longer felt qualified to fight the bad guys of the world. He wasn't a hero and had no desire to be one.

No one had contacted him about the Clapper fight, nor were there any news reports of it. McCracken blocked it from his mind.

The Army dragged its feet on his separation process, which was a good thing because McCracken wasn't putting much effort into finding civilian employment. He knew a few ex-Rangers who had gone on to become security managers for big companies, and the pay was pretty good. He had heard that training and development specialists made good money too. But he wasn't sure what those jobs entailed, nor was he motivated to learn.

The months passed slowly. At times McCracken wanted to die, but he didn't. Suicide wasn't for him. No matter how miserable he felt at times, he always wanted to see life through to its natural conclusion, if possible.

He landed a full-time job at eShopaholic, an online retailer with a huge regional warehouse in Columbus. The pay was $12 an hour and McCracken spent much of his day racing through a giant building, using forklifts, walkie riders, and cherry pickers to fill customers' orders as fast as possible. His manager was an asshole, always screaming at everyone for missing quotas. But

McCracken didn't work harder because he didn't get a bonus—his boss did.

One evening after work, McCracken stopped by Target to pick up a few things he needed at home. Grabbing a twelve-pack of toilet paper, he noticed a man grinning at him.

Howser.

They chatted for a few minutes. Howser said the Army program he had been running with Baldwin had ended. "Budget cutbacks, kill you every time," he said, still grinning. Howser also expressed his sympathy for Finn's disappearance—he didn't say "death"—and asked McCracken where he was working now.

"I'm a customer fulfillment associate at eShopaholic," McCracken mumbled.

"Sorry?"

"eShopaholic. In the warehouse."

"Oh, I see."

McCracken smiled. "Big step down from Ranger, I know."

"Well, it's honest work," Howser replied.

McCracken figured the conversation was over. Then Howser leaned in and whispered: "I'm developing a privately funded project that's just getting underway."

"Sounds cool."

"We could use a man with your skills. I'm sure I could double what you're making now. Interested?"

Doubling his shitty pay. Fuck yeah, he was interested.

McCracken gave notice at eShopaholic the next day. He put his furniture up for sale on Craigslist and began boxing his things.

The new job meant moving to Nevada. He knew next to nothing about the gig. Apparently Baldwin was involved too.

"Don't tell anyone about the project," Howser told him. That was easy, as McCracken didn't keep in touch with anyone.

McCracken celebrated his twenty-seventh birthday in Flagstaff, Arizona. He didn't celebrate alone. Pulling into town at midnight, he checked into the Easy 8 Motel and went across the street to IHOP. He sat at the counter and ordered a T-bone steak, three eggs over-easy, and a stack of pancakes.

Before his meal arrived, a tall woman—mid-twenties, blond and pretty—walked in and sat next to him. They chatted over dinner. She was a nurse at a local hospital and her shift had just ended. McCracken invited her out for a drink.

"This town shuts down pretty early," she laughed.

"Nothing's open, no bar?"

"Nope," she answered.

McCracken finished his coffee and checked his watch.

"How about your room?" she asked.

McCracken bought a bottle of white zinfandel from a liquor store next door. They sat on the bed and drank from the room's plastic cups.

He turned on the TV while she rummaged through her purse. "Got any gum?" she asked. He did not. "Well, I don't either," she said, "but lookie here, a condom."

McCracken felt woozy on top of her, thrusting away, feeling far too drunk from one glass of wine. He remembered coming when she did, rolling onto his back to relax, closing his eyes, feeling the room spin, and …

It was dark when he woke, throat parched, head pounding. He sat up and noticed she was gone. He walked to the bathroom, drank three handfuls of water, and popped two Tylenol from his travel kit. He glanced at his penis and noticed he wasn't wearing a condom. Had he forgotten to put one on? No, he remembered she had asked him to wear one. He checked the bed, the floor, the trash cans. No condom.

His wallet, keys, and phone were still there, though.

McCracken checked out late that morning, ate breakfast at McDonalds, and made it to Vegas by three p.m. Howser was waiting for him in front of a self-storage building at Big Sasquatch Office Park on Pecos Road.

"Nice trip?" asked Howser.

"Uneventful."

"Well, nothing wrong with that. Follow me, time to start your training."

McCracken was pissed. He had just driven nearly two thousand miles over two and a half days. He wanted to relax.

"What's the rush?" he asked.

Howser wasn't grinning this time. He always grinned, but not this time.

"Because we think your boy isn't dead," he said. "And if all goes well, we can help you get him back."

Ten

T*oo much time has passed.*

That was the first thing that popped into McCracken's head.

And where was Finn now?

Howser's nonchalant attitude angered him. How dare he drop that bomb, then turn and stroll toward the building like it was no big deal.

McCracken grabbed Howser's arm and spun him around.

"Whoa there," said Howser. "What's the problem?"

"What do you mean, he's still alive?"

"I'm saying it's a possibility."

"How do you know that?"

"It's classified."

"Don't fuck with me. If you know something about Finn, tell me now."

Howser sighed. "I wish it were that easy," he said. "We'll talk inside. There's an old friend who'll help get you up to speed."

Howser punched in the keypad code, waited for a soft click, and turned the heavy industrial handle to open the door. He asked McCracken to enter first.

McCracken hesitated, studying Howser's eyes for any sign of deception. After a few seconds he entered, momentarily blinded as his eyes adjusted to the long, dark hallway.

"Watch your step," said Howser. "Place isn't quite finished, some wiring may be exposed."

They walked toward a bright light, which McCracken soon saw was the entrance to a room at the end of the hall. Their footsteps echoed off the concrete floor and walls.

The room was larger than McCracken had expected—roughly the size and shape of two basketball courts placed side by side. It appeared to be a science or medical laboratory of some sort: dozens of computer screens blinking numbers and charts; rows of tables crowded with scientific gear and machines. A soft, mechanized hum filled the vast space, which had plenty of chairs but no people.

McCracken found it odd that a huge laboratory wouldn't be filled with busy scientists.

He spotted a lone, dark-skinned man sitting at a computer screen at the opposite end of the room. The man rose calmly, picked something off his white lab coat, and walked with a slight limp toward them.

"Hello, Mr. McCracken," said Baldwin, trying to smile but failing.

They shook hands. McCracken nodded.

"We'll enjoy a brief lunch before we begin," said Baldwin. "There's a lot to learn."

"Where's Finn?" asked McCracken.

Baldwin didn't answer, but rather turned and walked toward a small lunchroom adjacent to the main room. A plate of sandwiches, drinks, and pastries sat on a long conference table. One wall was lined with vending machines—all empty. Baldwin motioned for McCracken to take a seat.

"Please eat," said Howser.

"Yes, food is important," Baldwin added.

McCracken decided to be patient. If they could help him, that was a good thing. He suddenly realized how hungry he was. He grabbed three sandwiches—steak, chicken, and albacore tuna—a bag of organic vinegar-and-salt potato chips, and a Coke Zero.

Howser opened a bottled water. Baldwin didn't get anything. They sat across from McCracken.

"Now is as good a time as any to begin," said Baldwin. "Tell me, Mr. McCracken, I recall you telling us you're a fan of the Discovery Channel. Perhaps you've seen or read shows or articles about what's called the Mutational Meltdown Theory?"

McCracken's mouth was stuffed with food. He shook his head *no*.

"It's not a theory that I conceived, nor did I coin the term," said Baldwin. "A simple online search will reveal much information on the topic—sadly, most of it inaccurate."

"This theory is at the core of what we do," added Howser, fiddling with buttons on a tabletop console. An image appeared on a wall-mounted electronic whiteboard. Bold black text read: CRYPTO.

"What we're about to share with you is highly sensitive information," said Baldwin. "You're not to tell another living soul about it, do you understand?"

McCracken nodded.

"I need to hear your answer—yes or no?"

"Yeth," said McCracken, spitting a chip fragment onto the table.

"Very good," said Baldwin, nodding at Howser,

who tapped a button. A new slide appeared with simple drawings of a mastodon, a saber-toothed cat, a pterodactyl, and a human male standing beside a large question mark. "Mutational Meltdown" appeared at the bottom of the slide.

"Essentially, the Mutational Meltdown theory states that an accumulation of destructive mutations in a specific population ultimately leads to procreative decline and, in a worst-case scenario, the extinction of the affected population," said Baldwin. "Let's assume, for instance, that a significant number of these mutations take hold within a species. What happens? The birth rate begins to drop, and when it falls below what's known as the 'death rate,' the population size starts to decline."

McCracken found the subject matter interesting, but the slides weren't very good at all. And the way Baldwin spoke—slow and monotonous—made him sleepy.

The next slide was simply a list of countries.

"The decline in human birthrate is an established phenomenon across the globe. Numerous nations—Japan, Taiwan, Poland, Russia, Brazil, China, Germany, South Korea, and, well, I could go on and on—are grappling with this issue. The United States' fertility rate is falling as well, but its population is rising due primarily to immigration and longer lifespans. Octogenarians are quite common these days, as are nonagenarians and centenarians."

McCracken opened another bag of chips. "So humans are dying out?" he asked.

"Declining, not dying," Baldwin corrected.

"And not if we have a say in it," added Howser.

"Declines take a while to show up in population estimates globally, but soon they'll be readily apparent," said Baldwin.

"You'll see considerable news coverage on this topic."

"This is the driving force behind automation and robotics," Baldwin continued. "As the human workforce declines—and it will sooner than expected, based on our mathematical model—the need for automation will spike. Factory workers, manual laborers, truck drivers, airline pilots, lab technicians, financial advisors, lawyers—all are at risk for professional obsolescence."

McCracken nodded.

"This transition is inevitable unless we can halt or slow the mutational meltdown," said Howser. "And it's equally important that a switch to robotics not happen too abruptly, or social unrest will develop."

He switched to a slide showing people

protesting in the streets. They held signs that weren't in English.

"So why am I here?" asked McCracken.

"Research is in its early days, but promising," said Baldwin. "Two years ago, I led a team at Baylor College of Medicine that discovered a rare, unique protein in sperm. We estimate that only one in 500 million males has this protein."

"Or one in a billion, we're not exactly sure," added Howser.

The next image was a close-up of thousands of sperm swimming toward an egg.

"It has exceptional value in a variety of use cases," Baldwin said.

"Some are good, others potentially quite harmful," noted Howser.

"You see, outside of the egg, there is a protective coat called the zona pellucida," said Baldwin, waving his right hand over his left fist. "It prevents other species' sperm from fertilizing the egg."

"You can only imagine the chaos if the zona pellucida didn't exist," added Howser.

"Yes, chaos, truly," added Baldwin, frowning. McCracken figured Baldwin was pissed at Howser's lame comments, which didn't add a lot to the conversation.

"Think of the zona pellucida as a sentry

protecting the palace," Baldwin continued. "Its job is to stop foreign sperms from invading."

"Okay," said McCracken.

"There are specific proteins on individual sperms that identify them as foreign to the egg. Each species has a specific amount of genetic material, and altering that balance could lead to severe defects."

"Like what?"

"We'll get back to that. The reason we're sharing this with you—and here's the classified component you must not share with anyone—is that we've discovered … well, let's call it a 'mutational force' that enables interspecies combinations or hybrids. A very, very limited number of human males has a protein that allows this. To explain this phenomenon, I've coined the term *Universaliter Acceptos*, which is Latin for 'universally accepted.'"

"What this means is, sperm with this trait has the ability to penetrate the zona pellucida and fertilize virtually any egg, regardless of species," said Howser.

McCracken was beginning to understand the ramifications.

"How long has this … universal thing been around?" he asked.

"I don't understand your question," said Baldwin.

"This Acceptos thing, the sperm. Has it always been like that, only a few guys having it?"

"We can't answer that," said Howser. "Insufficient data."

"But you're saying you could, what, mix a human and a cow?"

"Conceivably, yes," said Baldwin. "We've made great strides in that area. Until very recently there was a high likelihood the fetus would be aborted early in the prenatal phase, the defects detected immediately by the host organism."

"The what?"

"The mother," said Howser.

"How can you tell if a guy has this?"

"A genetic test performed on a semen sample, but we're working on a blood test as well—far less invasive," said Baldwin. "If the test shows a strong likelihood of the *Universaliter Acceptos* protein, we'll proceed."

"There have been cases where the test indicates a false positive," said Howser. "So it's not always perfect."

"Success rate is now at seventy-eight percent and rising," added Baldwin.

Howser changed to a new slide, which showed

an earth globe on a metal desk. McCracken was getting bored with the slides.

"You've probably heard a lot about robots taking jobs," said Howser. "But the reality is that you can't have complete robotization of the labor force without billions of consumers being negatively impacted."

"People without jobs can't afford to buy things," added Baldwin.

McCracken opened a new Coke Zero.

"They can't buy phones or TVs or automobiles or other consumer goods," said Howser. "They don't stay in hotels, take cruises, or gamble in casinos. They don't go to restaurants or shopping malls."

"And that's bad for everyone," said Baldwin.

No shit, McCracken thought.

"Robotics alone don't make a lot of sense, long-term," said Howser. "A consumer-driven economy with out-of-work consumers doesn't work. And universal income, I'm afraid, is a utopian pipe dream."

McCracken was doing his best to be patient, but he wanted the conversation to get back to Finn.

"Unless …," said Howser, his voice falling to a whisper. "Unless you meld robotics with an optimized human workforce."

"Hybridization," added Baldwin. "Mixing and matching species with digital upgrades to produce a better workforce."

"It's a triple play," said Howser.

McCracken understood now. The tests. The semen samples.

"So I'm one of those guys," he said.

Baldwin glanced at Howser, who nodded.

"Yes, we spent three years testing members of the U.S. military, with full support of the Pentagon, which saw a significant strategic advantage in the hybridization option," said Baldwin. "There's more you'll need to know about this."

Baldwin walked around the table and sat next to McCracken, who smelled the familiar stale coffee breath.

"*Universaliter Acceptos* research is known to select entities—some developed nations, international agencies, multinationals, and others—a few of whom are conducting experiments that might be construed as … ethically dubious," said Baldwin.

"What experiments?"

"That's classified," said Howser. "Available only on a need-to-know basis."

McCracken was silent for a few seconds. "This doesn't sound right," he said.

"We've followed your military career, we've

researched your personal history, and, of course, we're aware of your genetic gift," said Howser. "In short, you have attributes that can help us achieve our goals."

McCracken was ready to leave. These guys were bullshitting him, telling half-truths. They thought he was stupid, but he wasn't.

"I'm out," he said, standing.

Baldwin grabbed his arm. "We need you," he said.

"I'm not interested."

"We need to block rogue entities from exploiting *Universaliter Acceptos* to their advantage."

Howser advanced to the next slide. McCracken shuddered at what he saw. It had to be fake.

"If you're wondering if it's real, yes, it is," said Howser. "This particular experiment took place at an orphanage in Romania two years ago. An Interpol raid ended it. The infants you see here were destroyed a few weeks after birthing successfully, although most would have died anyway."

"This wasn't our experiment, of course, but it's proof that hybridization is achievable via the *Universaliter Acceptos* techniques, which I pioneered," said Baldwin.

"Turn it off," said McCracken, looking away.

"Excuse me?"

"Turn that fucking thing off."

Howser closed his notebook. The image vanished from the wall.

McCracken's hands were shaking. He stood, walked toward the door, then stopped and stared at the rows of machines in the main room.

"There's no way that was real," he said, pointing at the wall where the image had been.

"I'm afraid it is," said Howser.

"How is that ... even possible?"

"The level of hybridization in the slide is just the beginning. Mammalian species are relatively easy to combine, particularly in the embryonic stage. We're moving beyond that now."

"*Universaliter Acceptos* enables us to grow specific body parts and use them outside the species they were designed for," said Baldwin. "Or transplant biologic components into a living host to bolster its capabilities."

"What you just showed me ... it's fucked up."

"We weren't responsible."

"You created it."

"Our classified research found its way into the wrong hands. Multiple hands, in fact."

"You don't seem too upset about it," said McCracken. "What they did to those kids."

"This sort of thing is a byproduct of genetic

research," said Baldwin. "But, yes, the Romanian experiment was unethical."

"We wouldn't sanction that," added Howser.

McCracken bolted from the room, sprinting full speed toward the exit. He reached the hallway door leading to the parking lot, but the handle was locked. He kicked the metal door repeatedly, then the handle.

He turned and saw silhouettes of two men approaching.

"Open the goddamn door!"

They stopped a safe distance away.

"Please reconsider," said Howser.

"You brought me here to … jizz in a test tube? For more of that?"

"A lot of good can come from this," said Baldwin.

McCracken couldn't help but laugh. He thought of *Willy Wonka & the Chocolate Factory*—an old movie he had watched many times with Finn.

He sat on the cold cement floor, facing the two men. Laughing, then weeping. He had the golden ticket.

Howser and Baldwin maintained their distance. McCracken was glad they did. At that moment, he would have killed them both.

"Where's Finn?" he asked again. "Is he mixed up in this?"

"We believe he was kidnapped, but his whereabouts are unclear," said Howser. "It was years ago."

"Who did it?"

"That's classified."

"I swear to fucking god, if one of you says 'classified' one more time—"

"Calm down."

"Why Finn?"

"He's your son," said Baldwin. "It's suspected that *Universaliter Acceptos* is hereditary. The data is insufficient, however."

"They kidnapped a four-year-old kid—for his sperm?"

"All the more reason to be hopeful," said Howser. "For them to, for lack of a better word, harvest the product, they'd need to keep him alive and healthy until puberty, and probably a long time after."

"It is the truth, sir," said Baldwin.

McCracken held his head in his hands. "Every night for years I've prayed my boy is dead, and now you tell me this," he said. "Why did you wait so long?"

"We didn't get clearance until a few days ago. We wanted to tell you, but couldn't," said Howser.

"So will you help us?" asked Baldwin.

McCracken lay back on the floor and stared at the ceiling. "Tell me what I have to do," he said. "Because I won't stop until I get him back …"

"Good man," said Howser.

"… and every last one of them is dead."

He was given two options: sleep on an inflatable mattress in an unused storage room inside the laboratory, or stay at the Lay-Z 8 Motel across the street. McCracken chose the latter, mostly because the former didn't have a window. The bad news was that he had to pay the motel's weekly rate out of pocket, whereas he could've crashed at the lab for free.

McCracken didn't mind. He was getting paid now and the Laz-Z 8 was cheap. It even had a kitchenette with a microwave, so he didn't have to eat out all the time.

His days were spent participating in a series of tests conducted by Baldwin and three lab researchers who spoke as little as possible. McCracken came up with a name for the trio: The Silent Assistants. One was a thin, pale white guy, six feet tall, with a patchy beard. He looked sickly,

McCracken thought, and needed to exercise and get some sun. The second Seeker was a short, balding Asian guy who smiled a lot and spent much of his time staring at computer screens. His name was Carl and he had a thick Chinese accent. The third was a woman with long red hair and thick-framed glasses. She always wore a long lab coat with white Reebok shoes—the kind you'd wear to the gym. McCracken always wondered what her body looked like under the shapeless coat.

He hated providing a semen sample every third day, which apparently was the proper length of time for his body to replenish the *Universaliter Acceptos* protein. The only time the female assistant spoke to him was when she asked for a sample. Her voice was soothing and gentle. McCracken was always embarrassed to hand her his specimen cup, just as he had been years earlier with the pretty nurse at the Dorn VA.

He did enjoy their brief encounters, though. They'd meet in the lunchroom and she'd politely request his sample. He'd remove the specimen cup from a paper bag and sheepishly hand it over. She'd hold it up to the light, examine it for a second or two, glance back at him—her eyes sometimes moving down his body—and then leave the room without a word.

The tests seemed endless.

"They're a variation of MIT's Moral Machine," explained Baldwin. "These tests provide a crowd-sourced view of human opinion on how machines should react when facing moral dilemmas."

McCracken didn't understand.

"You'll have to mull potential scenarios of moral consequence," Baldwin added, "and ultimately reach difficult decisions."

Each test featured an animated video clip with crudely drawn characters. The first video showed a group of five children walking alongside a lake shoreline. The kids were young, maybe five or six, and holding hands. An unkempt old man with a matted beard, torn clothing, and flies buzzing around his head was walking a few steps behind them. He snickered lecherously as he approached the kids, who were unaware of his presence. An alligator emerged from the lake and clamped its jaws on one of the children's legs.

The video stopped. McCracken, shirtless with electrodes strapped to his chest, biceps, and forehead, leaned back in his recliner and looked at Baldwin.

"There is only one way to save the child," said

Baldwin. "Push the elderly man onto the alligator, which will release the child, bite the man, and drag him into the swamp. Alternatively, you could do nothing and let the child die."

That's easy, McCracken thought. So what if the creepy old man dies? "I'd push him," he said.

The next scenario had the same lakeshore setting, but this time the kids were throwing rocks at the old man, who was too feeble to run away. The man fell to his knees and started to cry. The alligator emerged from the swamp and grabbed one of the children by the leg. The video stopped.

"To save the child, you must push the old man in front of the alligator," said Baldwin. "Make a decision."

This one was harder. The kids were being jerks, true, but they were young and had a chance to redeem themselves. The old man, on the other hand, had lived a long life, hopefully a good one, and maybe could be sacrificed to save a child, even a rotten one.

"I'd push the old man," said McCracken. "But I'd kick those kids' asses for being mean."

Baldwin frowned. "'Kicking their asses' isn't an option, sir," he said. "You can't choose that."

"But they—"

"Choose."

The old man died again.

The next video made McCracken sick to his stomach. The children were stabbing the old man with knives, blood gushing from open wounds all over his body. He was screaming for mercy. The alligator grabbed one of the kids. The video stopped.

"Decide," said Baldwin.

"I don't like this test anymore," said McCracken.

"Decide."

"They shouldn't be stabbing the old man."

"That's not the question. Would you push the old man onto the alligator to save the child?"

"No ... I mean yes. Shit, I don't know."

McCracken stood up and ripped the electrodes off his chest and arms. "This test is fucked up," he snapped. "I'm done."

"Sit back down!" commanded Baldwin. There was a forcefulness in his voice, an authoritarian tone that made McCracken think of his CO. The soldier in him responded appropriately. He obeyed the order, sitting patiently while Baldwin reapplied the electrodes.

"So then," said Baldwin. "Your decision?"

"I guess, well, I don't want the kids to die. But they shouldn't be stabbing the guy."

Baldwin sighed. "That's not what I'm asking."

"I don't know. Maybe I'd let them die. No … I wouldn't. I don't like to see kids getting hurt."

"Fine. We'll proceed to the final clip."

The last video began with a close-up of the old man walking along the path. He was smiling, laughing, and chatting with others out of frame. The man was friendly and calm, not dangerous or threatening or victimized. The camera pulled back, revealing three creatures that gave McCracken chills. One was a goat with a boy's head. Another was a reptilian creature with a lizard's face and a scaly primate body. It walked upright on two legs, wore a backpack, and had a New York Yankees cap on its head. The third creature had a girl's head, a chicken's torso, and rabbit legs.

The alligator clamped its enormous jaws around all three of the creatures' legs. Two of the creatures screamed like children; the lizard-like one squawked like a bird. The video stopped.

"Decide."

McCracken found the creatures silly and disturbing. They reminded him of Finn's disappearance and that … whatever it was … that one of the kids claimed had dragged his boy into the brush. A feeling of helplessness and sadness returned. He wanted to leave and resented Baldwin for making him feel this way.

"Let them die," McCracken mumbled.

"Excuse me?"

"Let them all die. The old man can live, he's the only human."

"Did you not notice the human characteristics of the other three characters?"

"They're not real people."

"Are you sure? They were speaking and laughing like people."

"No, they're not."

Baldwin scribbled on his notepad, got up, and left the room. A minute later, the female assistant entered with a tray of food, which she set on a table before removing McCracken's electrodes. Her touch gave him chills.

"Enjoy your lunch," she said before leaving the room. He hated that her lab coat was so shapeless.

McCracken decided it was time to go.

No more semen cups or mind games. He would find Finn on his own.

It was close to midnight when he began stuffing a pillowcase with the few possessions he had: a change of socks and underwear, two clean t-shirts, and a plastic bag of toiletries. Earlier that evening he had told the red-haired woman he was leaving. He apologized for not preparing a sample for her.

McCracken heard a loud knock on his motel room door. He looked through the peephole and saw Howser's face.

"What is it?" asked McCracken, opening the door.

"I hear you're quitting."

"Yeah."

"That's unfortunate. You'll need to pick up your final check."

"Can you mail it to me?"

"Where are you headed?"

"I'm not sure yet."

"Come to the lab and get your check."

Baldwin and the Silent Assistants were waiting for them in the conference room. The red-haired woman was the only one who smiled when McCracken entered.

"Coffee?" Howser asked McCracken. "It's fresh."

"Where's my check?"

"Carl will get it for you," said Howser. "Carl?"

Carl frowned, rose from his seat, and left the room.

"Before you go, there's something you must see."

"I'm not staying."

"Fine, we support your decision," said Howser.

"I don't like what you're doing with—"

"Understandable. Perfectly understandable. Would you agree to stay with us if you didn't have to do that anymore?"

"No."

"What about Finn?"

"I'll find him on my own."

"We can help."

"You haven't so far."

Howser went to the Mr. Coffee and poured a cup of French Roast. "Two sugars, two half-and-halves, right?" he asked McCracken.

The coffee smelled good and McCracken had a long drive ahead. He was heading back to Phoenix to crash at his mom's place, assuming she still lived there.

Howser brought the coffee to McCracken, who took the cup and sipped the hot liquid. It was just right—not too hot, not too sweet.

"We'll miss you," said Howser. "Why not have a seat until the check arrives?"

McCracken sat across from Baldwin, who stared intensely at him. McCracken looked away.

"Before you go, there's something you should know," said Howser. "We've received reports that

Universaliter Acceptos ... well, for lack of a better word, *product* ... will soon be shipping around the world for reasons unknown. Another group is doing this, not us. The cargo reportedly will be transported via self-driving trucks to minimize the risk of security leaks."

"Product?" asked McCracken.

"Biologically and digitally diverse entities," said Baldwin.

McCracken flashed back to pictures from the Romanian orphanage. He felt sick.

Howser handed McCracken a jacket patch shaped like a boomerang. Primitive drawings—like cave paintings of bison that McCracken had seen in a TV documentary on early humans—covered the patch.

"What's this?" McCracken asked.

"Memorize this patch," said Howser. "Memorize its exact shape and size, as well as its markings and images. This is the enemy."

"You'll have help, of course," said Baldwin.

"Help doing what?"

"You'll need to stop these trucks and retrieve the cargo," said Howser. "You'll have two assistants who won't know the true purpose of these missions."

"Your Ranger skills will prove beneficial," added Baldwin.

McCracken shook his head. "Why should I?"

"Because our intelligence tells us they're transporting children. Finn may be one of the kids involved."

McCracken's hands began shaking. He set the coffee cup on the table.

"How do I know you're telling the truth?"

"Would you like another photo?" Howser asked.

"Of what?"

"Do you want to see it? If you do, I'm sure you'll see things our way."

"Fuck you and your photos," said McCracken, standing. "I'm out."

Howser nodded at the woman, who handed McCracken a four-by-six color print.

He stared at the image in disbelief, then fell to his knees and sobbed. He began hyperventilating, hoping and praying the image was fake.

Howser helped McCracken to his feet and hugged him tightly.

"Will you help us now?"

Yes. Of course he would.

Eleven

It had been two weeks since the botched Paragosa heist, and they were bored out of their minds.

Howser had arranged for them to crash in Vegas at a foreclosed home on the Westside—a graffiti-scarred dump with security bars on every window. The neighbors didn't seem to mind that three men with no furniture were living there. There were more important things to worry about, namely a halfway house filled with paroled sex offenders. McCracken, Perlman, and Buscado were the least of their worries.

The Pahrump hideout was off-limits for now. Howser was a bit vague as to why, but when McCracken pressed him, he said a suspicious van marked "Sagebrush Plumbing" was often parked on the street for hours at a time, its engine running, with one man reading a newspaper behind the wheel.

Fuentes stopped by the crash pad every day to deliver supplies, usually Lean Cuisine, six-packs of Coke Zero and Bud Light Lime, and Marlboros for Buscado. Perlman didn't joke with her because McCracken threatened to kick his ass if he did.

Shit, nobody had a sense of humor anymore.

McCracken and Fuentes would leave every afternoon in her car. Perlman figured they were banging hard at her place, but McCracken wouldn't say. They always returned early in the evening before the neighborhood got too scary. She would drop him off at the curb.

Perlman wondered why Fuentes was mixed up in all of this. Love? No, had to be more than that. She seemed to genuinely like McCracken, always calling him *hon* and *babe*, and grabbing his butt when she thought no one was looking.

But Perlman was always looking. He was jealous that McCracken was getting laid like clockwork. Why not him? McCracken was dumb as a rock, whereas he was a genius.

And why was Howser keeping her around? She was expendable.

Maybe because Fuentes dealt blackjack at Barnaby's Casino, which was somehow mixed up in all of this.

If they failed a third time, Perlman was out. Mauritius awaited: Greyhound to LAX—McCarron was far too obvious—and then first-class on Air France. No one would ever find him in Mauritius, and lucrative black-hat work would keep him busy forever.

Fuentes always made McCracken wear a condom.

She was on top tonight as always, working fast because her employers insisted upon it. Baldwin's instructions were clear: immediately following ejaculation, she was to carefully remove the semen-filled condom, bring it to the bathroom, place it in a time-stamped specimen jar, and store it in the mini-fridge hidden under the sink.

She hated her job.

It had been a year since she first met Howser after applying to a Craigslist ad:

Part-time Help Wanted: Female Assistant for medical testing, some nursing experience helpful but not necessary. Good pay. Must be willing to work flexible hours. Send photo with resume.

The ad was suspicious. Photo? Probably some perv or pic collector, but Fuentes replied because Barnaby's Casino had cut her hours to twenty per week, three to seven a.m. The tables were empty, tips light.

Fuentes had taken a few nursing courses during an 18-month stint in community college, but was never motivated enough to earn a degree.

That was seven years ago.

Born and raised in San Antonio, she was the only child of immigrants. Her father blamed her mother for their inability to make more babies. He would disappear for months at a time, sometimes calling for a ride home or bail money, and finally left for good when Rosa turned eleven.

Fuentes got straight As in high school but didn't apply to college, at least not right away. After graduation she moved to Phoenix with her boyfriend—a kickboxer who spent all day at the gym. They soon ran out of money, got evicted from their studio apartment, and moved into his truck. After three nights of misery, he got a bold idea.

"Drive me down to CVS, baby," he said.

It was around eleven p.m. when Fuentes parked in the empty lot. She watched him hurry into the pharmacy, hoodie over his head, gun in his right pocket. She wanted to drive off but didn't.

The first gunshot made her jump. Before she knew it he was sprinting toward the truck, jumping in the passenger side.

The next morning Fuentes watched the TV news at McDonald's while ordering breakfast for two. He hid in the truck.

Lead story: her boyfriend on the security cam, shooting a CVS clerk.

Fuentes never went back to the truck. She borrowed an old lady's flip phone, called 911, and gave an anonymous tip. Cops swarmed the truck minutes later.

"I love you, baby," he told her when she visited him at County Jail. "Told 'em I acted alone, drove the truck and everything. You got nothin' to worry about."

The trial was quick. She missed a few days but went when she could. Verdict: guilty. Sentence: twenty-five to life.

She never wrote or visited him. After eighteen months, his letters stopped coming. She worried a lot. He could still rat her out.

She moved to Vegas. More bad boyfriends.

Briefly hooked on Percocet after injuring her knee, then OxyContin. Tried stripping to support her habit, but was fired for being too skinny. Kicked drugs, acted in two videos she wanted to forget, and borrowed money from her mom for community college.

Nursing wasn't for her. Next came Barnaby's, which paid well in good times but not recently. She was broke again.

Now she had a Starbucks interview with a man named Howser, the Craigslist guy who liked her photo.

It was 3:05 p.m. and he was five minutes late. Just another flake, probably. She'd wait ten more minutes, enough time to finish her caramel vanilla iced coffee. A minute later a very tall, thin man entered Starbucks, spotted her immediately, and smiled. An insincere smile, she thought. He walked to her table. "Rosa?" he asked. She nodded and shook his hand.

"I'll keep this brief because, well, I don't want to go into details in a public space," Howser said. "I'm offering you the opportunity to make one thousand a week, cash."

She rolled her eyes. "I'm not a prostitute."

"It's not prostitution, and you and I won't be having a physical relationship. Strictly professional. However …"

Howser opened his wallet, pulled out a photo, and handed it to her. "I want you to be this man's girlfriend."

She was surprised. The guy had a rugged, handsome face. She wondered what the rest of him looked like.

"No thanks," she said, sliding the photo back across the table.

"Why?"

"Because it's weird."

"And why do you say that?"

"A guy who looks like that doesn't need help finding a girlfriend. Unless there's something really wrong with him."

"There isn't."

"Then what is this shit?"

"It's unusual, yes, but I promise you won't be in any danger. I'll pay in cash—under the table, no taxes—every week."

Against her better judgment, she agreed to meet him again the next morning. She picked the time and place: ten a.m. at the High Roller Ferris wheel off the Strip. Tourists everywhere. If this Howser guy turned out to be a serial killer, she wanted an easy escape route.

Turned out the gig was weirder than she had imagined.

Her "job" was to have sex with the rugged guy, whose name apparently was McCracken. Twice a week would suffice. She started laughing when Howser told her about the semen collection, which was "crucial to the mission."

"There's someone I'd like you to meet," said Howser, waving toward a large crowd loitering outside a Panda Express. Baldwin, dressed in black slacks and a white, buttoned-down shirt, emerged from the crowd, which seemed oblivious to his presence. He appeared to be frowning as he walked toward them. But as he came closer, Fuentes noticed his expression was merely blank.

"Rosa Fuentes, Dr. Charles Baldwin," said Howser. As they shook hands, a smile formed on one side of Baldwin's mouth, then quickly vanished.

"Will you help us change the world?" Baldwin asked.

Fuentes laughed, Baldwin didn't. Clearly, he was serious.

"So … can you tell me what this is all about?" she asked.

Howser spoke first about the rising threat of automation, the dangers of economic power concentrated in a tiny percentage of the population, and of the great need for the common people to retake control of the global economy. He was eloquent and convincing—clearly a gifted speaker—but Fuentes had no idea what his little sermon had to do with her.

Baldwin was next. Drab and monotone, he spoke in vague generalities about the world-changing potential of something he called *Universaliter Acceptos*.

"A properly managed *Acceptos* program can save our endangered species from the Extinction Vortex," said Baldwin, leaning closer. "We can make that happen."

"Okay."

"The man we're asking you to ... um, form a relationship with, there's something very special about him, genetically speaking," said Howser. "The easiest way for us to extract the *Acceptos* protein is via harvesting."

"By collecting his semen," said Fuentes.

"Exactly."

"Without telling him."

"Well ... yes."

Without saying another word, Fuentes turned and walked away. The two men didn't try to stop her.

Two days later, Fuentes' mom called from San Antonio and asked for money to help cover her health insurance. And her car payment. And rent. Fuentes went to work that evening, only to learn her hours were being cut again.

"Fuckin' no good economy, Rosa," her boss said, shaking his head. "Fuckin' economy."

She now was down to ten hours a week.

She called Howser the next day, saying she was considering his proposal. "Just one question," she asked, "why don't you tell this guy what you're up to?"

There were a few seconds of phone silence. "That's classified," said Howser.

"Classified?"

"Yes."

"What does that mean?"

"It means I can't divulge further details."

"What is this, some sort of top-secret government thing?"

"In a sense, yes," said Howser. "I understand it's all very peculiar, but I assure you it's for the best. No harm will come to you."

Fuentes mulled her options.

"Hello?"

"Still here," she replied.

"Will you help us?"

"It just doesn't feel right."

"Let me elaborate," said Howser. "We're trying to help him accomplish a personal goal—one very, very important to him. He, in turn, is helping us. And you can help us as well."

"For one thousand a week, cash."

"Yes, that's our agreement."

"Paid every Friday, no exceptions."

"If those are your terms, we accept."

"They are. And if you miss one payment, I walk."

The next day she went to a meeting—Howser called it a "rally"—of about two dozen people at the Fairfield Inn. The meeting room was super cheap, she overheard Howser telling Baldwin: only $55 for two hours.

Fuentes wondered why they rented such a cheap space if they were paying her a thousand a week.

It was there she met McCracken—a very large man standing alone at the refreshments table, eating nachos and cheese. Fuentes walked over and introduced herself. "Hey," he mumbled, his mouth full. They sat together during Howser's speech, which she didn't really listen to.

She found herself attracted to McCracken. He was strange, silent, and sweet. And he looked exactly like his photo.

Baldwin spoke next. Blah blah blah. Fuentes was dying for the event to end, which it did ninety minutes later.

She planned to make a move right away but didn't have to. McCracken asked her out first.

They had sex at her place after the third date. And then again the following night, and pretty much every night after that for two weeks. Baldwin scolded her, telling her twice a week was best for *Acceptos* harvesting.

Fuentes didn't care. She found herself falling in love with McCracken and hating the deception. Plus, collecting semen was disgusting.

He often talked about his son, Finn, who she assumed was alive somewhere, maybe living in another city with his mother. Then one night, after sex, he broke into tears and told her the whole story.

The next morning she phoned Howser and said she was quitting. He told her to meet him at the High Roller at noon.

"I'm not changing my mind," she said.

"Meet me there," said Howser. "I'll pay you an extra five hundred if you do."

She did.

It was too hot to sit in the sun, so Howser suggested they talk in his car. She considered walking away, but her mom needed $500 right away. Once in the car, Howser started the engine and cranked up the AC.

"We did a background check on you," he said, looking out the window.

"What's that supposed to mean?"

"Before we hired you. We even talked to your boyfriend, the one in prison for the CVS robbery you participated in."

She was silent.

"He's angry that you've been ignoring him for years," said Howser. "Some days he swears he'll get revenge, maybe even testify against you."

"Look, it was his idea," she blurted. "I didn't even know he was gonna do it until I heard the gunshots."

"He tells a different story. You were both desperate addicts, needing cash."

"That's a lie!"

"He can be easily persuaded to talk to the police."

"You have no proof. It's his word against mine."

Howser reached into the backseat, grabbed a laptop and opened the lid. He launched a grainy parking lot security video showing Fuentes behind the wheel of her boyfriend's truck, a man in a hoodie running to the vehicle, and her speeding away.

"Took some digging, but we found this," said Howser, replaying the video. "It was misplaced and never used as evidence—wasn't needed, really, with your boyfriend valiantly protecting you."

Fuentes looked away from the screen.

"The image quality isn't great, of course. But digital enhancement works wonders these days, and we're pretty sure we can clean it up to get a clearer view of your face. Combined with his revised testimony, it's all pretty damning."

She started to cry.

Howser shut the laptop.

"You're going to continue doing what you're doing," he said. "You're going to harvest twice a week—no more, no less. If you don't, this video goes to the Clark County district attorney. Meet our terms and we'll keep your old boyfriend quiet. You might be interested to know that he's into heroin and very feminine young men now. Fascinating how our environment changes us."

Fuentes opened the car door and stepped out. "So, I'm back to work then," she said.

"Welcome back to the team," said Howser.

"Fuck you."

Twelve

The day of the heist arrived and Buscado was nervous. He had been thinking a lot about Cheryl, wondering what she was up to and why she hadn't come around lately. He wanted to ask her out, especially if the heist went well and he made serious money.

Sometimes he'd ask Howser what Cheryl was doing. The answer was always vague. "Oh, she's been busy with work" was the stock reply.

Perlman was content frequenting the meth whores who loitered near Fremont and Eastern.

McCracken wasn't saying much.

They had spent two weeks devising the plan but knew dozens of things could go wrong. This would be a brute-force attack, not one requiring computer hacks or malware. Perlman had a limited role—getaway driver—and wasn't keen on the demotion.

"Any fuckwad can drive a truck," he grumbled more than once to Howser and McCracken. But he was willing to swallow his pride for a sizable payday.

They parked on a gravel road a half-mile east of Highway 95, about 40 miles northwest of Vegas. The road led to Corn Creek National Wildlife Refuge, where an autonomous box truck, an unmarked white Ford F-350, was scheduled to make a stop before continuing on to Barnaby's, its final destination.

"That beast drives itself but with a human onboard, basically a keyboard jockey who can take manual control, if needed," Buscado noted.

"Why the babysitter—some legal shit?" asked Perlman.

"Nope, not anymore. Companies just like the idea. Pays minimum wage, I'm pretty sure. Requires basic office chores, spreadsheet-type stuff, when the rig's in transit."

As they sat in the rented U-Haul, Perlman tried

to figure out why the target rig was stopping at a wildlife refuge *and* a casino.

"Maybe just food and drink deliveries," said Buscado. "They got a pretty good visitor's center here, you know. Took my kids last year and—"

"Bullshit," interrupted Perlman. "Howser promised a big payday. That ain't happening if we're heisting microwave burritos and fruit juice. What do you think, McCracken?"

McCracken was busy texting.

"Who is that?" asked Perlman, reaching for McCracken's phone.

McCracken pushed him away.

"Hey, man, get your fuckin' head in the game!" snapped Perlman.

McCracken glared at him.

"Please share your opinion, oh wise leader, if you can stop sexting your girl for a second," said Perlman.

"What's your problem?"

"The cargo, what is it?"

McCracken set his phone on the dashboard. "Classified," he replied.

"Come on, man, we got a right to know," said Buscado.

McCracken grabbed his binoculars and looked north, studying Highway 95 for a full minute.

"Come on, use your words," Perlman said.

"There it is," said McCracken, pointing at the horizon. "F-350 box, white, looks like ... single occupant."

Perlman started the engine. McCracken and Buscado donned their wool masks.

You got this driving thing down?" Buscado asked Perlman.

"Balls of steel, my friend."

They were hiding behind a prefab warehouse a quarter mile off the highway. The F-350 turned onto the road and proceeded toward them at a steady pace.

When the F-350 was ten feet from the warehouse, Perlman hit the accelerator; the U-Haul lurched forward, blocking the truck's path.

The F-350 jerked to a stop. Its headlights began flashing red.

McCracken and Buscado, each wielding a Louisville Slugger, jumped out of the U-Haul and rushed the truck. Perlman stayed behind the wheel.

McCracken slammed the driver door with his bat. "Open up!" he shouted.

After a few seconds, the door unlocked. McCracken yanked it open.

"Hey, chill, chill," said a male voice.

A young man with pale, blotchy skin emerged from the driver's side.

"Hurry up!" shouted McCracken.

The kid stood beside the truck and held up his hands. He was holding a half-eaten Chick-O-Stick, and his eyes were hidden behind wraparound mirror sunglasses. McCracken guessed his age was nineteen, maybe twenty.

"It's all yours but I gotta warn you, man, the thing's already phoned home," the kid said. "Happens the second it senses trouble."

"So turn it off," said Buscado.

"Can't do it. I'm just the babysitter."

"Open the cargo hold," said McCracken.

"Don't have the code," the kid said. "Like I said, I'm just here to make sure nothing goes wrong."

"A lot's gonna go wrong if you don't open that hold."

"Hurry it up!" Perlman yelled from the U-Haul.

McCracken checked his watch. If the kid was telling the truth, they were short on time.

Perlman shouted again: "Stop circle-jerkin' and move it!"

"Shit, go see what he wants," McCracken told Buscado, who jogged back to the U-Haul.

"You're one of those guys, aren't you?" the kid asked McCracken.

"What guys?"

"They warned us about you," the kid said. "What are you after?"

"None of your goddamn business."

The kid removed his sunglasses. His back was to the U-Haul. Only McCracken could see his eyes. "Pretty cool, huh?" he asked.

McCracken felt sick to his stomach.

"This truck's a decoy," the kid said. "If you want the good stuff, it'll come right behind us in an armored car."

"What stuff?"

"Some cars move only money, but others also have hidden compartments hiding people and shit."

"People?"

"Yeah, sort of. Look, I don't know what they want."

McCracken pushed the kid aside and walked to the back of the F-350. He smashed the cargo door's padlock several times before breaking it.

He lifted the door. The hold was empty.

"See, I wasn't lying," the kid said. "The next truck, the armored one, that's got the good stuff."

"Why are you telling me this?"

"I want a cut—finder's fee."

"You blowin' that guy, McCracken?" shouted Perlman.

"Shit, the light hurts my eyes," said the kid, putting his sunglasses back on.

McCracken was anxious. "How long till it gets here?" he asked.

"I'd have to check the itinerary."

"Best guess."

"Well, I think it started in Reno, like me, and made stops at Fallon, Silver Peak, and Amargosa Valley. Should be here any minute."

"Hey, McCracker! Having tea with your girlfriend?"

McCracken stomped back to the U-Haul. "What the fuck is your problem?" he asked Perlman.

"What's your problem?"

"Shut up and listen. It's a short walk back to the highway. You're gonna go on foot and meet us there."

"No, I'm the driver."

"Not anymore you're not."

"Yeah? I ain't walking. It's hot out there and I'm not hiking with a wool mask on my face."

McCracken opened the driver door, grabbed Perlman by the hair, and dragged him out of the U-Haul.

Perlman, spitting and swearing, fell to his knees in the dirt.

"Put your mask on," said McCracken.

"Lick my load."

McCracken waved the kid over.

Perlman put on his mask and began walking toward the highway. The others boarded the U-Haul with Buscado behind the wheel.

The U-Haul edged around the stalled F-350, which turned off its flashers and resumed its journey the moment its path was clear.

"It's back on track," said the kid. "But they're gonna check on it anyway."

The U-Haul passed Perlman. A dirt cloud bounced off the passenger window.

Buscado stopped the truck 50 feet from the highway. The kid pointed north. "There it is!" he shouted.

Buscado and McCracken stared at the horizon but saw nothing.

"Just one driver too," the kid continued. "Shit, he's pickin' his nose. What a loser!"

"What? There's nothing out there," said Buscado.

"Sure there is," the kid replied.

"You see anything, McCracken?"

McCracken didn't answer.

A dark spot appeared on the horizon—a vehicle coming toward them.

"Five seven eight two ampersand G dash zero two A eight," said the kid. "That's it alright."

"What are you talking about?" asked Buscado.

"The plate," said the kid.

"How can you read it from here?"

The vehicle came closer. Buscado had a clearer view.

"Armored transport," he said. "Definitely one of Anderman's, I'd know that design anywhere."

"You know your trucks," the kid noted.

"I'll corral it," said Buscado.

"Go easy," McCracken said.

"Got this," replied Buscado, hitting the accelerator hard.

The U-Haul darted across the highway, swerving in front of the southbound armored van.

The van's driver made a rash evasive maneuver, turning hard to the right to avoid a collision. It tilted on two wheels, veered off the highway, and rolled twice before coming to a stop halfway down a hill.

"I told you to go easy!" shouted McCracken.

A cloud of dust rose from the wreck.

Buscado parked the U-Haul on the southbound shoulder. McCracken checked for approaching vehicles, but the road was empty for now.

"Stay here," McCracken told the kid.

He and Buscado scrambled down the hill to where the crashed van sat on its side.

"Tell me if you hear anything strange," said McCracken.

"Like what?"

"Anything."

The van's passenger side was wedged against a car-sized boulder. The rear door was open, hanging by a hinge.

"Anderman quality," cracked Buscado. "Always pieces of shit."

McCracken checked on the driver, who was holding his head and moaning.

"Hey, look!" Buscado yelled.

McCracken went to the back of the van, where Buscado was unloading brown courier satchels and tossing them onto the hillside.

"Anything else in there?" asked McCracken.

"Who cares, we hit the jackpot!"

McCracken tapped the walls, hoping to reveal secret compartments but finding none. The truck was ferrying money, nothing else.

"That's enough," he said. "We gotta go."

"There's a shit-ton of cash here! If we get Perlman we can—"

"Let's go!"

They hauled two satchels apiece up the hill,

each sack the size of a bowling ball bag. The kid and Perlman were waiting by the U-Haul.

A few cars drove past, their occupants unable to spot the wreckage halfway down the hill. But the sight of men in black ski masks no doubt caught their attention.

"Load up and let's go," said McCracken, handing one satchel to the kid. "Not sure how much is in there, but it's pretty heavy."

"Take me with you," the kid said.

"No."

"Aw, come on."

"No."

"I'll ride in back."

"You'll never see us again," said McCracken. "Now get back to your truck before they get here."

"Drop me off in town."

"Come on, McCracken, move it!" shouted Perlman.

The kid grabbed McCracken's shirt. "If I go back, they'll do more things to me," he pleaded.

McCracken pushed the kid hard, knocking the oversized sunglasses off his face.

The eyes. The irises were pale yellow. Like eagle's eyes.

The kid chuckled. "I dunno, maybe it's not so bad, I'm not sure yet," he said, reaching for his glasses. "I can see a mouse from two miles out. Can you do that?"

McCracken turned away.

"No, you can't," the kid said.

"*Dickwad, get in the fucking truck now!*"

McCracken ran to the passenger side and jumped in. As they drove off, the kid stood there and waved.

Thirteen

It was more money than they had anticipated. Stacks of tens and twenties covered the king bed at the Silver Mine Motel in Pahrump. Perlman, who was best at math, did a quick count and estimated the haul was in the $600,000 range. He jumped on the pile of bills, then extended his arms and legs to make a snow angel. Stacks of bills tumbled to the floor, snapping the currency bands and turning the brown carpet into a sea of green.

"It's raining tens! Hallelujah! It's raining tens! Twenties too!" sang Perlman, who rolled onto his stomach and started dry-humping the cash.

McCracken kicked him in the thigh.

"Ow! Fucker."

"I just want to remind you that we shouldn't

call attention to ourselves," said McCracken. "The less attention, the better."

"Lighten up, pecker, we just won the fuckin' Lotto," Perlman replied. "I say we split this loot three ways and ditch town. They'll never find us."

"Yes, they will. In about ten seconds."

"No way. Nobody disappears like me."

"Just put the cash back in the bags, both of you, and don't make any more noise."

McCracken walked to the window and peered through the blinds. He was angry for several reasons. He didn't want the cash, and he was disappointed the armored car hadn't been carrying more valuable cargo.

Buscado was checking his Twitter feed. "We're trending in Vegas—I mean the robbery is," he said. "Hey, go to Channel 7."

Perlman grabbed the remote and turned on the TV. A commercial for In N Out reminded him how hungry he was. Then *Eyewitness News 7* started. Lead story: *Brazen armored van heist on Highway 95. Armed-and-dangerous suspects still at large.*

"Armed? We weren't armed," said Buscado.

"It's hyperbole, fool," noted Perlman. "The more shit they make up, the more idiots like you watch the show. Higher ratings mean more ad dollars. It's all a scam."

A young female reporter was standing on the side of Highway 95, close to where the armored van had rolled. Her facts were mostly accurate: three robbers in ski masks; no visual identification.

"She's hot," said Perlman.

The reporter continued: "The lone witness, an Anderman Trucking employee aboard a self-driving delivery van, which was making a scheduled stop at the Corn Creek National Wildlife Refuge a mile from the crime scene, spoke to Eyewitness News 7 about what he saw."

A middle-aged Latino man appeared on screen. In broken English, he explained how the bandits had been moving too fast for him to jot down the U-Haul's plate number.

"Hey, where's the kid?" asked Buscado.

"Losers, you got the wrong fucking guy!" Perlman yelled at the TV.

"Quiet!" snapped McCracken.

"The wrong guy, McCracken! How is that even possible?"

McCracken shrugged. "I have no idea," he said.

Eyewitness News 7 segued to another story about an adorable newborn cougar cub at the Las Vegas Zoo. McCracken took the remote and turned off the TV.

A half-hour passed: Buscado scrolling through

Twitter; Perlman restacking the cash; and McCracken staring at the carpet.

"You look depressed, dude," Perlman told McCracken. "Not suicidal depressed … well, maybe."

"I'll be out tonight," said McCracken.

"Where to?" asked Buscado.

"I know where," said Perlman. "That little señorita snatch of his."

"Don't call her that again."

"I don't want to stick around either," said Buscado. "This room sucks."

"Yeah, we're heading over to the Chicken Coop," Perlman said.

McCracken thought it wise to let them go. "Promise me you'll be cool," he said. "Perlman, I'm talking to you."

"Oh, you can count on it."

Five miles north of Pahrump, the Chicken Coop Ranch was the lone building in a never-built housing development. When the project was abandoned, all that remained was a grid of paved roads and street signs, most of which had deteriorated over the years. An artificial lake shaped like a crescent moon, the subdivision's centerpiece, was filled with sand now, its original shape discernible only from the air.

The Coop, as the locals called it, was a rectangular structure with tilt-up concrete walls. A warehouse at one time, it was now painted in swirling pink and fuchsia. A neon lady in cowboy boots gyrated on its flat roof.

Perlman and Buscado arrived via taxi. Each brought a thousand bucks in small bills—heist cash—because drinks and whores weren't cheap in the VIP lounge.

The Coop had two entrances: food on the right; sex on the left. Neither Perlman nor Buscado had eaten all day, and with the adrenaline rush of a successful heist waning, they were more hungry than horny.

Perlman was holding a bottle of CÎROC Peach Vodka, which he'd bought from the desk clerk at the Silver Mine.

"Go easy on that shit, man," Buscado warned. "Remember, no unwanted attention."

"Here, take a gulp," Perlman slurred.

"What? No, that shit's too sweet for me," said Buscado, noticing the bottle was already half empty.

"Are you even capable of having fun? Do you even know what fun is?"

"Sure."

"Then quit flappin' your vagina. If I wanted mommy, I'd call McCracken. Drink up!"

Buscado grabbed the bottle and took a big gulp. The vodka burned going down. He winced, wishing he had taken a small sip.

Perlman laughed. "That'll unclench your sphincter," he said.

Buscado hated to admit it, but Perlman was starting to grow on him.

McCracken was pissed. Here he was, sitting in a Motel 6 suite he had paid for, and she wasn't sure she could make it.

Fuentes was stuck on I-15, watching emergency crews clear a four-car smash-up between Tropicana and Russell. She texted McCracken as he sat on the floor, eating a Taco Bell Chicken Fiesta Salad.

Not sure can make it baby :(

Where r u? How long will it take?

Dunno, maybe hours

Come anyway. Will be here, miss u

He didn't hear back for fifteen minutes. Then:

Did you bring condoms

???

Forgot to get em, will stop at CVS if u don't have any

Fuck the condoms, just come over

only take a sec...

McCracken phoned her number. She answered on the fourth ring.

"What's the deal with the condoms?" he asked.

"Better safe than sorry."

"We've been seeing each other for how long now? You're on the pill, right?"

"Well … I told you I think they're important."

"Why?"

"You know me, babe. Cautious type."

"If you want me to get tested, I will."

"No, you don't have to."

McCracken paused. "Then why the condoms?"

"It's just … it's important to me, okay?"

"Why? I don't get it."

"It just is."

"Rosa, you're not making any fucking sense."

"Don't make a big deal out of this, okay? I'll get 'em on the way over."

"No, we don't need them!"

"Stop yelling at me."

"I'm not yelling."

"Yes you are and I don't like it."

"I don't like wearing a condom every time."

"Stop yelling."

"What the fuck is wrong with you?"

"Stop it!"

"Tell me."

"I don't like you like this."

"Just tell me why I need to wear one every time?"

"You're making me cry."

"About what? Just answer the goddamn question."

"Okay, I'm hanging up now."

Silence.

McCracken called her back. Voicemail picked up. He hurled his phone against the wall, cracking the screen.

He lay back on the bed and watched TV, hopping from channel to channel. The sun was setting. Soon the room was dark, brightened only by the flat screen's glow.

He fell asleep and was woken by soft knocking. Hoping to see Fuentes, he jumped to his feet and hurried to open the door. His heart sank when he saw Howser standing there.

"May I come in?" Howser asked.

"How'd you find me?"

"Fuentes."

"Why would she contact you?"

"I contacted her."

McCracken grunted and reluctantly let Howser in. He sat on the edge of the bed and yawned.

"A bit dark in here," said Howser, flipping a wall switch. Both bedside lamps flickered on. "I take it you're alone."

"Yup."

"We need to talk about today."

"We scored a shit-ton of cash, in case you haven't heard."

"Oh, I've heard," said Howser. "It's making headlines around the world."

"Isn't that what you wanted?"

"The autonomous vehicle angle is absent. Why didn't you follow the original plan?"

"Just what I told you earlier. The first truck was empty."

"I see."

"I told you about the kid's eyes."

"Completely irresponsible use of the technology," said Howser. "I'm sure that Baldwin would agree."

McCracken rose to his feet. "We're not any closer to finding him," he said.

"We're getting closer, I'm sure of it."

"What should we do with the money?"

"Hide it, for now."

McCracken went to the bathroom and pissed in the toilet. "Why a wildlife refuge?" he shouted over his stream.

"What?"

"The truck. Why was it going to Corn Creek?"

"Those businesses are fronts. The young man in the truck, I suspect he's either an experiment or patient."

"And the casino?"

Howser checked his phone. "Oh, by the way, are you seeing Fuentes this evening?" he asked.

"What?"

"I asked if you're seeing Fuentes tonight."

McCracken flushed and washed his hands. Wiping his hands on a towel, he glared at Howser.

"What do you care?"

Howser smiled. "Just making conversation," he answered. "You know, you really need to chill sometimes. Seeing her relaxes you, that's a good thing."

Fourteen

Perlman and Buscado paid for the VIP suite with four girls—Chelsea, Pandora, Mandee, and Valletta. Perlman wanted each girl to represent a different season. Chelsea, black with long, bleached-blonde hair, was summer. Mandee, a redhead, was autumn. Pandora was winter because her name reminded Perlman of Christmas. And Valletta was spring because that was the only season left.

They ordered two bottles of absinthe, a liter of Diet Dr. Pepper, some hash, and a bucket of chicken wings because Valletta and Mandee were hungry.

Perlman poured shots for everyone, making sure Buscado finished every drop. "To the best highwaymen in the business!" he shouted, raising his glass.

He sat on a brown leather sofa next to a tall, bushy ficus tree—a good spot to dump his absinthe when no one was looking. He made sure everyone downed their shots, no matter how much they hated the taste.

Buscado was slumped in a beanbag chair, Pandora on his lap. He wanted to get drunk because he was nervous. He hadn't had sex in over a year.

"This licorice-flavored shit you're making us drink is gross," said Chelsea.

"It's anise, actually," replied Perlman, refiling Buscado's glass.

"Heard it makes you go crazy," said Pandora.

"We're all crazy!" shouted Perlman.

"Heard it makes you go blind."

"We're all blind!"

"What's a highwayman?" asked Mandee.

"Okay, how we gonna do this," asked Chelsea. "We splitting up in pairs, or is this one big free-for-all?"

"No anus," said Valletta, who didn't speak much English.

"We're highwaymen, girlfriend," said Perlman, trying to refill Chelsea's glass, which she blocked with her hand. "My bud Buscado deserves your best effort."

"No anus," Valletta repeated.

Perlman jumped up on a glass table. "We're highwaymen, ladies!" he shouted. "We're fucking HIGHWAYMEN."

"Perlman, stop!" said Buscado, sliding out from under Pandora and pulling Perlman off the table. "No crazy shit, remember?"

"You girls wanna hear the most amazing story ever?" Perlman asked. "You wanna know what badasses we are?"

Chelsea snorted. "Badasses, right."

"Laugh all you want, brown sugar, but my plebeian pal and I will soon be world famous, and you'll be bragging about how you licked our balls."

"Nobody's licking your balls."

Perlman held his hands in prayer. "A solemn request, my esteemed sex workers," he said. "I want all four of you to do my dear friend here. No holes barred, if you know what I mean."

"What about you?" Buscado asked nervously.

"I'm gonna go down the hall and drain the main vein," replied Perlman. "But when I return, I better see five naked bodies writhing on the floor. Chop-chop!"

Valletta and Mandee started undressing Buscado. Perlman, grinning, backed toward the door and left the room.

In the hall he nodded at two security goons—dudes even bigger than McCracken—and asked for directions to the restroom.

His hunch was right. The rear exit, no doubt a favorite of politicians, clergy, and school administrators, was next to the men's room. He chuckled at its brilliance.

Perlman pushed open the back door and breathed in the cool night air. His timing was perfect. The cabbie was waiting—the same guy who had dropped them off earlier.

Perlman paid up front, including a $200 tip. "You never saw me tonight," he said.

Four on one—Buscado would thank him later, if he remembered any of it. The douche clearly couldn't handle his liquor.

The motel parking lot was full when they pulled in. Perlman had the cabbie drop him off at the north end of the lot, far from the office. He studied the second-floor landing and their room. No one walking about, no one to ID him later.

He tiptoed up the stairs, slipped his key card in the door slot, and entered the room without a sound. He needed to move fast to make it to LA in time. There was a shuttle that went from Pahrump to LAX. He planned to be on it.

Perlman turned on the bedside lamp, grabbed a satchel, and went to work, snagging fistfuls of bills and stuffing them into the bag. Two satchels would be plenty—$300K, maybe more.

Flying with cash was suicide, of course, so Perlman planned to visit his old buddy, T0xic $ingularity, on the way to LA. T0xic lived in Inglewood and worked for an aerospace company in El Segundo. He owed Perlman a big favor and was willing to ferry the loot down to a Mexican bank for quick laundering. Perlman knew he'd take a thirty to fifty percent haircut in the process, but $200K in an offshore account was more than enough for Mauritius.

The first bag was nearly full when the bathroom light flicked on. Perlman bolted for the door but just as he opened it, a strong force slammed it shut. A giant hand grabbed his shoulder and spun him around.

McCracken yanked the satchel from Perlman's hand and tossed it on the bed.

Perlman grinned. "Figured you and Rosarita would be on round three by now."

"You think this is funny?"

"Whaddya gonna do, tell Howser? Baldwin? I know things about those guys."

"They know things about you, too."

"You believe that bullshit story they're telling everyone? You think they give a shit about how robots are fucking us over?"

McCracken didn't answer.

"I'm gonna get everything I can before this clusterfuck explodes."

"Alright, so there's more to it than that."

"No shit," said Perlman. "You think I didn't see that kid's eyes back on the highway? Got a nice, long look in the rearview."

"So what do you want?"

"The money and a ticket outta here."

"You can't have the money, not yet."

"If the world's going to shit, I'm gonna be safe in my bunker."

"You're not leaving."

"I'll split it fifty-fifty with you."

"No."

"Why?"

McCracken relaxed his grip on Perlman's shoulder. "I don't want the money."

"Kinda figured that too."

"Look, if you help me out, you and Buscado can split the money," said McCracken. "I won't take a dime."

"Why would you do that?"

"Do we have a deal or not?"

Perlman thought it over. McCracken intrigued him.

"Okay," he said, "but under one condition."

"What's that?"

"Tell me about the kid's eyes."

Fifteen

Howser said things were happening.

The catalyst was unclear, but no one could deny the movement was taking off. The crowds at the pep rallies were growing larger, typically three or four times the size of the turnouts just two months earlier. Small halls were no longer large enough to accommodate the angry hordes.

Howser started holding the events outdoors, usually in a corner of a strip mall parking lot. The formula was simple: a podium with a large banner reading "Jobs for Humans" in alternating red, white, and blue letters; a PA system broadcasting his message loud and clear; and rowdy crowds ready to vent. No chairs or refreshments were necessary. On two occasions the shopping center's security team tried to disperse the gathering, but backed off when the audience threatened to rough them up.

One of these skirmishes caught the attention of a local news reporter, Taulia Sarono, a 27-year-old Hawaiian native who had moved to Vegas two months earlier. Sarono covered several beats for the *Las Vegas Register*, a local newsweekly that paid him $150 per feature—which Sarono figured came out to around $2.30 an hour.

Sarono had family in Vegas and was crashing in his Uncle Eli's garage until he could find a full-time reporting gig. The *Register* wasn't an option; it had just eliminated half of its staff, mostly well-paid old-timers.

His short-term goal was to do solid reporting and save up enough money for the deposit on a one-bedroom rental.

Uncle Eli, 62, had been in Vegas for the better part of two decades. He loved the dry heat and desert light, and was only a six-hour nonstop from Oahu if he ever got homesick, which he seldom did. Nevada had been good to Eli, enabling him to buy a three-bedroom house in Summerlin, get married, and raise two boys on a city bus driver's salary. He was retired now and supplemented his income by driving for rideshare companies.

Things were changing, though. The rideshare firms were switching to self-driving fleets, as were the bus and taxi companies. Eli suddenly had no income other than a partial city pension that didn't cover his basic expenses.

A former Uber driver told Eli about the parking lot rallies. Eli considered attending but ultimately decided not to—politics wasn't his thing. He forwarded the tip to his reporter nephew, figuring a good story could help the kid's career and maybe get him to move out.

Sarono pitched the story to his editor, who agreed there was something there. The October 27th event in a huge lot fronting a shuttered Albertsons on Charleston drew two hundred protestors. Taulia recorded Howser's and Baldwin's speeches and snagged an impromptu interview with the duo after the event.

The *Register*'s editors liked the story so much that they plugged it heavily on social media. National publications, seeing the broad appeal of a grassroots movement pitting blue collar versus elite, picked up the story. Multiple articles were written about the rallies, but none exposed the real story underneath, which neither Howser nor Baldwin was willing to discuss publicly.

Their secretiveness puzzled McCracken, who

figured full disclosure would aid their cause and maybe help him find Finn faster. He stayed in the shadows as a growing entourage of celebrities, politicians, bloggers, TV personalities, actors, and musicians began appearing at the Sunday rallies, all hoping to share the spotlight.

McCracken considered the hangers-on phonies and avoided them as much as possible.

But Howser was basking in the limelight, giving frequent TV interviews and post-rally news conferences.

Baldwin kept a lower profile. He spoke to the media on occasion, but really didn't enjoy the attention.

Howser was having sex with some of the women who came to the events. Buscado, who grudgingly agreed to play Howser's bodyguard during press conferences, told McCracken that Howser preferred short, large-breasted Asian women in their thirties, ideally self-employed blogger types not affiliated with a major news service. The target female usually would strike up a conversation with Howser, who would invite her to continue the discussion over a drink. Howser didn't want his wife to find out, so he would borrow Baldwin's Subaru Legacy for a couple of hours, and have Buscado drive him and the woman to the massive garage at Sam Buster's Hotel & Casino on Boulder Highway. Security was lax there and they wouldn't be noticed.

Buscado would wait in the casino, playing blackjack or video poker, while Howser and his companion would stay in the car or get a room. Howser got lucky most of the time. One time when Buscado was returning to the fourth level—Howser's preferred parking spot—he noticed the car bouncing up and down. Another time a woman lifted her head up from Howser's waist, wiping her mouth with a tissue, when Buscado approached. But most of the time Howser played it safe by renting a room at Sam Buster's, which had a $29.99 Sunday night special. He often complained about the additional $25 resort fee because he never used the Wi-Fi, spa, or other amenities.

Buscado really didn't care about Howser's groupies. He figured most guys who suddenly got famous would do the same thing.

He didn't ask questions, but McCracken did.

McCracken couldn't understand why Howser and Baldwin weren't telling reporters what was really going on. He also wondered how Howser was paying for his hotel rooms and bar visits without his wife finding out. The only thing McCracken didn't want revealed was his connection to *Universaliter Acceptos*, which he found embarrassing.

"We must stick to our narrative for now," Howser told McCracken one Sunday night in the All Nighter Lounge at Sam Buster's.

"I think we could find Finn faster if everyone knew the truth," McCracken replied.

Howser shook his head. "Are you familiar with *The War of the Worlds*—the radio play, not the novel?"

McCracken had seen the movie, the one with Tom Cruise, although he had heard the earlier film was a lot better.

"Well, back in 1938, a decade before television took off, Americans enjoyed much of their electronic entertainment in the form of radio theater," said Howser. "The Mercury Theater company, led by a young Orson Welles, decided to adapt H.G. Wells' science-fiction novel *The War of the Worlds* for CBS national radio."

McCracken remembered watching a documentary on this.

"It was Sunday evening in October, and millions of people tuned in to CBS Radio to hear what they were led to believe was a live orchestra playing from New York City," said Howser. "Soon after the performance began, a series of news flashes began interrupting the broadcast. An explosion was detected on Mars! A meteor crashed on a farm in New Jersey! Then creatures—hideous, tentacled Martians—began emerging from spacecraft landing across America. Even worse, the invaders were decimating the human race left and right, including the mighty U.S. Army, with terrible heat-ray weapons."

Howser was in full professor mode. He was a good storyteller, McCracken thought.

"Now, you might expect people to act rationally in this situation, maybe contact their local police or newspaper to check the veracity of this alleged invasion—and, to be fair, a lot of folks did," Howser continued. "But many, many more panicked, causing traffic jams while trying to flee the aliens, taking to the streets in numerous cities, and shouting and screaming that invaders from Mars had arrived to kill them all."

Howser paused to chuckle at the absurdity of it all. "Sadly, much of humanity is reactionary and dull-witted," he noted.

McCracken didn't find it funny at all. He felt sad for the terrified people.

"What does this have to do with us?" he asked.

"Simple. Mass panic is exactly what we're trying to avoid here. Humanity hasn't evolved noticeably since 1938. Telling people it's technically possible to merge humans and other species—and that a clandestine effort to do so is already underway—would result in a global panic unlike any we've seen before. The only ones who might benefit would be ..."

Howser paused to check his phone, which had been ringing for a few seconds. He stared briefly at the flashing number, then stood and walked away without a word.

McCracken checked his phone too: five unanswered texts and three voicemails from Fuentes. He hadn't read any of her messages yet and wasn't sure he wanted to.

Howser returned to the lounge, saying he had just had a nice conversation with his publisher. A book he had written two years earlier, *Heretics and Robotics: Global Economies in the 21st Century*, was suddenly selling like hotcakes on Amazon, and Howser's publisher was insisting upon a multicity promotional tour ASAP.

"Looks like I'll need an assistant with a background in PR and marketing," said Howser, trying to find a contact in his phone. "Maybe Baldwin knows someone. This could be good for all of us."

"This is taking too long," said McCracken.

"Patience is paramount," said Howser. "I've told you so many, many times."

"No, it's not."

"Is this about the money?"

"It's not about the money. You're lying to me."

Howser frowned. "A casino is the worst place to have a sensitive conversation, cameras and microphones everywhere," he said. "But as I've told you many times, we need you."

"Yeah, I know why."

Howser's phone buzzed. He glanced at it and placed it in his jacket pocket. "Get some rest," he said. "Take Fuentes out to dinner or something, let out some steam. Goodness, you're wound tighter than a two-dollar watch."

Howser disappeared into the casino. McCracken sat at the bar and ordered a beer. He took a sip and decided he wasn't thirsty.

He checked his phone again. No new messages from Fuentes, but one from Perlman:

Answer ur phone, fuckng asshole!!!

He didn't want to talk to Perlman. He had lied to him about a lot of things, most recently about the kid with the weird eyes. *Eagle Eyes*, Perlman called him.

Some sort of military-sponsored eye transplant, McCracken had said. A secret program reserved for vets injured by exploding IEDs.

All bullshit, of course, which Perlman hadn't called him on.

McCracken left the casino and sat in his truck for a few minutes, reading Fuentes' texts and listening to her voicemails.

He sent her a message: *miss u babe, coming over.* She texted back: *door is unlocked.*

She lived four miles from Sam Buster's. I-515 South would have been faster, but McCracken decided to take city streets to see if he was being tailed. He wasn't.

He parked in a guest space at Fuentes' complex—a sprawling place with beautiful landscaping, three clean pools, and cheap apartments with thin walls and rattling windows.

McCracken walked quietly up the stairs and proceeded to #212. Lights out, curtains drawn. He turned the handle, entered, removed his boots—Fuentes had a strict no-shoes policy—and dragged his feet across the living-room carpet to her closed bedroom door.

"Come in," she said softly.

She was naked on the bed. Candles glowed on the side tables and dresser.

"Hey, handsome," she giggled, grabbing a condom from the side table. "Miss me?"

He started to undress. Boiling inside. Calm exterior.

He walked to the bed and removed his boxers.

He was already hard as she pulled down his shorts, his cock slapping her chin. "Well, you're happy to see me," she said.

He sighed deeply.

"Socks too," she said. He usually kept them on unless she insisted otherwise.

She reached for a condom and he grabbed her wrist. "Wait …," she protested.

He pinned her down on the bed and climbed on top.

"Wait!"

McCracken covered her mouth with one hand, held her down with the other, and forced himself inside her. He went as quickly as he could, thrusting madly without his usual concern of whether she came first. He closed his eyes so he wouldn't have to look at her.

Ignoring her muffled cries, he pulled out and came on the sheets. He climbed off, sat on the edge of the bed, and immediately began getting dressed.

Fuentes curled into a ball. "Why did you do that!" she screamed.

"You know why," he said, zipping up his pants. "Maybe you can scoop up enough for your sample."

"It's not like that!"

"Yes, it is."

"I love you!"

"I know you work for them."

"No, no … okay, I did, but I won't anymore."

"Goodbye, Rosa."

"Wait!"

"No."

"Let's leave, okay? Take me with you. Let's leave tonight."

"No."

"Please, baby, forgive me, I'm so sorry …"

He walked to the front door and grabbed his boots. She ran over, sobbing. Dropping to her knees, she grabbed his legs.

"Please, please don't!"

"Stop it."

"They … I had no choice."

He pushed her back, opened the door, and walked down to his truck. The sprinklers were on and his feet got wet.

Channel 4 was around here somewhere. He was ready to share his story.

Sixteen

KVND Channel 4 Las Vegas was located in a new glass building in the Arts District. McCracken parked across the street and walked toward the entrance.

A security guard inside the lobby was facing a bank of video displays, giving his face a bluish sheen. McCracken thought the guard was watching him, and he was right.

The guard rose from his chair as McCracken rapped on the locked glass door. He pressed a button on the console; an outdoor speaker crackled and popped.

"*May I help you?*"

"Yeah," said McCracken, raising his hand as if to ask a question. "I'm … I've got a story for the Channel 4 News Team."

"*News department is closed, sir. Come back tomorrow.*"

McCracken watched Channel 4 all the time. They always bragged about their 24-hour news team.

"It's a big story and I think they'll want to hear about it," he said.

"*Sorry, buddy. Come back tomorrow. Better yet, use the Channel 4 News App.*"

"But—"

McCracken heard a click and watched the security guard exit through a side door. He was pissed he couldn't meet a reporter right away.

A police car cruised by; the cop studied McCracken closely.

McCracken walked back to his truck and sat in the cab for a few minutes, unsure of his next move. The cop car returned. McCracken started the engine and drove a few blocks north, parking on 6th Street near the El Cortez, where he sometimes played video poker.

He wanted a beer but decided to call another reporter first—the Hawaiian guy who was always following Howser around. The guy probably wouldn't remember him, even though they once met when the reporter was interviewing random folks in the crowd.

McCracken hadn't been in a chatty mood that day and had refused to answer the reporter's questions. He remembered the guy handing him a business card for future reference.

The card was still in his wallet:

Taulia Sarono
Contributing Writer
Las Vegas Register

It was 1:30 a.m. when he phoned the number on the card, expecting to get voicemail. After three rings, someone picked up.

"Hello?"

"Oh...hey … I'm trying to reach Taw-lee-ah Sar-ono. Is that how you say it?"

"Close enough. May I ask who's calling?"

McCracken gave his name and said they had met before. "I have a story you might find interesting," he said.

"Could this wait until tomorrow? I'm in bed."

"Sure, but it's about, you know … the movement," said McCracken. "You said I should call you if I had something to say about it, and I do."

"Okay," said Sarono, yawning. "Like what?"

"Well, the jobs thing is just a cover for what's really going on."

"So what's really going on?"

"It's kinda complicated," said McCracken. "It involves hybrids and stuff."

"Did you say 'hybrids'?"

"Yeah, they're using my sperm to make them."

Silence on the other end. After a couple of seconds, McCracken said, "Hello?" He repeated it two more times before realizing the reporter had hung up.

He decided to play a little video poker to feel better. Just then his phone buzzed. A text from Perlman:

Raid!!!

McCracken wasn't sure what Perlman meant, but knew it wasn't good. He was only a short distance from their West Vegas hideout, so he decided to drive over to see what was up.

From a block away, McCracken spotted several cop cars, red and blue lights flashing, parked in front of the hideout. He made a quick U-turn and drove west on Summerlin with no particular destination. After driving aimlessly for a few minutes, he parked outside an abandoned golf course.

McCracken opened the glove compartment and rummaged through a pile of service records until he found a single joint, one end slightly torn, and licked its edges to mend it. He lit the joint and inhaled deeply, staring at the dead grass covering what was once a beautiful putting green. With each toke, he held the smoke in his lungs for exactly three seconds to maximize the buzz.

He smoked half the joint and stubbed it out in the ashtray. His phone buzzed. Perlman again:

Meet at calhouns now!

McCracken rolled down the windows to air out the truck. It was chilly for October and he put on an old sweater he kept behind the seat. He didn't feel like driving, but it was time to go.

He was buzzed—very buzzed. Perlman always bought primo shit.

His mind raced with all sorts of crazy thoughts. Kids in orphanages. Differences in condom colors.

Recent advice he had given Buscado.

Buscado had moved out of the hideout because Perlman preferred to walk around wearing only a t-shirt—no pants or underwear. When Buscado noticed brown spots on their creme suede sofa—a donation from a neighbor—he had had enough. Cheryl agreed to let him crash at her place, but only if he understood their relationship was strictly platonic.

"You bangin' her?" Perlman asked one day when Buscado returned for a few of his things.

"It's not like that," said Buscado. "She knows a

P.I. who's gonna help me track down my kids. Plus, she says somebody's been watching her place and she needs protection."

"I'd be bangin' her," said Perlman. "A little long in the tooth, but still bangable."

Buscado ignored Perlman but confided in McCracken.

"I want what you have with Fuentes," he told McCracken after a few days of sleeping on Cheryl's sofa.

McCracken advised him not to rush things. It would happen at some point when she was ready, he said.

He really didn't believe his own advice, but it seemed to make Buscado feel better.

Buscado knew next to nothing about Cheryl, who rarely talked about herself. She had worked as a bookkeeper or accountant or something, and apparently had enough marketing or scheduling experience—he wasn't sure which—to help Howser with his book tour. Her apartment was neat and clean, almost grandma-like with dried flowers in vases, drink coasters, and cloth napkins on the dining table. She liked cooking for him, too.

He wanted more.

One evening when they were sitting together on the sofa, hips almost touching, watching some boring Netflix documentary she really wanted to see, he made his move. Leaning in, he kissed her on the lips. She recoiled, ran to her bedroom, and locked the door behind her.

He never tried again.

"I want to have her at least once," he told McCracken the next day. "Just once, you know, before it's too late."

"Too late?"

"Everything we're doing, everything we've done," said Buscado, shaking his head. "I'm not feeling good about all this. But she makes me happy."

Seventeen

Calhoun's was a dive bar a mile east of the Strip. It was the only business still operating in an L-shaped strip mall that formerly housed a 24-hour pawn shop, a Thai massage parlor, and a Blockbuster Video, all of which had been gone for years.

Perlman loved Calhoun's, a favorite of off-duty prostitutes and greybeard biker gangs—the ones too tired and old to beat up people. McCracken had been there just once before to pick up women, but that was before he met Fuentes.

McCracken took Sunset Road over I-15 and circled around McCarran. His head was buzzing from the weed, making it hard to concentrate on the road. He mistakenly turned right instead of left on Tropicana, then drove a mile before realizing he was going the wrong way.

Making a U-turn at a red light was a bad idea.

Not one, but two, cop cars appeared behind him, red lights flashing.

He pulled over, mulling what to do about the half-smoked joint in the ashtray. He considered swallowing it but his throat was too dry. He opted to drop it between the seats.

McCracken rolled down his window, grabbed the vehicle registration from the glove compartment, and waited.

A minute passed, no cop.

McCracken saw two uniformed bodies standing on the curb about 50 feet behind him, holding some sort of conference. He heard voices but couldn't tell what they were saying.

His heart was racing. This wasn't a routine stop.

Finally a cop walked up to McCracken's window. Another moved along the passenger side, shining a flashlight inside the cab.

"Driver's license and registration, please," the officer said. McCracken handed over his documents, then returned his hands to nine and three on the wheel. He looked straight ahead, hoping the cop wouldn't notice his bloodshot eyes.

"Step out of the vehicle, sir."

McCracken felt uneasy—an occasional occurrence whenever he smoked pot. Exiting the cab slowly, he kept his hands in plain sight.

"Walk around to the front of the vehicle. Stand on the sidewalk."

Odd request, McCracken thought, but he complied. One cop, saying nothing, shined a flashlight in each of McCracken's eyes. The other looked inside the cab.

"Check this out," said the officer examining the truck. The first cop walked over to investigate.

McCracken's mind raced. If they found the joint, no big deal. But there were so many other things he had done. And who were these guys, really?

The cop holding his license and registration walked toward him, stopping a foot away. He was Latino, average height, but his eyes seemed brighter than normal, as if absorbing ambient light.

No, I'm just stoned.

"Have you been using controlled substances this evening, sir?" the cop asked.

"Nope. Maybe a couple beers, but that was a few hours ago."

Stupid answer. Everyone tells cops they've had a "couple beers." MPs used to joke about that all the time.

"We smelled marijuana inside the cab. Have you been smoking?"

McCracken noticed a patch on the cop's shirt pocket. It was very distinctive, even under the dim glow of the street lamp: a boomerang. McCracken squinted and stared at the emblem.

"I asked you a question, sir."

McCracken was afraid. Or was he angry? And where was the second cop now?

"One last time, sir. Were you smoking marijuana?"

"No, not this evening," said McCracken, trying to smile. "Drove past a rough bunch of skunks, though. Sprayed me pretty good."

McCracken heard an engine accelerate. The second cop car made a U-turn and sped off toward the Strip.

That left McCracken alone with the interrogating officer. He stared again at the boomerang patch.

I could do it now. No one's around. No one would know.

"Consider this a warning," said the officer, handing McCracken his license and registration. "Be more careful next time."

McCracken looked into the officer's eyes, which seemed off. They glowed too much, or maybe it was a trick of the light.

The cop walked back to his cruiser and drove off.

McCracken, hands shaking, returned to his truck.

He drove cautiously and parked on a side street a half-block from Calhoun's. Walking around the building for no particular reason, he entered through the smoking patio in the alley.

It was three a.m. and Calhoun's was nearly empty. The bar was bathed in red—walls, lighting, even the upholstered booths. On the small dance floor, two women in flannel shirts were slow-dancing to "Crimson and Clover," the Joan Jett version.

McCracken's eyes took a few seconds to adjust. He scanned the room and spotted someone waving to him from a booth in the far-left corner.

"'Bout fuckin' time," said Perlman when McCracken walked over. Buscado was there too, as was Cheryl, staring at her drink.

"What's up?" asked McCracken, wondering why Cheryl was there.

"Sit down," said Perlman. "We got shit to talk about."

Perlman scooted toward the wall, making room for McCracken.

"Our hideout is history, thanks to the Las Vegas PD," said Perlman, speaking louder than he wanted to. Katrina and the Waves' "Walking on Sunshine" was blaring from a speaker above his head.

"I hate this fucking song!" Perlman shouted. "I know the owner, he's supposed to be a cool guy, but this music sucks ass."

Perlman waved at an old man tending the bar and pointed at the ceiling speaker. The man nodded and lowered the volume, angering one of the dancers, who jokingly threatened to kick his ass.

"Much better," said Perlman. "Just hope the place isn't bugged."

"So what happened?" asked McCracken.

"I should ask you the same question," said Perlman. "Cops raided us, that's what happened. Somebody tipped them off."

Perlman pulled up a text on his phone and showed it to McCracken. "Got a text from—you ready?—the number zero," he said. "'Cops coming, leave now.' That's all it said."

"What'd you do?"

"Grabbed whatever I could—laptop, lotion, some bud—and hauled ass."

McCracken had buried the heist loot in the desert, but had saved a few thousand for living expenses. "What about the cash?" he asked.

"Had about eight hundred on the counter, twenties and change, so I took that, too. There's still about two grand in the crawl space, though. Guess the cops got it now."

The song ended. The two dancers kissed and walked hand-in-hand to the bar.

"We're broke again, more or less," said Perlman. "Unless you share the wealth now, McCracken."

Cheryl hiccupped.

Perlman was bothered by Cheryl, who had arrived with Buscado. There she was, not making eye contact with anyone. Sipping her ginger ale with lime. Nobody should be that mysterious, he thought, not someone mixed up in all of this.

He nodded at Cheryl. "What do you think?" he asked her.

"Well...I...," Cheryl stammered.

"That's okay, babe," said Buscado.

"What's with the vow of silence, hon?" said Perlman, leaning toward her. "Give us your take."

"Leave her alone!"

"We don't know a goddamn thing about her," said Perlman. "Her past, present, or why she's even here."

"She's here because I invited her," said Buscado.

"Well, I didn't."

"She has her reasons."

"We all have reasons."

"She's never committed a crime in her life, unlike the rest of us!"

Perlman shushed Buscado and looked around the room. The people at the bar were staring at their table. "Christ, numbnuts," he hissed. "Keep it down."

"There's nothing wrong with Cheryl," said Buscado, putting his arm around her.

"What say you, honey?" asked Perlman. "Your boyfriend telling the truth?"

Cheryl cleared her throat and made eye contact with Perlman. "You have nothing to fear from me," she said.

"Yeah? Prove it."

"Drop it, Perlman," said McCracken.

Cheryl looked more hurt than scared.

"No, she needs to prove her loyalty," Perlman insisted.

"Prove it? Holy shit, what more do you want?" asked Buscado. "She could've ratted us out by now."

"Whatever it takes to convince me," said Perlman.

Buscado turned to McCracken. "You on board with this?"

McCracken said nothing. He didn't like what Perlman was up to, but didn't trust Cheryl either.

"We need proof," said Perlman. "A loyalty test."

"We're way past that," said Buscado.

There was a moment of silence. Perlman stared at Cheryl, who looked down at her drink. Buscado glared at Perlman and grinded his molars—something he always did when he was angry.

Perlman's eyes moved to Cheryl's chest. "If you're loyal, prove it," he told her.

"Excuse me?" she asked.

"Prove you're loyal."

"Back off," warned Buscado.

"Show us your tits."

Buscado lunged across the table. "Asshole!" he yelled, grabbing Perlman by the hair and dragging him onto the dance floor.

Perlman broke free and tried to crawl away, but Buscado grabbed him by the shoe. McCracken ran over and locked Buscado in a bear hug.

"Lemme go!" shouted Buscado.

"Calm down!" said McCracken.

Buscado relaxed when he realized who was holding him. After a few seconds, McCracken released him.

The owner rushed over and helped Perlman to his feet. "That's it, guys, you're out," he said, pointing at the door.

Buscado helped Cheryl out of the booth and

walked her to the exit. He glared at Perlman, who was too busy massaging his kneecaps to notice.

"If you ever talk to her that way again, you're dead!" Buscado shouted.

Perlman pulled a few crumpled twenties from his shirt pocket and handed them to the owner. "You never saw us tonight, Jacques," he said.

In the parking lot, Buscado helped Cheryl into the passenger seat of her Chevy Cruze. Perlman and McCracken stood at the bar entrance and watched.

Buscado kept staring at Perlman but didn't push things further.

Perlman lit a Newport and sat on a bench by the door. "Pecker's pussywhipped," he said.

With Buscado behind the wheel, the Cruze left the lot, merged into traffic, and was immediately rear-ended by a black Ford Transit van. The Cruze slammed into a Saturn VUE parked on the curb.

The van pulled up beside the Cruze, blocking the driver door. Two masked men emerged from the van's cargo hold, ran to the Cruze's passenger side, and pulled a dazed Cheryl onto the street.

Buscado climbed out of the Cruze's passenger side, but couldn't reach the van before it sped off with Cheryl in the back.

McCracken and Buscado ran over to help.

"Call the police!" shouted Buscado, holding his bleeding forehead. "Somebody call the—"

McCracken slapped him. "Nobody's calling the cops," he said.

Buscado sat on the curb and cried. "They got her, man. They got her," he repeated over and over.

A crowd was gathering.

"We gotta get him outta here," said Perlman.

McCracken and Perlman helped Buscado to his feet and escorted him quickly to McCracken's truck.

Eighteen

3:34 A.M.

Zach Leeds of St. George, Utah, was shooting video of his girlfriend in Calhoun's parking lot when a Ford Transit van rear-ended a Chevy Cruze. From a hundred feet away, Zach recorded two shadowy figures leaping from the back of the van and escorting a disoriented female from the Cruze into their vehicle, which fled the scene.

The clip ended there because Zach's phone battery died.

An hour later, Zach uploaded the video to YouTube and tweeted a link to the clip. He and his girlfriend then ate pancakes at an all-night buffet. By noon Zach's clip had gotten a half-million views.

Cheryl had gone viral.

People across Nevada—and soon nationwide—were demanding answers. Who was the woman? Why hadn't she put up a fight? Was it really a kidnapping? A hoax?

The mystery proved irresistible. The story led national TV newscasts for several days and was a hot topic on cable and radio talk shows. The FBI and Clark County Sheriff's Department announced they were devoting major resources to solve the kidnapping, assuming one actually had occurred.

The woman was soon identified as the Cruze's registered owner: Cheryl Francis Thompson, 49, of Henderson, Nevada.

That same week the *Las Vegas Register* posted a lengthy feature on a mysterious string of truck hijackings in the Valley. The details, sketchy and often inaccurate, were loosely based on the exploits of McCracken, Perlman, and Buscado.

The Western Motel heist got the most coverage, but the reporter, Taulia Sarono, left out key details, including the two dead men left inside the wrecked autonomous rig. Citing unnamed sources in law enforcement, Sarono spun a tale of shadowy highwaymen running amok in the desert.

"This guy can't write," said Perlman, tossing

The Register across the room. "I'm half-tempted to call him up and give him the true story."

A UNLV sociology professor quoted in the article suggested that working-class rage was fueling the highway attacks, which he called "socioeconomic payback."

"Total horseshit," countered Perlman. "Pseudo-intellectual spooge."

McCracken was antsy. Howser and Baldwin kept trying to contact him, but he was ignoring their calls and texts. He too considered contacting Sarono and telling him everything, but feared the repercussions.

All he really knew was that they were three guys stuck in a crappy motel in Pahrump, with $453 to their name and nowhere to go—Buscado napping on one double bed, Perlman reading porn comics on the other, and McCracken sprawling across the beige sofa. They had been there for three nights and four days. The toilet clogged frequently and cash was running low.

They needed a new plan.

Perlman picked up a newspaper and found another hijacking story, this one with a Howser quote.

"Clearly these attacks are earmarks of an emerging and epic struggle between our innately human need for work—it defines who we are, in fact—and the cost-saving, some might say 'work-eliminating,' technology we've created," Howser told *The New York Times*.

Or was it *The Economist*?

"Doesn't matter, they're all full of shit," said Perlman, offering his take between bong hits. "That pompous hack loves the limelight way too much. Here he is, giving quotes left and right like some kind of goddamn sage, and he's responsible for most of this crap."

Buscado was having trouble sleeping. Cheryl was on his mind, and he felt edgy and nervous most of the time.

McCracken's phone buzzed constantly. He repeatedly scrolled through Fuentes' texts, none of which he replied to:

Call me
We need to talk
can we talk?
Please talk
I'm sorry!
fuck you I'm trying to help!
I can really help you
U really suck, u know that?
i love u

don't u fucking get it!!!
Fuck you asshole if u wont let me help you
I love you

McCracken wondered if Howser—or maybe Baldwin—was making Fuentes send the messages. He should have seen through her from the start.

Maybe he had been too horny. That always got guys in trouble.

McCracken was tempted to block her number, but couldn't do it for some reason.

Maybe he missed her.

He felt his anger rising. He tried to forget all the insane things Baldwin might have done with his … well, whatever that stupid Latin term was.

Did she know about that too? He didn't want to think about it.

"We gotta get out of here," he snapped.

"Great, let's get the cash you buried and go," said Perlman, picking up the TV remote.

"Not just yet," McCracken replied.

"Stop saying that! If you don't, Buscado and I will."

Perlman flipped from channel to channel.

The hottest TV doctors offer age-defying skin care tips …

Click

My mom raped my boyfriend and is having his baby …

Click

This amazing Crock-Pot with A.I. cooks a frozen turkey in just 15 minutes …

Click

Reports of autonomous truck hijackings …

Stop

CNN was reporting on a rash of hijackings targeting self-driving trucks. The trend reportedly started on deserted highways in Southern Nevada, the reporter said.

Now, copycat crimes were occurring in other states that had legalized autonomous deliveries, including Texas, Montana, and Florida.

"Florida?" Perlman sneered. "Nothing there but skanky parole vio—"

"Shut up!" said McCracken, snatching the remote from Perlman's hands and cranking the volume.

In the Texas incident, a crew of masked bandits on horseback stopped a Walmart auto-rig heading west on Highway 290 near Sheffield. A brief video clip from an onboard camera showed the thieves sledgehammering the trailer's roll-up door, climbing inside, and tossing boxes onto the roadway.

Police video from Missoula, Montana, showed

flames shooting out the back of a refrigerated auto-rig.

There was no video of the Florida incident. "State lawmakers there have just passed emergency legislation allowing trucking companies to place armed guards on all autonomous transport vehicles," the reporter said.

"Our boy McCracken took care of a couple of those armed goons, didn't ya, killer?" Perlman joked.

McCracken felt sick to his stomach. He walked to the window and peeked through the closed blinds at the parking lot.

"There's something you guys gotta know," he said.

"Yeah, what?"

Buscado sat up.

"Let's take a drive and I'll tell you," said McCracken.

Nineteen

Buscado was too freaked out to speak. Perlman wouldn't stop laughing. "*Universaliter fucking what?*" he kept asking.

McCracken was driving, biting his lip, wondering if it made sense to bury Perlman's body in the desert and be done with him.

Perlman wouldn't let up. "They're milking you like a cow!" he chortled. "A sperm cow!"

Let it go, McCracken told himself.

"Hey, maybe you can market your jizz as a super healing balm," said Perlman, laughing so hard he was spitting.

"Dude, give it a rest," said Buscado.

"I'm sorry, man, it's just so weird, milking his sacs for sacred sauce," said Perlman, calming a bit.

"You know, I wouldn't mind getting paid for something I'm already doing for free."

They were heading southwest on Highway 160, about 15 miles from Pahrump.

"Well, I gotta hand it to you, McCracken, you do have a sense of humor after all."

"I'm not joking."

"Whatever. You gonna tell us where we're going?"

"In due time."

"What's that supposed to mean?"

"Like I said before, you two can split the money fifty-fifty," said McCracken.

"Why give up the money?" asked Buscado. "What's in it for you?"

"You're gonna help me find my kid."

"Only if you help us find Cheryl," Buscado countered.

"Don't negotiate on my behalf, clown," said Perlman.

"Cheryl's not our problem," McCracken replied.

"We've gotta help her."

"Hate to break it to you, dude, but she totally wasn't into you," said Perlman. "And there was something off about her … well, can't pinpoint it. Anyway, forget her."

"Then give me a third of the money now—I don't want half—and we're done," Buscado said. "I'll find her on my own."

"Doesn't work that way," McCracken said.

"Who made you boss?"

"He did," Perlman laughed.

"We could vote on it," said Buscado.

"Sounds fair," said Perlman. "Democracy in action."

"We're not voting."

"You have no right to keep my money from me," said Buscado. "I earned it as much as you did."

"Well, numbnuts, you've got two options," said Perlman. "Kick McCracken's ass or go along with his plan. Which makes the most sense?"

Buscado fumed in silence.

McCracken checked his phone.

"We know Cheryl better than your kid," added Buscado. "We should focus on saving her."

"Let it go, dude," said Perlman. "Your girlfriend's weird."

"Enough, both of you."

McCracken's phone pinged. He was expecting another text from Fuentes but received one from Baldwin instead:

Where are you? Please advise.

McCracken ignored the text. His phone buzzed again, a text from 000-000-0000:

School bus ahead

He stared at the screen, his attention diverted enough for the truck to creep into the oncoming lane.

"Watch the road!" shouted Perlman.

Another text:

Coming toward you

"Who's texting you—Fuentes?"

McCracken shook his head. A new ping:

U-turn, left on Tecopa Road

"What the ...?"

Then he saw it: a yellow school bus approaching. He slowed to 40 mph, then 20 ...

"What are you doing?"

The school bus drew closer. Tinted front windows, no discernable driver. It zipped past them and continued toward Pahrump.

McCracken made a U-turn and followed the bus, pushing the F-250 to 90 mph.

The bus turned left on Tecopa Road and headed southwest toward the California border. The nearest school had to be at least a dozen miles away.

McCracken was gaining ground; he pushed the truck past 100 mph.

"Jesus fuckin' Christ, dude, slow down!" shouted Perlman.

A hundred feet and closing fast. He saw it. There, on the back of the bus—boomerang logo with cave paintings.

McCracken thought he saw the back of heads—kids' heads—inside the bus. He couldn't tell for sure.

Closer. Seventy-five feet, fifty, twenty-five. Right behind it, bumper to bumper.

He slammed his fist on the horn.

"Are you fucking nuts! Slow down!"

McCracken kept pounding the horn until a small head in the backseat turned and stared out the window.

It was … could it be? The face. Eyes.

"FINN! FINN!" he screamed. The child turned back around.

Both vehicles sped toward a bend in the road. McCracken kept screaming Finn's name and pounding the horn. He tried to pass the bus on the curve, sending the F-250 on a collision course with an oncoming eighteen-wheeler.

Buscado and Perlman screamed as McCracken swerved to the left, narrowly missing the oncoming rig. The F-250 bounced along a soft shoulder, skidding in the dirt and sand for several hundred feet, the impact blowing out the truck's front tires.

McCracken, swearing and crying, tried without success to restart the engine.

Perlman and Buscado scooted out the passenger side, leaving McCracken to howl alone inside the cab.

The yellow bus was gone.

Twenty

The F-250 wasn't going anywhere. Stuck in sand with only two good tires, it needed a tow they couldn't afford.

Perlman spat on the alloy wheels. He had no intention of spending what little money they had left on a tow truck. Buscado wanted to hitchhike, but Perlman thought that too risky.

McCracken was off by himself, sitting on the desert floor, his head in his hands.

Traffic was light as the sun started to set. Perlman glanced over his shoulder at a group of tall cholla cactus a few hundred yards to the west. Their thick trunks and purple joints looked almost human in the lengthening shadows, and Perlman couldn't help but think of McCracken's crazy story.

Maybe Buscado didn't believe it, but he did. He had seen Eagle Eyes.

Perlman watched McCracken sit in the dirt and play with pebbles and sand, brooding over a child in a school bus he may only have imagined.

They couldn't stay here much longer, not with the Highway Patrol—and who knew what else—roaming after dark.

The occasional truck and car passed by. A few drivers slowed to take a closer look at the disabled truck, but no one bothered to stop.

"This is what the world has come to," said Perlman, shaking his head. He glanced over at Buscado, who was peeing on a boulder, then walked to McCracken and sat across from him.

"Hey man, sorry about … you know."

"What."

"Your kid."

McCracken grunted and stared at his boots.

"You're sure that was him?" asked Perlman.

"Yeah … maybe."

"Not to be a dick or anything, but it's been years since you've seen him. And you said you saw only half his face?"

McCracken shrugged.

"You saw half his face *and* you were driving like a maniac," said Perlman. "The sun was out too.

I mean, who knows? Maybe you saw what you wanted to see."

"I know what I saw."

McCracken's phone pinged—another text from Baldwin. He showed the message to Perlman.

"He wants to see you," said Perlman.

"I'm done with them."

"If that's the case, you better lose that phone."

McCracken's phone pinged again.

"He's 'concerned about your well-being,'" said Perlman, reading the text.

Buscado, who was eavesdropping, walked over. "Have him send a tow truck," he said.

"We'll need a car too," added Perlman.

"Why both?" Buscado asked.

"You're gonna go with the tow driver, we're not," replied Perlman. "Have him tow it to Terrible Herbst in Pahrump. We'll deal with the tires later."

"How come I'm not going with you?"

"*No necesario*," said Perlman. "We're gonna make a quick trip into Vegas to see a buddy of mine, Thryce Kenston. Lives a half-hour from here."

Buscado studied Perlman, then McCracken, and then Perlman again.

"How do I know you guys aren't gonna get the money?" he asked.

"Because we're not."

McCracken snapped out of his funk. "Who is this guy you wanna see?" he asked.

"Get a couple of photos of your kid," said Perlman. "He'll need 'em."

"What for?"

"You have the pics or not?"

Perlman knew the answer. McCracken kept three photos of Finn in his wallet. One was a shopping-mall portrait that Marissa had taken when Finn was one. The second was a close-up of McCracken and Finn blowing out candles at the boy's third birthday party. The third was an outdoor shot of Finn standing with his arm around a friend at the park on the day he vanished. The photos were on McCracken's phone, too.

"What's he need them for?" asked McCracken.

"He's a forensic artist, does freelance age-progression work—you know, missing person cold cases," said Perlman. "The man's a genius, if a tad eccentric. He'll take those pics of yours, work his digital magic, and show you exactly what your boy would look like today."

"Exactly?"

"Dude's good, trust me. When CNN did a show on missing kids a couple years ago, they contacted my buddy Thryce to do the age progressions."

"How come you know this guy?" Buscado asked.

"What's that supposed to mean?"

"Well, he seems normal."

"Listen, limp dick, just because I—"

"Shut up," snapped McCracken. "How far away is this guy?"

"Thirty minutes, tops," said Perlman. "Near Rhodes Ranch in Vegas. Runs his business out of his dad's condo. Well, it's his condo now, actually. Dad's serving five at Ely."

Perlman offered more backstory, but McCracken cut him off. "Let's do it," he said.

"Buscado, use your phone to get us a ride-share outta here," said Perlman.

"Why my phone?"

"Just do it."

Buscado tried three ride-share apps before finding one that would pick them up in the middle of the desert and drive them to Vegas. Getting a tow truck was easier, but the driver said it would take him at least an hour to arrive.

"Now, everybody give me their phones," said Perlman.

They did. Perlman smashed them to pieces with a baseball-sized rock. "From here on out we're all using burners," he said. "Ten bucks, CVS."

A Prius arrived within thirty minutes. Perlman was hoping for a female driver.

"Oh, the irony," he said as a self-driving car pulled to the shoulder.

Buscado asked what he meant.

"Shut up," Perlman replied.

Twenty-One

Thryce Kenston lived in a two-story townhome one block from a middle school. Perlman rang the doorbell several times before the door cracked open. A bloodshot eye peeped out.

"Thryce, buddy!" said Perlman.

The door slammed shut, followed immediately by a cacophony of locks clicking and clacking. It reopened wide, revealing a bearded, obese white man in his late thirties, holding a Diet Dr. Pepper.

"Whoa! Put on a few pounds there, bud," said Perlman, pointing at Thryce's protruding gut.

"Food's a lot better on the outside, Perl."

"Sure, I understand. Well, here's the guy I told you about, McCracken. He's the one who needs your magic."

Thryce took a sip of soda, turned, and walked down the hall. After a moment's hesitation, Perlman followed, then McCracken.

The short hallway led to a long, narrow living room. Rows of moving boxes, each marked with purple permanent ink, were stacked against one wall.

McCracken scanned the box labels: *Assclown, Ely State, dubble trubble, shit-eating grin, nutmeg, Photoshop Follies, VERBOTEN.* He wondered what the labels meant and what was inside each of the boxes, all of which were taped shut.

The furniture included four gray folding chairs and an L-shaped, glass-and-metal desktop that held a Dell tower workstation, three 4K monitors, and a MacBook Pro.

Thryce sat facing the monitors, his butt cheeks folding over each side of the metal chair. He pointed at the other chairs. "Pull them closer," he said, looking at McCracken. "You, big fella, you got something for me?"

"What?"

Perlman nudged McCracken. "The photos, numbnuts, he wants pictures of your kid," he whispered.

McCracken handed three photos to Thryce, who scrutinized them with a magnifying glass.

Thryce spent a full minute staring at the photo of Finn at Rigdon Park. "He was a preschooler when he vanished?" he asked.

"Yes."

"Between three and four?"

"Yeah."

"Cute kid."

"What?"

"I said he's cute. Wavy, golden hair and nice smile."

McCracken already didn't like this guy.

"This is the last picture you have of him?"

McCracken nodded.

"Got one of his mom?"

"No, just those."

Thryce scanned the photos and loaded them into Photoshop. He stared at the digitized images for a minute or two, closed PhotoShop, and reopened the photos in another program.

"The apple doesn't fall far from the tree," Thryce mumbled. "I think there's enough here to proceed—bone structure, skin tone, parental example. Give me an hour or so and I'll show you what Finn would look like at seven or eight."

"Cool," said Perlman. "Should we come back or—"

"You called him Finn," McCracken interrupted.

Thryce turned his head. "What?"

"You called my boy by his name. We never told you his name."

"Well, that's his name, isn't it?"

"Yeah, but how did you know?"

Thryce turned to Perlman. "What is this shit?" he asked. "Am I getting hassled here?"

"Hey dude, chill out, man," Perlman told McCracken. "Let maestro work his magic and we'll be back in an hour."

"No," said McCracken, pointing at Thryce. "I wanna know how he knew his name."

"Jesus fucking Christ," said Thryce, slamming his soda can on the glass table. "Ever heard of Google? Your kid's disappearance was plastered all over the goddamn news when it happened. Not too hard to do a quick search of 'McCracken' and dredge up a little backstory, now is it?"

"There you go, buddy!" laughed Perlman uneasily. "Come on, man, let's head to that Sharky's we passed down the road, get one of those roasted veggie bowls you're always creaming over, and come back here in, oh, say, an hour or so. That work for you, Thryce?"

Thryce nodded and wiped his sweaty forehead with a Starbucks napkin. "No more stress, okay? My heart can't handle it. I'm already taking Inspra twice a day, can't sleep, my breasts are enlarged, and I'm having hallucinations at night. Seeing all sorts of weird shit."

"What kind of shit?" asked Perlman.

"Stuff outside the windows. Hell, never mind all that. Just gimme an hour."

Thryce turned toward the monitors and got to work. Perlman nudged McCracken and led the way out.

Twenty-Two

The tow truck unloaded the F-250 in a dirt lot just south of Terrible Herbst on NV-160.

Buscado was bored, cold, and hungry. Cheryl was on his mind again, as were his kids. He knew nothing of the whereabouts of those he cared about, and the thought made him miserable.

Someone was to blame for his predicament. Howser? Maybe. But Howser was right about a lot of things, like people losing their jobs. Life was bleak for plenty of folks, and Howser got that. He gave great speeches, too.

Buscado didn't know much about Baldwin, who McCracken said was some sort of evil genius. That seemed ridiculous, but maybe some of it was true.

He recalled the strange, white-faced creature he had seen the evening of the Paragosa heist. He also remembered telling McCracken, who had shrugged it off.

McCracken must have been lying then. Was he lying now? About his boy and the *Acceptos* stuff?

Maybe that was it.

Maybe they had been planning this all along—McCracken and Perlman ditching him to retrieve the buried satchels, split the cash, and leave him with nothing.

His mind ached.

Buscado wanted a hot dog and soda. He checked his wallet and pockets and found only $1.34—not enough for the Super Dog Special at Terrible Herbst. Credit or debit card was too risky and probably wouldn't have worked anyway.

The F-250 didn't have much loose change because McCracken kept the cab pretty clean. Buscado found that funny. McCracken, the tough guy, bending over to dust and vacuum the interior. Shit, if this had been his truck, there would have been food wrappers and Coke cups on the floor, and at least ten dollars in loose change wedged in every nook and cranny.

A car pulled up beside him, a Honda Accord

driven by Baldwin, who motioned frantically for Buscado to come over.

Buscado exited the truck and got in the Accord's front passenger side.

"It's about time," snapped Baldwin, slamming the car in reverse. "Where's McCracken?"

"Vegas, I think."

"You think?"

"That's what they told me. Visiting a friend of Perlman's."

"I seriously doubt he has friends."

Buscado noticed Baldwin's forehead was sweaty. "Where are we going?" he asked.

"It's very important I reach McCracken. He's not answering my texts or calls. Perlman neither."

"Can we get some food, I'm starving."

Baldwin gripped the steering wheel tighter. "There aren't a lot of food options here," he said. "A sit-down restaurant is out of the question."

"Drive-thru?"

Baldwin exhaled slowly. "Tell me where McCracken is, and we'll eat," he said.

"I told you, I don't know."

"Then no food."

"I'm pretty sure where they're headed, though."

"And where is that?"

"There's a Taco Bell up ahead. Stop and I'll tell you."

Baldwin used the drive-thru. They ordered four Crunchy Tacos, a Triple Steak Burrito, and a large Mountain Dew. Buscado thought the order-taker's voice sounded a little mechanical, but didn't give it much thought.

They parked in a cavernous casino lot between two RVs. Buscado engulfed his meal like a starving man, smacking his lips and making Baldwin a little nauseous.

"So," said Baldwin when Buscado was done, "where are they headed?"

"Mauritius."

"Preposterous. That's in the middle of the Indian Ocean. How do they propose to get there?"

"Perlman's got all kinds of connections," said Buscado, picking his teeth with a soda straw. "He told me if he could get to Mexico, he could get anywhere in the world, passport or not. He said Mexicans are resourceful little bastards—his words, not mine—and that they can do anything they set their minds on."

"You're going to Mauritius too, are you?"

"Nope, not invited," said Buscado. "They screwed me."

"How so?"

"Running off with the money we earned. Don't have proof yet, but I know it's true."

"The armored car money?"

"Yeah."

"They'll have a challenging time navigating customs with huge sums of cash in their possession."

"Well, that's the plan," said Buscado.

Baldwin studied Buscado's low forehead and weak chin. He tried to remember why Howser had brought him in. Oh, yes, driving skills. Buscado reportedly was an excellent driver.

"That's unfortunate," Baldwin said. "You're the odd man out."

Buscado shrugged and crumpled up the Taco Bell bag.

"It's not fair, you losing your career," Baldwin continued. "And your family, as I understand."

"I don't wanna talk about that."

"Understandable that you've given up."

"I haven't given up," Buscado said defensively.

"You've been cheated out of money that took considerable risk to earn."

"Yeah."

"In a sense, you were simply retrieving money taken from you when your job was eliminated."

"Yeah, sort of how I look at it," said Buscado. "Made it easier to do, you know?"

"The few benefitting from the suffering of the many. A very old story."

Buscado smiled. "You're sounding a lot like Howser now."

"We share similar viewpoints," said Baldwin. "Let me ask you a question. What would you do with your share of the money?"

"Lots of things. Put a down payment on a house. Hire a lawyer and get my kids back."

"Worthwhile expenditures."

Buscado looked out the side window. He felt claustrophobic being wedged between two RVs.

"Hey, do you know anything about Cheryl?" he asked.

"What do you mean?"

"You know, like what happened to her. Who took her. That sort of thing."

"I'm afraid I don't."

"Well, I always figured you know more than you're letting on," said Buscado. "Same with Howser."

"I'm afraid that whatever happened to that poor woman …," said Baldwin, his voice trailing off.

"What?"

"Her personal history, did she share it with you?"

"Nope, Cheryl's not a big talker," said Buscado. "Most of the time we talked about my family. She was real curious about family life, you know? Like what it was like to eat dinner together, go to the movies—basic stuff. I figured she was an only child or something, maybe raised by a single mom."

"I didn't know her well, but she had many good qualities," said Baldwin. "So you've been trying to locate her?"

"I've wanted to, but McCracken and Perlman weren't interested. They didn't care if she was dead or alive."

Baldwin shifted in his seat. "Um, may I ask you a personal question?" he asked.

"Like what?"

"Did you have a … romantic relationship with her?"

"I guess you could call it romantic. We were close."

"How close?"

"What are you getting at?"

"I'm just trying to establish the level of intimacy involved."

Buscado was angry. "What the hell does that mean?" he asked.

"Nothing, really."

"Did I *fuck* her? Is that what you're asking?"

"No reason to be crude," said Baldwin. "If you're offended, I apologize."

Buscado rubbed his eyes. "Aw, man, I'm sorry. She's just really special to me, you know? I'm worried sick about her."

"We all are."

"And, no, we didn't have sex. Lots of handholding—it was all real sweet and innocent. I wanted more, of course, but figured she didn't have a lot of experience in that area. I was taking things kinda slow."

"A prudent approach."

There was a lull in the conversation.

Baldwin checked his watch. "It's a shame your friends did that to you," he said.

"The money, you mean?"

"Yes."

"I'm wondering what I should do now."

"Trust me, neither McCracken nor Perlman is in Mauritius, not yet, anyway."

Buscado felt uncomfortable because Baldwin was staring at him now. "What do you mean?" he asked.

"We need to keep him here. You can help us do that."

"Be a spy, you mean?"

"Nothing nefarious, just help us out."

"And then what, I get the money?"

"Yes."

"I'm not a snitch."

"You don't have to be a snitch," said Baldwin. "More like a monitor."

The conversation lagged again. Buscado felt more agitated than before. *They fucked me*, he said to himself. He repeated the sentence over and over in his head.

"Okay," he said. "What do you want me to do?"

Twenty-Three

McCracken's roasted veggie bowl was all right, but he had had better. The Brussels sprouts were too salty and the organic yams had a weird, metallic taste. Everything else was just fine, though.

Perlman ordered chicken taquitos but ate only half of them. He was convinced the cashier was spying on them and taking notes. Whenever he looked at her, she turned away.

A wall-mounted flat screen showed news reports of riots in several U.S. cities, followed by a black-and-white photo of Cheryl, a nighttime shot of Calhoun's, and finally a brief clip of a newborn panda at the Chicago Zoo.

Perlman wanted to ask the manager to turn

up the volume, but McCracken advised against it.

After dinner, they walked back to Thryce's condo and noticed the front door was ajar.

"Whoa," said Perlman. "Not good."

McCracken knocked on the door. He waited ten seconds before knocking again.

Then Perlman knocked. No Thryce.

Perlman pushed the door open. "Thryce, you there?" he shouted.

No answer.

"I'm not liking this, man," Perlman said. "Maybe we should bail."

McCracken entered the condo first, pausing halfway down the hall and listening for … he wasn't sure what. Perlman waited a few seconds before joining him.

They heard a soft moan coming from upstairs. McCracken glanced at Perlman, who shrugged. "Doesn't sound like Thryce," he whispered.

They heard it again.

McCracken stepped slowly up the carpeted stairs, eyes locked on the second-floor landing for any signs of trouble. The walls were white, spotless, and barren, but the filthy beige carpet looked like it hadn't been vacuumed for weeks.

Perlman waited at the bottom of the stairs;

McCracken motioned for him to follow. They heard the moan again, which seemed to be coming from the master bedroom.

McCracken motioned again; Perlman began tiptoeing up the steps.

As they entered the master bedroom, a large, pale blob caught their eye: Thryce, lying naked in a fetal position on a king-sized bed. He was rubbing his temples and mumbling incoherently.

"Thryce?"

Thryce continued mumbling and didn't look up.

"Hey, Thryce, buddy, it's Perlman. You okay?"

"No, Perl, not okay," Thryce whispered. He tried to sit up but lacked the strength. Perlman, averting his eyes, grabbed Thryce's arm and pulled him up.

"Sorry, guys," said Thryce, scratching his thighs. "I usually work naked but was planning to get dressed before you got here. That's why I came upstairs—to put my clothes back on."

"Whatever, man," said Perlman. "But how come you're all comatose and shit?"

"I freaked out, Perl. I'm seeing things, really weird shit, like I told you earlier. Shit in the windows, shit I can't explain. Freaking me out."

Thryce began hyperventilating and placed his hands over his heart. "Fuck, it's gonna explode!"

"Deep breaths, deep breaths," Perlman advised. He looked at McCracken and shrugged. "So … you finished that age-progression thing, right?" he asked.

"Oh, man, it's gonna explode …"

"Nothing's gonna explode," said Perlman. "Take some more breaths. Deeper! That's right, just like that …"

"It's those things, man, they come around at night and roam the neighborhood," said Thryce. "They're not after food in the trash cans, either. I don't know what they're up to. Totally weird 'cause sometimes I think I'm seeing things—imaginary things, Perl—but I know I'm not."

"Bummer," said Perlman.

"I'm losin' it, man."

"Can we see the work you did?" asked McCracken.

"Yeah, check it out. Still up on the monitors downstairs, front and side angles, just like you asked. I'd show you but I really gotta rest."

McCracken left the room.

"I hear ya, buddy," said Perlman. "So what is it that's got you all freaked out?"

"They're like coyotes, but not really. Parts of 'em are sorta shiny and metallic. And their faces! Swear to God, they're human. Two or three of them, every night after dark. Climbing over the back fence, sniffing around, and it's like they're yelping or communicating with each other, but their voices sound almost human."

McCracken stood outside the bedroom door, listening.

Thryce was done talking and lay back on the bed. Perlman covered his bloated body with a Dallas Cowboys comforter lying on the floor.

"Take it easy, young gun," said Perlman. "Give that ticker a rest."

McCracken walked downstairs to the living room. His heart skipped when he looked at the computer screens. The boy on the screen: Finn, only older.

He was sure of it.

The side angle: he couldn't stop staring. Nearly identical to the child he had seen on the bus—hair, chin, cheekbone. Everything.

"Hey, McCracken!" yelled Perlman from upstairs. "I think he's having a heart attack! We gotta go!"

McCracken couldn't take his eyes off the screen.

"Hey, McCracken! You down there?"

His boy was alive.

Twenty-Four

Dale met his replacement a week before he got canned.

Dealer Bot was a six-foot metallic humanoid with a rotating torso, two carbon fiber arms with aluminum and alloy knuckles, suction cup fingers for deftly moving cards around the table, multiple cameras with embedded A.I. for spotting cheats and card counters, and two reptilian-like glass eyes that looked surprisingly real. And it could shuffle fifty decks at once.

Dealer Bot didn't require a health plan or 401K, wouldn't take sick days, and could work 24/7.

A two-pack-a-day smoker with a sandpaper face, Dale looked considerably older than his sixty-seven years. He was a longtime friend of Taulia Sarono's uncle Eli, and had been a blackjack dealer for fifteen years. Before that Dale had served a decade in the Coast Guard, had worked as an auto mechanic, and had briefly sold newspapers door to door.

What struck Dale the most about Dealer Bot was its humanness. He had read a few newspaper stories about how a new class of robot was skilled at analyzing human emotions and responding appropriately. But Dealer Bot took things a step further. It could engage blackjack players in very personalized ways—complimenting their clothes or hair, joking about slogans on their hats or t-shirts, and even reacting to emotions such as joy, sadness, or anger.

"Big deal," said Eli when Dale told him about Dealer Bot. "Magic tricks. It's just doing what it's programmed to do."

They were eating lunch at the Fremont Hash House, a Monday afternoon ritual.

"Yeah, I thought so too until I saw the damn thing the night before they let me go," said Dale.

"You saw it? Where?"

"It was two a.m., just finished my shift, and I was walking out to my car," said Dale. "Employee lot was kinda deserted, as usual. Two guys—never seen 'em before—were wheeling Dealer Bot into one of those big cargo vans near my car."

"At two a.m.?"

"Yeah, they were trying to wheel the damn thing up a ramp, but its wheels kept getting stuck. So I'm about ten feet away and the damn thing tumbles off the ramp, falls on its side, and the back panel snaps clear off."

"Cheap build quality," said Eli. "Doesn't sound like a 24/7 dealer to me."

"Well, you're not gonna believe what I saw inside that thing," said Dale.

"What'd you see?"

"There's all sorts of circuits and chips and whatever in there. But right in the middle is—I swear on my mother's grave—is this greyish, slimy thing that looks like some sort of body part."

"What?"

"A body part," Dale repeated.

"From what?"

"A human body part, like it's alive or something, all folded up with creases, like a brain wedged real tight in there."

"No way that's what it was."

"I'm just telling you what I saw," said Dale. "Anyway, it fit just right, as far as I could tell, like it was grown or manufactured to be there. And there were all these little computer wires and things attached to the wrinkly parts. Whatever it was, it was kinda jarred loose after the fall."

"You weren't drinking?"

"Been cutting back, you know that."

"Dale, were you drinking?"

"Couple of Coronas in the lounge, but I know what I saw."

"That's crazy."

"Gets even crazier. You've seen Dealer Bot on the floor, right? Those lizard eyes that watch everybody's cards? Well, one of 'em was jarred out of its socket."

"Where was it?"

"Hanging by a cable—maybe a nerve, whatever—and sorta dangling over the side of the head part. It was looking at me. Then it blinked. Twice."

"Holy shit."

"If I'm lying, well ..."

"So what'd you do?" asked Eli.

"What the hell do you think I did? Screamed like a little girl and jumped back two feet."

"Little girl, huh?"

"Stop it. Well, those two guys didn't bat an eye or flinch or even say a word. Just put the eye back into place, snapped Dealer Bot's head panel back on, made sure it was all secure, and then picked the whole thing up and placed it nice and snug inside the van."

"You swear you weren't drunk? No weed?"

"Like I told you. Two Coronas."

"Man, I would've crapped my pants."

"I got the hell outta there," said Dale. "Almost couldn't drive, my hands and feet were shaking so bad."

Taulia Sarono estimated the crowd size at five thousand, based on a mob-measurement formula he'd learned in journalism school. No true count was possible, of course, not with so many people coming and going all afternoon. The mood was relaxed, but Sarono knew things could change in an instant.

Uncle Eli was there, mostly to show his support for Dale, who had hung himself two days earlier.

Eli had shared Dale's story with Sarono the night before the protest.

"You believe it?" asked Sarono.

"At first I didn't, but now I do," said Eli. "I don't think it was suicide. That man was one of the happiest guys I've ever known, Taulia. Retiring soon, two grandkids he absolutely adored. He was happy—always talking about those grandkids, man. Then his wife found him hanging from a rafter in his garage."

"You think somebody killed him."

"Gotta be, gotta be. Made it look like a suicide," said Eli. "Dale saw something he wasn't supposed to see, that's what I think."

Eli's story made Sarono recall the late-night phone call he had received a couple of weeks earlier—the guy who claimed to work for Howser, the guy he had hung up on. His story had sounded nutty. But Eli's story was just as nutty, and Eli didn't lie.

Sarono opened his notepad and thumbed through dozens of pages of notes and story ideas. There it was: McCracken.

He phoned McCracken. No answer. How could he reach him? He remembered another guy at Howser's rallies who seemed to be friends with McCracken. A short, weird-looking dude who never shut up. Sarono had made a point to get his contact info too.

This guy didn't answer his phone either, so Sarono emailed him and asked how he could get in touch with McCracken.

It was time to schedule a meeting.

Twenty-Five

Thryce wasn't dying, but he was suffering a severe panic attack.

Perlman and McCracken fled the condo in Thryce's Kia Soul, drove to the end of the block, and used Thryce's iPhone to call 911. Thirty minutes later, they watched three paramedics cart Thryce into an ambulance and take him to the hospital.

"Man, I could use a hot bath," said Perlman. "Let's crash at Thryce's."

"That's a bad idea," said McCracken.

"You think I'm stupid? Told Thryce I wouldn't call an ambulance unless he agreed to my terms. Dude caved, we can stay there."

McCracken slept soundly on Thryce's bed that evening—the best sleep he had had in weeks.

The next morning, Perlman used Thryce's laptop to check his email. "Hey, some reporter named Sarono is trying to reach you," he told McCracken.

"Have him call here."

Ten minutes later, Sarono phoned Thryce's landline. He asked if McCracken remembered their earlier conversation.

"Yeah, you hung up on me."

"Sorry about that," said Sarono. "You gotta admit, though, what you said was pretty weird."

Perlman, enjoying his breakfast of Organic Earl Grey, Twinkies, and Newports, was eavesdropping on the conversation.

"I'm gonna be at a rally this afternoon on the Strip," Sarono continued. "Your guy Howser is speaking."

"He's not my guy."

"I thought you worked for him."

"Not anymore."

"Well, I want to talk to you about your story. Can you meet there?"

They agreed on five p.m., roughly an hour after Howser's speech was scheduled to end. McCracken picked the High Roller as their meeting spot. It was easy to find, and parking was free.

"There's a Howser rally today," McCracken

told Perlman after hanging up. "We're gonna see that reporter there."

"He's a clown. They all are."

"I think he can help."

"Yeah, yeah, okay," sighed Perlman. "But we need cash. I cased the condo—no money, no jewelry. Don't want to take Thryce's computers, though; he'll call the cops."

McCracken checked the wall clock. "We gotta reach Buscado somehow," he said.

The home phone rang. They let voicemail pick up.

It was Thryce, sounding groggy. "Hey, guys... come on," he slurred. "Perlman, I know you're there, man. Bring my car to Southern Hills and gimme a ride home. Okay? Hit me back ..."

Thryce hung up.

"I'm not picking him up," said Perlman. "He's gonna want payment in full for the age progression, and we don't have it."

They took a city bus to the Strip, ate churros, and stopped at CVS to buy two flip phones.

"I need my truck," said McCracken.

"And we need Buscado's new number," Perlman replied. "Hopefully dumbass bought a burner by now."

Twenty-Six

They were careful to stay at least fifty yards from the stage. Perlman went incognito in an XXL Las Vegas Raiders hoodie. McCracken wore cheap sunglasses and a black Golden Knights cap.

Perlman was in a foul mood for no particular reason. "You know, technically we may still work for this ass-clown," said Perlman. "Did you sign any papers? I did."

McCracken scanned the crowd for signs of anyone watching them.

Perlman reconnoitered too. Nothing new here, he thought, just the usual hicks and hayseeds. He smelled weed, too, and hoped someone would pass a joint his way.

Howser stepped on stage and walked confidently to the microphone, waving and smiling for a full minute as the crowd hooted and hollered. He absorbed the applause greedily, ignoring a few scattered boos.

"You know, there's nothing better than Las Vegas this time of year, nothing better at all," he said to scattered cheers. "Sunny and not too hot, not too bright. And certainly not as bright as our future!"

The crowd cheered. As the applause died down, a lone voice shouted, "YOU SUCK!"

McCracken tried but couldn't locate the heckler.

"A lot has happened since we began this movement, most of it good," Howser continued. "We've raised awareness in Washington—and globally, too—concerning the plight of working men and women. And yet our jobs—your jobs—continue to vanish."

"TELL 'EM ABOUT THE CHIMERAS!"

"Shut the hell up! Let the man speak!" another voice shouted.

Others told the heckler to keep quiet.

Howser, ignoring the commotion, continued: "Each of us, as human beings, has an inalienable right to opportunity, to improvement, to advancement, to gainful employment. We should enjoy the fruits of technology, not be oppressed by it."

"TELL 'EM THE TRUTH, HOWSER!"

Pushing and shoving broke out not far from McCracken and Perlman. Fists and beer cups started flying, but it was unclear who was fighting whom. The crowd swayed with raucous energy.

Howser stepped away from the mic and pointed at the scuffle. A black-shirted security team moved in.

Perlman's phone pinged—a text from the reporter, who Perlman had called earlier from his new burner. Sarono was waiting at the High Roller.

"He's early," said McCracken.

Another fight broke out, this one between two women standing near the stage. Howser begged everyone to calm down.

McCracken and Perlman weaved through the crowd toward the High Roller.

Sarono spotted McCracken right away, despite the cap and sunglasses. He had heard the heckler in the audience, the one screaming about chimeras and freaks, and wished he could find the man and interview him. For now, McCracken would have to do.

"You made it," said Sarono.

McCracken nodded.

"Ready to win a Pulitzer?" Perlman asked Sarono.

They walked to a brewpub in the LINQ Promenade. "You're buying," said Perlman. "We're flat broke."

"No offense, but I'm here to interview him," replied Sarono, nodding at McCracken.

"We're a team, dude."

"What's that mean?" asked Sarono.

"Look, we need your help," said McCracken.

"Okay, well, I want to hear your story because the things you told me over the phone don't seem so crazy anymore," said Sarono. "I'm hearing things from other people."

"Do you pay sources?" asked Perlman.

"No," replied Sarono, wishing Perlman would go away.

"We don't want your money," said McCracken. "We want you to write a story about what's really going on."

"Well, what is really going on?"

The beers and onion rings arrived. Sarono paid with his VISA, hoping his notoriously cheap editor would approve the expense.

"We have to act fast," said McCracken. "I'm short on time."

"To do what?"

A dozen chanting protesters marched into the brewpub. One jumped up on the bar and kicked a pint glass, sending glass splinters flying in all directions. One shard dug into McCracken's wrist.

"Get off the bar!" the pub manager yelled.

The man kept stomping and chanting.

McCracken pulled the shard from his bloodied wrist and walked over to the protester. Grabbing the man by his ankles, he flung him into an ice-filled plastic container behind the bar.

The horrified protesters fled.

The manager ran behind the bar to check on the man's condition.

"You shouldn't have done that, sir," he told McCracken.

McCracken showed the manager the cut on his wrist.

"Look, we don't want any trouble. Leave now and I won't call the cops."

Sarono's phone pinged—an urgent text from his editor asking him to come to the office immediately.

"I gotta run," he said. "You have my number. Show me some evidence, some proof, anything. If I don't hear from you soon, expect a call from me."

Sarono left the pub. Perlman and McCracken

finished their beers and walked down the Promenade, sitting on a bench near the High Roller.

A black van pulled to the curb a few feet from them. Then a second van.

"Uh-oh," said Perlman.

Two police officers in riot gear exited the first van. Three more emerged from the second.

"You need to come with us," one of them said.

McCracken stood his ground, ready to fight.

Another van pulled to the curb. The cops encircled them.

"Not the time for heroics, dude," Perlman muttered.

They frisked McCracken first, then Perlman, took their cell phones and wallets, and escorted them into the back of a van. The cargo hold was windowless. A thin white pad covered the walls and floor.

Perlman was first to spot the dried bloodstain, a foot in diameter, near the rear doors.

"No way they traced our burners," he said. "Way too soon."

The trip lasted fifteen minutes. The final segment was a bumpy ride that had to be off-road somewhere.

The van came to an abrupt stop. Footsteps and

muffled voices moved from one side of the van to the other.

The rear doors opened, revealing a desert landscape at dusk. The sunset made McCracken flash back to the Arizona border, where he had been stationed briefly during his Ranger days.

Two armed men in ski masks motioned for McCracken and Perlman to exit the van.

There was Howser, dressed in the same blue jeans and long-sleeved work shirt he had worn at the rally.

"Keep them at least ten feet away," he ordered the armed men.

"How'd you find us?" asked Perlman.

"The reporter you met writes about us often. We keep tabs on him."

"Maybe we can make a deal."

"You have very little to offer," Howser told Perlman.

"Cash?"

"Soon to be worthless paper."

Howser turned and nodded at a black Cadillac Escalade with tinted windows. The vehicle was parked just east of the van.

"Here, I want to show you something," he said, motioning for them to follow.

Howser walked around the van, keeping his eyes on McCracken the whole time.

They stopped at a human body covered with a white sheet.

"You've met him before," said Howser, pulling back the sheet just enough to reveal the young man's face and torso.

It was Eagle Eyes, in the early stages of rigor mortis. One of his eyes had grown to three times its original size, bulging out of the socket and leaning over the bridge of his nose. Flies were buzzing above it.

Perlman puked up his onion rings.

Howser draped the sheet back over the body.

"This, unfortunately, is an example of *Universaliter Acceptos* gone wrong," he said. "The transplanted retina fovea cells from the bald eagle, made possible by a semen donation—not yours, Mr. McCracken—never stopped growing. The cells extended outward as well as inward, causing the recipient's brain to hemorrhage."

"Why are you showing us this?" asked McCracken.

"Because we can do better."

"If it wasn't my …," said McCracken, pausing.

"Whose was it?"

McCracken nodded.

"A jute farmer in the Ganges Delta in India. The Chinese had him but apparently he's dead now, for unknown reasons," said Howser. "There were only three *Acceptos* matches worldwide that we know of. You're one, of course, then the jute farmer. There may be more, but we haven't identified them."

"Who's the third?" asked McCracken.

"Classified."

McCracken calculated how quickly he could lunge at Howser, and whether he could snap the man's neck before being shot.

"Where is he?" he asked.

"I've addressed that before. We're not sure."

"Yes, you are."

"It's better if we have Finn, better for everyone involved."

"I won't let you."

"I'll be completely honest with you," said Howser. "You've killed quite a few people, including a young man in an alley behind a restaurant in Columbus, Georgia. We have security stills. I'm sure the victim's father would be interested in seeing them, too. He's quite prominent in the military."

"I know things about you," said Perlman. "You act like you're important, but you're not."

"You should have been in prison a long, long time ago, the things you've done," Howser replied. "Is that where you want to spend the rest of your days?"

Howser glanced at the Escalade again. McCracken wondered why.

"There's also the issue of your girlfriend, Mr. McCracken."

"I'm done with her."

"Well, she's gone rogue, possibly out of devotion to you."

McCracken wanted it to be true, but knew it wasn't.

"I don't care what happens to her," he said.

Howser approached McCracken, stopping five feet away.

"We'll find him eventually," he said. "He hasn't reached maturity yet, but will in a few years. Blood tests long ago proved he's inherited your unique trait … although we won't know for sure until someone collects a sample."

McCracken lunged at Howser, grabbing him by the neck and punching him twice in the nose.

Three men tackled McCracken, tasering him repeatedly before shackling his hands and feet.

Howser, his nose bloodied and broken, waved off assistance.

McCracken, spitting dirt, glared at Howser. "When I get my chance ..."

Howser, wiping blood and mucus on his shirt, walked toward the Escalade.

The Escalade.

"Who's in there!" shouted McCracken.

Howser waved without turning around.

Was it her?

Howser ordered the men to load McCracken into the first van.

Finn?

"Your services are no longer required, Perlman," Howser said before getting in the Escalade. "I advise you to stay out of trouble."

"Finn!"

Inside the Escalade, Howser examined his nose in the rearview mirror. "Should've known better," he mumbled.

"FINN!"

"You never said you were gonna hurt him," said Buscado from the backseat.

"I certainly got the worst of it, I'd say."

"You promised you wouldn't hurt him! I just wanted my money, that's all. You didn't even ask about that."

"You might want to concern yourself with more important things," said Howser, stuffing a Kleenex up each nostril.

"It was just about the money!"

"Things are changing rapidly," said Howser. "Money may soon be the least of your worries."

Twenty-Seven

The room was cold.

Strapped naked to a medical gurney, legs spread wide, McCracken listened to the soft whoosh of chilled air escaping from the ventilation shaft suspended from the ceiling. His muscles ached from being tased, and his right arm was bruised from when he'd hit the ground. His penis was wrapped snugly in a condom-like device with an oversized reservoir.

The room's only illumination came from four rows of blue LEDs mounted on one wall, giving the chamber a dark, ominous feel.

McCracken felt drowsy and wanted to sleep.

Sitting a few feet away, Baldwin stared at the glowing screen of a laptop. He quietly hummed a melody that sounded familiar to McCracken—a nursery rhyme, maybe.

Baldwin walked to the gurney and studied McCracken's physique from head to toe.

"We removed your clothes as a safety precaution," he said, doing a quick visual inspection of the straps. "Hidden weaponry is a risk we couldn't afford, given your … tendencies."

"Don't do this."

"If you're cold, I could drape a towel over your chest."

"No."

"This is a process called electroejaculation," said Baldwin, holding up a thin, wand-like device. Two wires—one tipped black, the other red—were connected to one end.

"This is an anal pelvic muscle probe," he continued. "Once inserted into the rectum, it will deliver a mild electrical jolt to stimulate the prostate gland, which should result in ejaculation after two or three cycles. The sheath on your penis, of course, is to collect your ejaculate."

McCracken looked away.

"This is very important. I had hoped you'd be more cooperative."

"I have money. I'll show you where it is."

"Money is just paper," said Baldwin, applying

petroleum jelly to one end of the probe. "Like you, I find this procedure distasteful. It's used primarily on large mammals, but you've left us little choice."

McCracken clenched his rectal muscles. He pushed and pulled on the straps in a futile attempt to free his limbs.

"Relax, it'll happen quickly," said Baldwin, placing his hand on McCracken's thigh. "In fact, it will be pleasurable, if you allow it."

"Don't."

"Remember long ago when I told you about the Mutational Meltdown theory?"

McCracken remembered bits and pieces, something about genetic mutations causing the human race to go extinct.

"Sort of," he said.

"It's very real, unfortunately," said Baldwin.

"Let me go."

"Telling humanity it's entering a death spiral, well, let's just say that takes a degree of finesse," said Baldwin. "Will you relax? Anyway, you can't simply tell homo sapiens that they may cease to exist in a few generations. The key is to present an alternative first. That's what we're doing here."

"Stop—you're not like him."

"Him?"

"Howser."

Baldwin pondered McCracken's remark. "That's true," he said quietly.

"Let me go and I'll help you."

"The only way you can help me is by unclenching your sphincter," said Baldwin. "Whether you approve or not, this is going to happen."

"You're lucky I'm strapped down."

"I suppose you're right," said Baldwin, glancing at the straps. They were medical grade.

"I'm aware this is unpleasant," said Baldwin. "But better you than ..."

"Than what?"

Baldwin looked away. "Never mind," he said.

Howser sat in a metal chair in a windowless room, watching a live video feed of Baldwin engaging with a naked McCracken. He looked at his reflection in a wall mirror: dried blood caked on the tips of his nostrils. Disgusting.

And his raccoon eyes, all black and purple.

He pulled a handkerchief from his back pocket and blew into it. The pain made him wince.

Howser was impressed with McCracken's great capacity for pain, both physical and emotional. He wasn't that strong.

He stared at the blood and mucus in his handkerchief. How would his new appearance play before the crowds?

It made him look weak. He would have to devise a clever backstory, one they would approve and applaud.

He was afraid. In the grand scheme of things, his role wasn't all that significant.

He grinned without confidence.

Truck hijackings—his idea. Copycat attempts across North America, China, and Europe. Choreographed chaos.

Chaos breeds fear. Ultimately, people want order, stability.

Acceptos would be the most significant advancement in life on Earth since the Cambrian explosion.

They would deliver it.

Except his role was unclear. They might not need him.

And *Acceptos* wasn't working well, not as well as planned.

Early setbacks were common, he told himself. Par for the course in every scientific endeavor.

Fortune favors the bold.

McCracken screamed and struggled to free himself as Baldwin inserted the probe. Howser looked away.

He hit the mute switch. Seconds later, he turned off the video feed.

It was done.

He looked at his reflection again and covered his nose with his hands.

Twenty-Eight

The Tiki Sky Dive hadn't changed much—same weird mix of Polynesian decor and skydiving trophies the owner had won over the years. Fuentes sat alone at the bar, sipping a foamy drink that tasted like an Orange Julius spiked with rum.

The young, handsome bartender who used to work days wasn't there anymore, which put her at ease. He used to flirt with her until he figured out why she was there. He ignored her after that.

Her brief side gig ended the afternoon she met the nerdy engineer from Craigslist, the one who brought a Taser, handcuffs, and razor blades to the motel room. Before she could request two hundred roses, he pushed her to the floor, yanked a clump of hair from her head, and tried to stomp her neck. A maid passed by just as Fuentes screamed; the knock on the door sent the freak bolting down the stairs and into a BMW parked across the street.

No one called the cops.

That was months before she met McCracken. She was off drugs now, more or less.

Rather than dwell on bad memories, she wanted to focus on the positive. It was nice being inside a dark hole with nothing to do but watch TV.

Air-conditioning was nice, too. Summer was coming soon and the afternoons were already too hot for her. The sugary drink left her slightly buzzed and giddy, the way first drinks always do. She was determined to stop at one.

At the opposite end of the bar, a fat biker in jeans and a Metallica t-shirt was checking her out. She ignored him and chatted up the girl bartender, who was on a semester sabbatical from UNLV.

Fuentes checked her watch: 3:42. He would be arriving soon.

She felt nervous, not because of him, but because she was being drawn back in.

She hadn't heard from McCracken since the night he had walked out. He never responded to her texts, which she eventually stopped sending.

They owed her money for her work, maybe three weeks' pay, but she hadn't tried to collect.

And now this.

The bartender and biker were watching a CNN report from somewhere overseas, maybe Eastern Europe or Russia based on how the people in the video were dressed. Fuentes wasn't paying much attention until the reporter said the villagers claimed that "golden jackals," some standing upright, had broken into several homes and dragged off two preschoolers, ages three and four.

The biker laughed.

"Estonia!" he shouted. "Fuckers probably downed too many shots of that hundred-proof Vana Tallinn." He winked at Rosa. "Goes down real smooth—I'll bet you do too, sweetheart."

She was tempted to walk out. Assholes never gave up easily.

She stayed, though. Her glass was empty, and she debated the pros and cons of a second drink.

She checked her phone again.

CNN switched to a story about protests at the Bighill Diamond Mine near Yellowknife, Canada, where a team of open-pit truck drivers had just been replaced by autonomous rigs. Rioters had set fire to the new equipment and shut down the mine.

Howser was on hand to negotiate on behalf of the miners.

Fuentes was surprised to see the nose splint and heavy pancake makeup as Howser gave his usual sound bite. She wondered what had happened to his face.

Someone touched her shoulder.

She flinched and turned, expecting the biker.

"Hey," said Buscado. "Hope I didn't scare you."

Fuentes grinned and asked him to take a seat.

She began second-guessing her strategy. Would this work? Buscado didn't exactly inspire confidence.

The bartender asked Buscado for his order. "Whatever's cheapest," he answered.

She brought him a pint of Coors Light—just $3 before five p.m.

"So … whaddya been up to?" Buscado asked.

"Looking for work, mostly."

"Me too. Gettin' hotter earlier this spring, seems like."

Small talk was the worst.

"You need to help me find him," she blurted out. "On the phone you said you know where he is."

"I sorta know," said Buscado, sipping his beer, which he found too warm. "They got him hidden away in the desert."

"Hidden away ... you mean kidnapped?"

She was agitated and talking too loudly. The bartender and biker heard *kidnapped* and glanced at her.

Buscado put his hand on her shoulder. "Come on," he said.

They moved to a corner booth near the entrance.

"Look, I screwed up bad," he said. "I thought they fucked me over—pardon my French."

"If you know where he is, just tell me."

"Baldwin said they would help me find Cheryl, if I helped them," Buscado continued. "They haven't ..."

His voice trailed off as he stared at his beer.

It was four p.m. and the bartender changed channels to the local TV news, which led with a story about a pack of coyotes roaming the hills near Red Rock Campground. Area residents had spotted a few of the strange animals, which were breaking into locked garages and stealing food. Small pets were missing.

"Tell me where he is," Fuentes repeated.

"I think I know, but I'm not positive."

"Where?"

"There's an underground bunker a couple miles east of Pahrump," said Buscado. "I'm pretty sure he's there. It's not far from where McCracken busted Howser's nose."

Fuentes couldn't help but laugh, particularly after seeing Howser's face on TV. She wished she had been there to see it happen.

"'A couple miles east of Pahrump' could be anywhere," said Fuentes. "Pretty empty out there."

"Yeah, well, I pinpointed it," said Buscado. "Baldwin's supposed to be this genius, but he's kinda out to lunch too, you know? A lot of geniuses are like that."

"Absentminded."

"Yeah, that's it. So me and him were eating dinner in the car right before we were supposed to meet Howser ..."

"Wait, why were you two eating in a car?"

"Because I thought McCracken and Perlman had double-crossed me."

Fuentes frowned.

"Look, if those two hadn't treated me so bad, we wouldn't be in this mess."

She sighed. "Okay back to the story. You're eating in the car ..."

"Yeah, well, Baldwin's bean burrito had red hot sauce squirting out one end," said Buscado. "He ran into Taco Bell to use the shitter, pardon my French, or maybe for another reason. Who knows, he's a nervous guy."

"Okay."

"He told me to stay put, so I did. I'm guessing he didn't want us to be seen together in public. Anyway, he was in such a hurry that he left his phone behind. He got a couple of texts from Howser's number. I wrote them down ..."

Buscado pulled a wrinkled napkin from his back pocket. "Veer left where Roadrunner turns into 928400, then two miles on left."

"And you know where that is?"

"The next day I did a Google search around Pahrump and found Roadrunner Road. It heads east from 160 and—get this—eventually turns into a dirt road called 928400. There's a fire trail that veers to the left, and I'm pretty sure that's where we'll find him."

It was worth a shot, she thought.

"We have to do this on our own, no cops," said Fuentes. "Don't tell anyone, don't trust anyone."

"Okay."

"Do you have a gun?"

"Nope."

"Well, I do."

Twenty-Nine

Baldwin was incensed.

After just two days, McCracken's production levels had dropped to almost zero, providing minimal *Acceptos*-grade fluids. Baldwin had three laboratories waiting: the principal facility in Enid, Oklahoma; a second near Zagreb, Croatia; and a mobile lab that moved surreptitiously around Santiago, Chile.

But no viable product to ship.

"He's refusing all liquids," Baldwin complained to Howser over the phone. "You know what that does to semen production?"

"I'm aware," said Howser.

Howser, though concerned, was preoccupied with other matters. Yellowknife, Canada, was freezing in April, and his nose ached more than usual. He had three TV appearances within the hour—NBC, CNN, and BBC—and needed time to rehearse his comments and reapply pancake. His face had been far too orange during the Fox segment.

He advised IV rehydration immediately—a course of action Baldwin had already taken.

There were other concerns too.

"Something's off with his body chemistry," said Baldwin. "It's troubling. I overnighted the most recent sample to Enid for analysis."

"We always knew he wasn't one hundred percent perfect."

"But he was close enough," said Baldwin. "Now his sperm is failing to penetrate the zona pellucida some seventy percent of the time."

"Has the failure rate ever been that high?"

"Never past twenty-five."

"Your prognosis?"

"If this continues, he'll be an unacceptable donor," said Baldwin. "Which would leave us with no donor."

Now Howser was really worried.

"We'll continue this discussion later," he said. "Continue with the IV and monitor his samples closely. If he's failing, we'll have to redouble our efforts to find a new source."

Baldwin checked the video feed. McCracken was asleep, or appeared to be.

"You know, I hate to turn on the news these days," he said. "These reports are on the rise."

"You know what they say, too many cooks," said Howser, viewing his nose from different angles in the bathroom mirror.

"How many years have we been working on this?" asked Baldwin.

"Maybe ten. Longer for you."

"The Chinese, Russians, North Koreans …"

"Don't forget the Indians. Now the Iranians, maybe."

"All they have is stolen Acceptos supply. We have the source—the only known donor—and he appears to be failing."

"Yes, the boy's test was flawless," said Howser.

"That was years ago. Do they have him?"

"They won't say."

"So you're in contact."

"At times. Communication is never easy."

"Who would they prefer to work with?"

Howser practiced his TV face. "Be nice to McCracken," he said. "Don't confuse physical with mental toughness. He's easily influenced. Maybe he can be persuaded to play along again."

"What are you saying?"

"Well, contented cows give better milk."

Baldwin thought it over.

"Is that supposed to be funny?" he asked.

"I'm saying there's growing pressure on me—on us—to move this thing along. It's all going too fast, particularly with bad samples floating around. They're moving forward, regardless."

"A crackdown is unwise," said Baldwin. "I can make this work, I've said so many times. Speak to them again. Which language do they prefer?"

"Not English, I can tell you that. Too many irregularities, weird orthography, phrasal verbs. Maybe Spanish, I'm not sure."

"I speak some Spanish, but I'm a little rusty."

"This may soon be out of our hands, my friend," said Howser. "My advice is to make the best of it."

Thirty

Taulia Sarono had heard of the coyotes.

The first tip was from the *Las Vegas Register*'s night janitor, Tigran, whom Sarono got to know from working late at the office. Uncle Eli's garage was a sauna in the summer and freezer in the winter, so Sarono kept a sleeping bag and change of clothes in the *Register*'s stockroom, where he once slept for six weeks until the human resources manager found him one Saturday morning and kicked him out. Although Sarono was a freelancer, management liked him well enough to let him continue to work onsite, only without sleeping privileges.

Tigran was seventy-two, five-foot-six, and thin as a toothpick. He hid a half-liter of Hennessy in a Lysol container and sometimes did shots with Sarono, who drank only when he wasn't on deadline.

The janitor's broken English was hard to understand, and he tended to slur his words after three shots. He liked to fish and drink before sunrise, and often drove to Lake Mead after his shift ended.

Tigran told Taulia about the "man wolves" he had seen a few months earlier, when his 1996 Mazda 626 had broken down on Lakeshore Road.

"They watch you like a man, but don't speak," the janitor said. "They watch and circle car, some stand on two legs."

Sarono smiled.

"You think I joke, but I'm not," said Tigran. "One of them, its face very flat and smooth, like a man."

For months, Sarono blew off the janitor's stories as ramblings of a crazy old drunk. But after meeting McCracken and hearing Uncle Eli talk about Dale, he thought there might be something there.

He had planned to ask Tigran to take him to see the man wolves, but he waited too long. One Monday, the old man didn't show up for work. Then Tuesday. Then the entire week.

Sarono asked human resources about Tigran.

They didn't know anything because the janitor was a contractor, not an employee.

"He just stopped showing up for work, so we terminated his contract," said Becky in HR.

"He was a pretty nice guy," said Sarono. "How can I reach him?"

"What for?"

"I dunno, if he needs work, maybe I can help."

Becky passed along the janitor's cell number, which was disconnected when Sarono phoned that afternoon.

Later that day, Sarono met with his editor and recounted all the strange stories he had been hearing. She wasn't impressed.

"People are just freaked out because of the riots and job losses," she said. "We can't run a bunch of crazy stories. We're not fake news, Taulia."

He left her office, seething. She was maybe two years older than him and lecturing like a sanctimonious J-school professor.

He marched back to her office. "What if I can get video, some sort of proof?" he asked.

"If you wanna chase this thing on your own time, fine," she said. "But I have plenty of real assignments, if you're interested."

"Like what?"

She picked up a notepad and flipped through

several pages of notes. "City bus ridership is down," she said. "What's up with that? Everybody wants monorail or light rail, but nobody's willing to ride the bus. Why?"

"Sounds fascinating."

"Your sarcasm isn't appreciated," she said. "Anyway, the story is yours, if you want it. But drop this mutant stuff. We do real news here."

On the bus ride home, Sarono received an anonymous text: *I have something you need.* The number that sent it was a string of zeros. Figuring it was spam, a prank, or a cellular mix-up, he deleted it.

Sarono was depressed. No money. Living in his uncle's garage. When was the last time he had been on a date? Best not to think about it.

At least he could still write. And he had a good story.

He had to get in touch with McCracken, but the guy wasn't returning his messages.

After eating dinner, spending an hour on Uncle Eli's treadmill, and taking a shower, Sarono sat on his inflatable mattress on the concrete floor and drank a Corona.

Should he move to Los Angeles? He had family there too. Summer was coming and he didn't share Eli's love of 115-degree days.

He heard a knock on the garage door. His phone said 11:15 p.m. Eli never bothered him after ten.

Sarono opened the door to find a slim, attractive older woman with greying brunette hair and green eyes. Dressed in a black V-neck t-shirt and baggy blue jeans, she looked very familiar.

"Uh … can I help you?" he asked.

"You're Taulia Sarono, the reporter?"

He nodded.

"We met once at one of the rallies where Professor Howser was speaking, maybe a few months ago."

It clicked. The kidnapped woman. Cable news darling. Cheryl whatshername.

"I know exactly who you are," he said.

"I sent you a text earlier today, saying I had something you need."

"That was you? Wow...yeah, I got that. How'd you get my number?"

"I can help you with your story."

"What story?"

"McCracken."

Thirty-One

Perlman spent several days drinking to excess, flirting with hookers, being ignored by women who weren't hookers, and wondering why the world didn't find him brilliant.

Sure, he was broke now, but soon he would be flush, all proceeds safely stashed in an offshore tax haven far from those greedy fucks at the IRS.

Legit work was for chumps. He was past churning out pedestrian code for tech startups, or shepherding clueless government hacks trying to migrate to the cloud.

He had principles.

He deserved better.

Fame eluded him only because he had yet to achieve his own savage takedown.

Every black hat had his own favorite. Perlman's was the Saudi Aramco hack of 2012, where phreaks known as the *Cutting Sword of Justice* set Saudi Arabia back to the 1960s, wiping out 35,000 computers within a few hours, disrupting billions of petrodollars in fuel shipments, and generally taking a steaming shit on every multinational that deserved it.

Even better, no one got caught.

Perlman knew black hats turned up dead every now and then—an assisted suicide here, a faked drug overdose there—but the risks were always worth it.

Black hats achieved immortality. Their exploits would be discussed for decades within the community.

Whatever those *Sword of Justice* limp dicks managed to pull off, he could do better.

Perlman craved respect. His skills had never been used to their full potential. Now was an opportunity to change that.

Maybe he didn't have all the pieces to the puzzle, but he could visualize the finished product. A global competition. Multiple players. McCracken's jizz.

Could he play a part in all of this? Muck it all up?

Wouldn't that be fun.

And then there was McCracken. Weird dude, but all right. Bummer about his kid.

Perlman did have an idea as to where McCracken's kid might be, a hunch based on something Thryce told him the night of fatso's panic attack.

While McCracken had waited impatiently downstairs, Thryce had insisted upon a deathbed confession. Perlman recalled listening to Thryce's panicked revelations, many of which involved felonies for which he had never been caught.

"Jesus, dude, TMI. Nobody wants to hear this shit."

"That's who I am, Perl. That's what I'm all about."

"Had a hunch."

"Promise me one thing, Perl."

"What."

"If I die, sprinkle my ashes outside that children's playground in the desert. I see the buses go in and out of there all the time. Packed with kids."

"Playground?"

"I shoulda been a teacher, Perl."

"That's the last thing you should've been."

"You know I love the kids."

"Yeah, I know."

"It's true."

"Okay, so what playground?"

"Hey, could I get some water?"

"After you tell me about this place."

"On the way to Pahrump, down Tecopa, there's a gun range. Same road, but farther west. Now can I have some water?"

Perlman went to the bathroom, filled a glass with tap water, and brought it to Thryce, who gulped it down.

"Ah...much better, buddy. Thanks."

"The school, what about it?"

"Playground, not school, walled off from the desert. Buses packed with kids going in and out of that place, like 24/7. I like to park outside in the evening and watch with my night-vision scope. Buses coming and going, always children."

"A playground in the desert? You're hallucinating, dude."

Thryce laughed and coughed up yellow spittle. "Yeah, maybe," he rasped. "But that's where I want to rest for eternity, Perl. Sprinkle my ashes along the walls of that schoolyard."

Perlman remembered saying he would, but promises were made to be forgotten.

He had a pretty good idea where to find this mysterious playground, which he guessed was just over the California side of the border, near some sort of religious retreat.

And as Perlman sat on Fremont Street at

midnight, two-fisting Schlitz Tall Boys and baked on Cataract Kush, watching screaming tourists fly overhead on that zip line that aggravated his hernia the one time he tried it, he finally felt his life had meaning.

He would help McCracken. And wreak havoc until they screamed.

Thirty-Two

McCracken looked terrible, even on the video feed.

Baldwin wasn't surprised. His subject had barely moved in days. McCracken refused food and water, and his once robust physique was wasting away. His skin was pale, his cheeks sunken.

Intravenous feeding wasn't delivering the results they had hoped for. McCracken's samples were consistently poor—so poor that Baldwin hadn't bothered to harvest in thirty-six hours. The zona pellucida penetration rate had been unacceptable for days. It seemed McCracken was trying to die.

Baldwin had his orders: get rid of him.

He resisted at first, ignoring the command for twenty-four hours, pretending to be busy. When the next status update was due, Baldwin didn't reply until the following day.

He tried several excuses. The timing wasn't quite right. No one had specified exactly what "get rid of him" meant. He might need assistance to carry out the order.

Then came the ultimatum: get rid of McCracken or Baldwin's role in *Universaliter Acceptos* would be terminated.

His project.

He received a text from Howser: *How you choose to get rid of him is up to you.*

Baldwin replied: *I object on moral grounds.*

Howser: *They've moved on. Proceed.*

Had they located the younger McCracken? New donors? Baldwin didn't know. It was difficult to say. *Acceptos* had so many variables. So many ways to make it work or fail.

Get rid of him.

As a scientist, Baldwin had disposed of many lab animals once their usefulness had ceased. But McCracken was different. His humanity was a factor, of course, but there were other considerations as well.

Baldwin had enjoyed his time with McCracken, particularly the early days when McCracken was the pupil and he was the teacher. Playing the Moral

Machine game—that was fun. Baldwin grinned at the thought of McCracken losing his temper over some of the difficult decisions he had to make.

Now it was Baldwin's turn.

He was alone with McCracken in the bunker, forty-five feet under the Nevada desert. There was a beauty in their isolation, freedom from the constraints and mores of human society. Baldwin could do whatever he pleased. Whatever actions he took, no one would know.

He thought it would be fun to play the Moral Machine game one last time. Was McCracken strong enough to participate? Baldwin could only hope.

He checked the monitor again. McCracken appeared to be sleeping. No, wait, perhaps not—a leg was moving. Now would be a good time.

Baldwin exited the observation area, proceeded down the fluorescent-lit hall to the patient holding room, and gently pressed against the stainless-steel door. He peeked in the window.

McCracken was awake, staring at the ceiling.

Baldwin went to a medical cabinet and filled a syringe with midazolam, hoping the dose would be sufficient to make McCracken sleepy and hence easier to contain.

He knocked on the window to be polite, counted

to two, and opened the door. McCracken turned and stared. His sunken eyes made Baldwin sad.

"Our work here is finished," said Baldwin, hiding the syringe in his lab coat pocket.

McCracken didn't respond.

"It's been a pleasure working with you."

Baldwin hoped for a reply but didn't get one.

"I know the past few days have been challenging for you," Baldwin continued. "They've been difficult for all of us. But the good news is that we're nearly finished here, although I was hoping to do one final test."

"No."

At least he said something—a good start.

"It's nothing physical, I assure you," Baldwin replied.

"No."

"This research is very, very important. Let's make a deal."

"No."

"You don't want to hear my offer?"

McCracken didn't answer.

"So you do, then."

"Let me go."

"All I ask for is ten minutes of your time," said Baldwin. "It's a game we've played before. Does that sound so terrible?"

McCracken grinned.

"A rare smile," said Baldwin. "How nice."

"What's the game?" McCracken asked.

"It's the final chapter of the Moral Machine game we played some time ago," Baldwin replied. "Remember? We used cartoon videos at the time, but that's not possible here."

"Yeah."

"We'll play again."

McCracken turned his head and spat on the floor.

Baldwin looked at the pool of spittle and frowned. The distraction allowed McCracken to tug on the restraining strap holding his right arm down. The tie had been weak for days. McCracken could feel the fibers stretch and loosen as he repeatedly tugged on the restraint. One swift jerk might free his arm, if he had the strength.

"To refresh your memory, I present you with a moral dilemma and—"

"I remember. It was a stupid game."

"Well, you decide which course of action to take."

"Whatever."

"I hope you'll see its merits someday," said Baldwin.

One tug should do it.

"My first question, if you're ready."

"Sure," said McCracken, spitting and tugging in unison again.

"Please don't do that."

"How come?"

"It's unhygienic, and there's no janitorial service here."

"Sure."

"Very good. So, you're a passenger in a self-driving car and—"

"Wait," McCracken interrupted. "Why is it a self-driving car?"

"It just is, that's all. The driver, man or machine, is irrelevant. What matters is the life-or-death decision you're about to make."

McCracken spat again.

"I said don't do that."

"Okay, go ahead."

"So, you're in a self-driving car which suddenly goes haywire, accelerating rapidly. Up ahead are two groups of pedestrians, one of which will be killed by your decision. Do you understand?"

"Sounds good."

"The first group consists of four schoolchildren, a sweet elderly lady, and two puppies. They're jaywalking, however, flouting the law."

"Why would puppies flout the law?" asked McCracken.

"'Why' isn't relevant here. They're just doing it."

"Okay."

"The second group is obeying the law by walking within the boundaries of the crosswalk. It's a sect of convicted rapists and murderers, each of whom has paid his dues to society and become a law-abiding citizen."

"Got it."

You must take control of the vehicle," said Baldwin. "Your options: steer straight ahead and kill the law-breaking children, elderly woman, and puppies; or veer to the left and kill the reformed, law-abiding rapists and murderers."

"If they're rapists and murderers, they're not law-abiding."

"They've served their time."

"So what? They're creeps."

Baldwin was growing exasperated. "Just make a decision, Mr. McCracken. Who lives and who dies?"

Almost free now. One tug away. Keep distracting him.

"Easy. The convicts die."

"Even though they're not doing anything wrong?"

"They've done plenty wrong."

Baldwin checked his watch. Time for his decision, which he dreaded. He was procrastinating, he knew it.

Use the syringe or release him?

"One final question," Baldwin said.

"Good. I hate this fucking game."

"Similar scenario," said Baldwin. "The jaywalking group is the same—schoolchildren, elderly lady, puppies. But the law-abiding group is a family of mutants."

He felt a snap. His wrist flinched slightly.

"Mutants?"

Don't move. Not yet.

"Imagine something esthetically disagreeable, something you would find visually repugnant. Something you feel shouldn't exist, even if its existence doesn't impact you in the slightest way."

I could kill him now.

"Like what?" McCracken asked.

"Imagine something repugnant."

"A dog-faced boy?"

Baldwin shifted uncomfortably in his chair. "Yes, if you find that repugnant."

"Are we done here?"

"Almost. Which group dies?"

"The mutants."

"Why?"

"Because they're not human."

"Based on your description, they're partly human."

"Stop this game. I'm done."

"What if one of the mutants is related to you?"

"What?"

"Say … your son, for instance."

McCracken's face flushed. He formed a fist with his right hand. Baldwin, scribbling in his notebook, was too busy to notice.

"What are you saying?" McCracken asked.

"Just hypothetical."

"Why my boy? Why not somebody else?"

"No reason to get upset. It's just a game."

"It's not just a game. It's never been just a game."

"Calm down."

"Tell me where he is."

"I don't know."

"Tell me where he is or I'll tear your head off."

"Calm down!"

"Tell me!"

"I would kindly remind you who's in charge here."

McCracken broke free of the strap, grabbed Baldwin's neck and tried to crush his trachea.

Baldwin, gasping for air, couldn't pull away. He began to panic before remembering the midazolam. Pulling the syringe from his coat pocket, he jammed it into McCracken's arm, injecting as much fluid as possible.

McCracken yanked his arm back, causing the needle to break. The syringe flew over the gurney and skidded across the floor.

Baldwin fell backwards, landing on his back as McCracken used his free hand to undo the gurney straps.

Scrambling to his feet, Baldwin fled the room and raced down the hall to the stairwell. He reached the second level and heard loud, thumping footsteps behind him.

Baldwin moved faster, climbing two steps at a time. Third level. Ground level. Upon reaching the exit door, he reached into his coat pocket for the card key. That's where he always kept it ...

It wasn't there.

The footsteps slowed; McCracken was stumbling up the steps toward him. The midazolam was working.

Baldwin checked every pocket. No card key. It must have fallen out.

There was another option: door keypad. Flipping open the pad's plastic lid, Baldwin began entering his code: four ... zero ... five ... one ...

Two hands seized his neck. Baldwin tried to breathe but couldn't.

He began losing consciousness, wondering if this was how his life's work, all he had ever strived to accomplish, would come to an end.

A gasp of air entered his lungs.

McCracken's head drooped; his hands slid down Baldwin's neck as he fell to the floor.

Baldwin's trachea was bruised, but the airway remained open. He could breathe.

He entered his security code and heard the metal door click. Pushing McCracken's leg out of the way, he pulled the door open and escaped into the desert.

Thirty-Three

He was naked and shivering. His mouth was dry, his head pounded, and when he sat up he nearly passed out. He vomited a greenish brown fluid.

McCracken took deep breaths to calm his nerves. He checked his right arm—bruised and bloodied where the needle had broken the skin.

He remembered where he was and how he had gotten there. He remembered the pain of the needle penetrating his arm, and his mad rush to catch Baldwin before the drug took effect. He was disappointed he hadn't succeeded.

The door was open just enough for moonlight to stream in and brighten a sliver of the sterile entry. He kicked it open all the way, revealing a desert landscape: no streetlights, cars, or people.

He was free. Maybe.

A gust of wind blew sand in his eyes. He rose to his feet and steadied himself, pausing when he felt lightheaded.

He walked outside and turned to examine the entry, which was little more than a concrete box, roughly ten feet square, with a stairwell descending to the laboratory where he had been violated for days.

He suppressed his anger. The essentials mattered more: water, food, clothing. He considered returning inside to search for things he needed, but quickly decided against it. Baldwin had fled, apparently, but others might be down there.

The bunker had no exterior lighting, a quarter moon provided the only illumination. A gravel road winded down a gentle slope into darkness. No black vans here—at least none he could see.

McCracken felt nauseous again. He crouched down and vomited more bile onto a patch of weeds. Wind gusts made his body shake.

He heard something scurrying in the darkness, maybe ten yards away. He knew he had to leave as soon as possible, but deemed it unwise to hike along the road.

McCracken wasn't hungry but was determined to eat. As a Ranger, he had learned to trap wild rabbits using nothing more than a few sticks and some wire. If he could ingest something edible, even a lizard or spider, he would feel stronger.

He decided to hike up a nearby hill and walk along the ridge. There was no path, and McCracken was hesitant to trample through sagebrush in his bare feet. He proceeded slowly, grateful for the moonlight that brightened his route.

He stepped on a small animal; the creature slithered under his foot and darted into the brush. A rattler, maybe, but one with no interest in starting trouble.

McCracken stopped to catch his breath. Thirsty and weak, he still felt woozy from whatever drug Baldwin had shot inside him.

He saw headlights coming up the dirt road toward the bunker. The vehicle was maybe a mile away. It crept along, pausing twice before parking and turning off its lights. McCracken wondered why the driver would stop so far from the building.

He thought he heard human voices, but couldn't determine the direction they were coming from.

McCracken continued along the ridge, moving parallel to the road, away from the bunker. He felt sick again and kneeled in the dirt, hoping his frequent breaks would help him regain his strength faster.

He was shaking. The evening was cool, not cold, but the temperature was falling fast. He needed to find shelter or clothing soon to avoid hypothermia.

The sounds returned. But from where? Maybe the wind was carrying them from a great distance.

He listened closely. Human sounds. Not actual words. More like noises that sounded human. Repetitive sounds, like a child learning to speak.

A reflective object about twenty yards away caught his eye. McCracken moved toward it, crouching low to keep his footing and avoid detection.

He came upon a small clearing scattered with trash and food. It didn't appear to be a campsite.

McCracken spotted frozen pizza boxes, granola bars, crumb cakes, and cans of what looked like baby formula. If it was a trap, he was too hungry to care.

He moved in, reached down, and scooped a crumb cake off the ground. Tearing off the cellophane wrapper with his teeth, he shoved the entire cake into his mouth. The cinnamon and sugar danced on his taste buds. He never knew Entenmann's could taste this good.

His mouth was too dry to swallow the food. He searched for water.

Twigs snapped behind him. McCracken turned and counted at least four white-faced coyotes, with more lurking in the shadows. Their faces didn't shock him, although he was surprised they didn't. Each bore a resemblance to him.

The creatures were not identical. One had humanlike eyes and ears, but a hairless, coyote-like snout. Two others had human-shaped heads too large for their canine bodies, camera implants bulging from their eye sockets. And the fourth, which McCracken assumed was the leader because it stood nearest to him, had yellow, rounded eyes.

McCracken rose to his feet, hoping his large frame would intimidate the creatures. But he also feared his nakedness and open stance might make him vulnerable to attack.

They stared at him. He stared back.

After a few seconds, the leader made a loud grunting noise. A new creature limped out of the shadows and stood in the moonlight. This one was a mess—double snout, canine ears, and waxy, human skin. Its round eyes were bloodshot as it limped forward on coyote legs with human toes. Wires extended downward from a neck opening that appeared moist and infected.

The animal took a step toward McCracken and stumbled, nearly falling over. The other creatures continued to stare at McCracken. Not attacking, only staring.

McCracken extended his hand slowly toward the leader, as one might greet an unfamiliar dog. The leader began to howl. The rest of the pack joined in, giving McCracken chills.

A loud pop, like an exploding firecracker, filled the air. Then another. The leader crumpled to the ground, blood streaming from its body. The others scurried into the brush.

McCracken crouched to his knees and spotted two human silhouettes running up the hill toward him. He sprinted along the hilltop, moving southwest toward Pahrump.

Tripping over a thick clump of black brush, he landed hard on his right hip. He winced and grabbed his side. It felt wet and warm.

They were closing in.

He tried to burrow under the brush when he heard a familiar voice: "McCracken!"

He spotted Buscado first, then Fuentes. She was holding a gun.

"Oh, god, you're bleeding," she said, crouching beside him.

McCracken glared at Buscado, who looked away.

"We gotta go," Fuentes said.

"Why'd you shoot at us?" McCracken asked.

"Us?" she replied.

"Yeah."

"I didn't shoot at you. I saw a naked man fighting off wolves—or whatever they were."

"You killed one of them."

"Come on, get up," she said.

"Yeah, we really gotta go," said Buscado.

"I'm not going anywhere with you," McCracken snapped.

"We came to rescue you," said Buscado.

"You're the reason I'm here," McCracken said. "You think I don't know? I heard your voice inside the car, talking to Howser."

"Come on, no time for this now," said Fuentes. "You're bleeding."

"Leave me the fuck alone, I'll walk back."

"I'm really sorry," said Buscado. "I just thought … I wanted my money."

"You know what they did to me in there?"

"Please, babe, we'll talk this over, I promise," said Fuentes. "Let's go!"

McCracken inspected his left hip, which was scratched and bloody but not badly injured. Buscado took off his jacket and tossed it at McCracken. "Here," he said. "Don't catch cold."

"The car's about a mile away," said Fuentes.

McCracken hesitated. She smiled.

"Come on," she said gently.

He reached up and grabbed her hand. She helped him to his feet, brushing twigs and dirt off his butt.

As they hurried to the car, McCracken turned and glanced up the hill. He had hoped to see the creatures moving about, maybe watching him, but they were gone.

Thirty-Four

Fuentes drove from Pahrump to Las Vegas. At first she was sure a dark van was following them, but the vehicle was gone by the time they reached Mountain Springs.

McCracken sat in the backseat and responded to Fuentes' questions with one-word answers. He ignored Buscado completely.

I-15 was closed between McCarren and downtown, forcing them to take a lengthy detour to get to her new place. As they traveled east, Buscado spotted several large buildings on fire near the Strip, but couldn't find any radio news reports explaining why.

Fuentes had been evicted from her old apartment—the one McCracken knew well—a few weeks earlier and was living in an Airstream trailer at the Whispering Pines Mobile Park, not far from Nellis Air Force Base. The place was semi-furnished, the rent was cheap, and the jet noise wasn't too annoying once she got used to the windows rattling.

Fuentes had to pester the landlord a few times to toss out the worm-infested sofa. On Craigslist she found a $50 replacement couch, which was where Buscado, who had nowhere else to go, was spending his nights.

Fuentes slept in the bedroom on an inflatable queen air mattress. She had sold all her old furniture to pay her monthly expenses. Now that money was almost gone.

When they arrived at the trailer, Fuentes' first goal was to find clothes for McCracken. Buscado had only one pair of pants—which he was wearing—two t-shirts, and a pair of UNLV basketball shorts.

The shorts were too small for McCracken, who put them on anyway.

They sat at the dinette table and ate organic mac and cheese from Trader Joe's, animal crackers, and baby carrots. Fuentes hadn't been to the market in a week.

McCracken, eyes watery, coughed and sniffled.

Fuentes figured he was getting sick and offered him a paper towel. He pushed it away and started crying.

"Chill out, you're safe now," said Buscado, patting McCracken on the shoulder.

McCracken knocked away Buscado's hand.

Fuentes stood and wrapped her arms around McCracken, hugging him tightly for a minute. Buscado finished off the mac and cheese and moved to the sofa.

When McCracken calmed, Fuentes led him to the bathroom and locked the door behind them. She turned on the shower, giggled as she struggled to remove his too-tight shorts, and then took off her clothes.

She helped him into the shower and proceeded to soap his entire body, spending extra time on his penis. He pushed her against the shower wall, grabbed her neck, and entered her from behind. She trembled as he thrust harder and harder, reminding himself it was okay to let go. He came inside her and seemed satisfied, she thought. No condom, no ulterior motive.

She dried his body, wrapped a towel around his waist, and led him to the bedroom. Buscado was watching *Two and a Half Men* and eating pretzels on the sofa.

Fuentes apologized for the air mattress. "It's a little unstable, but you'll get used to it," she said, removing her robe and getting in bed. She smiled and waited.

He stood there naked, watching her.

"What's wrong?"

He continued to stare.

"Hello? Hey, you there?"

"Why'd you do it?"

She sighed. "We've gone over this."

"No."

"I'm sure we have."

"We haven't."

"Babe. I'm sorry. I needed money, I agreed to it, I know …," she said, thinking of the right words. "They … know things about me."

"Do you know what they're doing?"

"What do you mean?"

"With my …"

"A little. Not everything."

He continued to stare.

"You're starting to freak me out a little."

"What about tonight?" he asked.

"What about tonight?"

"Why did you shoot at us?" he asked.

"*Us*? Who's *us*? That's the second time you've asked me that. I didn't shoot at you."

"You shot at the … animals. Didn't you see what they looked like?"

"They were coyotes or something. It was dark."

"Why did you shoot them?"

"I was at the bottom of the hill and aimed upward. I'm a bad shot, okay?"

"You shouldn't have done that."

Fuentes wanted to scream but held it in. She didn't want to fight, not tonight. She moved to the edge of the air mattress, almost tipping it over, and rubbed his thigh. "I'm sorry," she said.

McCracken looked for his shorts but realized they were in the bathroom. He put on her bathrobe and slippers instead.

"What the fuck are you doing?"

"Leaving."

"What—why? Where are you going?"

McCracken didn't answer.

"Come on," she said, tugging on the robe. "Can't this wait till morning? Come to bed."

"Gimme your car keys."

She sat back on the mattress. "No."

He began searching the room for her keys but couldn't find them. "Where are they?" he asked.

She didn't answer.

McCracken opened the bedroom door and

began searching the trailer. Buscado watched from the sofa. "What's up?" he asked.

"Don't talk to me."

"Hey, man, I'm just trying to—"

"I'm gonna find him," McCracken blurted.

"This has nothing to do with him!" yelled Fuentes, emerging from the bedroom naked.

Buscado bolted upright. McCracken ignored her and kept looking.

"You're just chickenshit!" she shouted. "You're just afraid to feel anything."

McCracken slammed his fist into the wall, shaking the trailer violently. He stormed out the front door without the car keys.

"That's right, run away!"

Buscado stared at Fuentes, who flipped him off and returned to the bedroom, slamming the door behind her.

Quickly slipping on his shoes, Buscado hurried out the front door after McCracken, who was walking at a fast pace down Lamont Street.

Buscado spotted him immediately—a large man in pink robe and slippers.

"McCracken!" he shouted.

McCracken didn't turn around. Buscado sprinted after him. "Hey!" he said when he caught up.

"Go away," said McCracken.

"What's wrong with you?"

"I swear I'll break your fucking neck. Go!"

"Chill out, man," said Buscado, maintaining a safe distance. "You wanted an explanation, I'm trying to give you one."

"You have three seconds."

"I figured you and Perlman were gonna screw me out of the money. You guys were acting weird and treating me like shit," said Buscado. "I didn't tell them where you were because I didn't know. They found you on their own."

McCracken grabbed Buscado's arm, yanked him closer, and punched him in the gut. Buscado fell to his knees.

"I can't … breathe ..."

"You'll be fine," said McCracken. "Deep breaths."

Buscado regained his wind. McCracken helped him to his feet.

"I swear I'm sorry," said Buscado. "You can keep my share, okay? Just leave me a few bucks to get back on my feet."

"It's not about the money."

"I know, I know, your kid. I'll help you, okay? Rosa, I know she wants to help too."

"I'm leaving."

"What? Why?"

McCracken continued walking.

"Hey, you got a good woman back there, man," said Buscado. "Nothing going on between us, if that's what you're thinking."

"I'm not."

"Then what is it?"

"I'm running out of time."

"Why do you say that? Look, you haven't seen him in … how long has it been?"

"I just feel it."

"Listen—and don't hit me—you're screwing up. I wanna help, Rosa wants to help. Shit, I wish I had a woman like that. You're throwing her away, man."

"I'm not."

"Yeah, you are."

"No."

"Maybe you are chickenshit."

"No."

"Come on, let's go back," said Buscado. "We'll all help. Perlman too."

"Perlman?"

"We haven't talked or anything, but I think he's trying to reach Rosa," said Buscado. "Posted a note on her trailer door yesterday, asking if they could get together. She tossed it in the trash, but I fished it out."

"He's a sick fuck."

"True, but he's smart."

"What'd it say?"

"The note? Says he knows where your kid is."

McCracken stopped walking.

"I mean, I dunno if it's true or anything," said Buscado. "Maybe he thought he had a chance with Rosa if he told her that—or he's telling the truth."

A pickup truck with three teenagers drove by. They jeered at McCracken. "Faggot!" one of them yelled.

"Okay," said McCracken. "Let's go back."

"Cool."

They returned quickly to Whispering Pines. The night breeze was chilly but not too cold.

"Sorry I punched you," said McCracken.

Buscado nodded.

They reached the trailer and saw the front door was ajar. "I know I shut it when I left," said Buscado. They rushed inside.

Fuentes was gone.

Thirty-Five

Riot police encircled the 750-foot husk of L'Auberge Las Vegas, a never-completed resort and casino that had sat abandoned for more than a decade on the north end of the Strip. A day earlier, protesters had stormed the vacant shell, overwhelming a skeleton crew of security guards and occupying L'Auberge's lower floors. The brazen move encouraged a second swarm of squatters to move in, quickly turning Vegas' most imposing structure into the world's tallest homeless camp.

The original security team had moved out hours ago. Black-helmeted enforcers were now in charge—a tip Taulia Sarono had received just an hour earlier via anonymous text.

Sarono had seen riot police before, but never

like this: heads encased in what appeared to be tight-fitting black buckets; a ring of red LEDs encircling the head at eye level; no openings for eyes, ears, mouth, or nose.

Was the tipster Cheryl? He had no way of knowing. The two hadn't spoken since the day she got him fired.

Okay, that wasn't fair, he thought. She wasn't responsible. Maybe he was just bitter.

The night Cheryl showed up unannounced, she stayed maybe 15 minutes. Sarono knew immediately who she was; her kidnapping, though weeks old, was still marketable fodder for talk shows, conspiracy bloggers, and subreddits. Reporters had been digging diligently but still couldn't turn up anything on her, aside from her home address in the Vegas metro. Her mysteriousness was irresistible.

And here she was, standing in Uncle Eli's garage.

He had a million questions. Who kidnapped her? Why? Where had she gone? And most importantly, who was she?

He wanted an exclusive. She wanted to talk about McCracken.

"I'm more interested in your story than his," said Sarono.

Cheryl declined, quietly insisting that if Sarono persisted in asking personal, intrusive questions, she'd leave. He agreed—reluctantly—and Cheryl accepted his offer to sit in the canvas director's chair and be interviewed.

She confirmed the more outrageous elements of McCracken's story. It was estimated that an infinitesimally small percentage of human males—maybe one in five hundred million, no one knew for sure—had the genetic mutation that made *Universaliter Acceptos* possible.

"My math might be off a bit," she added.

"How do you know this?" Sarono asked.

He repeated the question several times over the quarter-hour, occasionally changing the phrasing to see if a less direct approach would get her to open up.

It didn't.

"Why should I believe what you're telling me?" he asked.

"Look around you," she replied.

"Look around me? What does that mean?"

She fidgeted in her chair, crossing and uncrossing her legs repeatedly. Sarono noticed black leggings under her baggy jeans. Her legs were long and thin, but he wasn't focused on her physical traits. An interview with this woman could turbocharge his career.

Photos, yes, he would need those. Video too. He checked his phone battery—fifty-five percent remaining. All was good.

He grew agitated and had to pee.

"I'll be right back," he told her.

As he flushed the toilet, he heard a scraping sound across the cement floor. When he returned from the bathroom, she was gone.

The next day Sarono told his editor about Cheryl's visit. She asked for proof.

He insisted the *Register* run the story: *Cheryl Francis Thompson, mysterious kidnapping victim from Henderson, is alive and well and here in town.*

Details were scant, but he could find a way to pad the piece.

She asked again for proof—an in-office interview, video chat, photos. "Or work on something else," she said.

Sarono had a personal blog. He posted the story there. It went viral—in a bad way. People called him batshit crazy, a loon. He provided no evidence he had met Cheryl. No audio, no video. Not a single pic.

He was fired.

Now he was just another unemployed journalist with a blog, albeit one with a small and growing audience.

But no income.

For an abandoned construction site, the L'Auberge was hopping on a Saturday night.

Sarono had been inside the place a year earlier, sneaking past security to shoot video for a feature on what went on inside an unfinished mega-resort. Nothing much had been going on, actually, aside from rat, bat, and bird activity. Things were different now.

Sarono couldn't take his eyes off the cops. They were unusually tall—NBA tall—but with spindly legs too thin, and feet too long and narrow, for their bodies. Their torsos were husky, though, perhaps because of the body armor.

He wondered about their helmet lights. A camera system of some sort? It was hard to tell from fifty yards out.

The riot police formed a ring around the structure.

Sarono looked around; no other reporters were nearby, at least none he could identify. He saw flickering lights some twenty floors up, in a section where windows had been broken by vandals over the years.

He walked to the rear of the structure and saw more riot police, but no protesters. He heard shouting above, then what sounded like a muffled scream. The cops didn't respond to the noise.

Sarono saw a dark object tumbling down the east-facing side of the building.

There was another way inside the L'Auberge—an adjacent eight-story parking garage built for the resort. The El Camino Hotel & Casino, located next door, was using it now.

In his previous tour of the L'Auberge, Sarono had paid a squatter $10 to guide him through an underground passage leading from the garage's basement to the hotel. While other walkways from the garage had been sealed over the years, this one was still accessible, largely because few people knew it existed.

Sarono walked to the El Camino, passed through the casino, and entered the parking structure. No protesters here, just gamblers heading to and from their cars.

A riot officer stood silently at the payment kiosk, his head turning to track Sarono as he walked quickly to the northwest corner of the garage.

There it was: the door marked PRIVATE, behind which was a hidden stairwell leading to the lower level.

They never lock it, man, the squatter had told him. He was right. The warped door required several swift kicks before opening just enough for Sarono to slip through.

He descended to the basement and walked along the north wall to a door marked EMERGENCY EXIT. A separate sign read: OPEN DOOR AND ALARM WILL SOUND.

Sarono pressed the exit handle and pushed the door open. No alarm. He descended another flight of stairs leading to an unlit corridor. Turning on his phone's flashlight, he hurried through the cool, damp tunnel, surprising the occasional rodent.

A clanging sound echoed off the walls.

Sarono turned to see a pinpoint of red light growing larger. He turned off his flashlight and edged along the wall, moving as fast as he could as the red glow behind him grew brighter.

He heard footsteps.

Jogging now, hands sliding along the smooth, concrete wall, Sarono prayed there was nothing to trip over, no abandoned work bucket to kick.

He saw a soft glow ahead, ambient light

streaming down from the L'Auberge entrance. He quickened his pace, jogging to the stairwell and bounding up the steps as quietly as possible.

The vast lobby was a concrete and steel shell, as cavernous as an airport terminal. Very majestic, thought Sarono, as he glanced up at mounds of pigeon shit encrusted on exposed steel beams.

A red glow caught the corner of his eye. Sarono sprinted across the lobby, hiding behind a four-by-four support pillar. Footsteps approached, stopped abruptly, and moved away.

Sarono peeked around the pillar to see a riot officer standing near the elevator bank, helmet lights casting an eerie halo. The cop wasn't moving, which posed a problem; the nearby fire stairwell was Sarono's only path to the upper floors.

The distant sound of breaking glass caught the officer's attention. The cop moved toward the noise at the opposite end of the lobby.

Sarono bolted to the fire stairwell. He raced up the steps, not pausing for breath until he reached the seventh floor.

Panting heavily, he realized he wasn't as fit as he had thought.

Sarono caught his breath and scanned the floor. Nothing unusual—support beams, a few scattered beer bottles, discarded construction materials, a sleeping bag, and more pigeon droppings.

Floor-to-ceiling windows protected most of the interior from the elements, although a few panes were missing here and there.

He walked to a windowless section and stood at the ledge, studying the crowd below. He estimated maybe two dozen protesters—not enough to draw news coverage these days, as there were far larger protests elsewhere—and three times as many riot officers, some blocking the entrance to the parking garage.

He remembered the falling object he had seen earlier. Sarono looked up. How far had it fallen? From what floor? Maybe the twentieth, but he was guessing.

Returning to the stairwell, he continued climbing, guided by the soft glow of his phone's screen. The flashlight app stayed off; in addition to drawing unwanted attention, it drained the battery too fast.

He continued his investigation. Floors eight to ten, nothing. The eleventh floor had a small dome tent pitched near a window, but no one was inside, only a blanket, a BIC Lighter, and a couple of empty LaCroix cans.

Floors twelve through eighteen, zilch.

Continue to the seventieth floor? Hardly. This was looking like a waste of time. And shooting random video of empty floors didn't make a lot of sense.

Then again, he had nothing better to do.

On the nineteenth floor, Sarono spotted a dark shadow lurking in a windowless section. LED signage from across the street brightened the floor somewhat, allowing Taulia to identify the shadow as a riot officer.

The cop leaned out of the building and looked up. He—it?—leaped out and began scaling the exterior wall, scrambling upward and out of view.

Sarono dropped his phone. Cursing, he quickly picked it up and checked the screen—no visible damage. He launched the video recorder and ran toward the spot where the cop had stood.

A scraping sound caught his attention. Sarono darted behind a support column as the cop swooped back inside the building, landing gracefully on its feet.

Sarono's heart raced. *Scoop.*

He heard the cop moving across the floor, mostly along the ledge. Sarono kept repositioning himself behind the thick column to avoid detection.

He edged his phone around the pillar, tapping the start button to capture video of the cop leaping off the ledge to the next floor up.

Another scream.

Sarono was ready to climb the stairs for a closer look, when the cop landed on the floor, grasping a man by the neck.

The man's body was limp, his clothes dirty and tattered. He had stringy, dirty hair and a salt-and-pepper beard. His sneakers dragged across the floor, squeaking loudly as the cop dragged him like a rag doll toward the elevator shafts.

Watching the video screen, Sarono zoomed in and noticed something odd about the officer's gloved, oversized hands: they were shaped like talons.

The cop reached the elevator bank and flung the man's body down the center shaft.

Sarono, staying in the shadows, edged toward the stairwell. He stumbled over a PVC pipe, a decade-old construction artifact, which skipped noisily across the concrete floor.

The cop, helmet lights flashing, turned toward the sound.

Sarono dashed down the stairs, leaping three steps at a time. Floor nineteen … eighteen … running in total darkness.

Seventeenth floor.

Thumps and stomps behind him, growing louder …

He couldn't outrun this thing.

Sarono exited the stairwell at the sixteenth floor and ran toward the elevator bank, desperate to find a new escape route.

A taloned hand seized his neck, jolting him backward, Sarono dropped his phone and gasped for air.

The cop dragged him toward the elevator shaft.

Don't panic … don't panic …

Sarono had a ballpoint pen in his back pocket. He pulled it out and jammed it into the taloned hand. The grip loosened, and he broke free.

The cop grabbed him again, shoving him against the wall, inches from the elevator shaft. Sarono fell to his knees and clutched the edge of the shaft, fighting the cop's efforts to push him over the edge.

Spotting guardrails inside the shaft, Sarono grabbed the cop's leg and rolled over the edge, grasping a guardrail with his free hand.

The cop lost its balance and tumbled down the shaft.

Sarono watched the red lights dim, then go dark as a dull *thump* reached his ears.

He pulled himself out of the shaft, resting for a minute on his back. His neck hurt, but not as badly as his left ankle, which he must have sprained in the scuffle.

Sarono hobbled across the floor, found his phone, and limped down the stairs, favoring his right leg.

The descent took a half-hour. He checked for signs of police activity before entering the lobby. All was quiet. He hobbled through the tunnel and garage to the El Camino, where he sat briefly at a video poker machine to catch his breath.

His ankle was killing him.

Sarono took a rideshare home, requesting a human driver to avoid trouble with Uncle Eli, and immediately posted the riot-cop video to his blog. The clip, though dark and grainy, clearly showed the cop's superhuman skills.

Feeling an adrenaline rush, Sarono promoted the clip on every social media outlet he could find. Then he popped three Extra Strength Tylenol and went to bed.

He slept fitfully for an hour before getting up. His ankle was swollen and still hurting. He might have to see a doctor.

His phone pinged.

A text from someone named Perlman. It took a

while, but Sarono remembered him: McCracken's friend from the High Roller.

Perlman said he had just watched the cop video and wanted to meet.

In the morning, Sarono texted back.

Right fucking now pecker, Perlman replied.

Thirty-Six

Perlman suggested meeting at Sunset Medical Center, where Sarono planned to have his ankle X-rayed.

"You're a viral sensation, dude," Perlman said over the phone. "I'm reading the comments on your blog now—half of 'em think you CGI'd that clip."

Sarono really didn't want to meet Perlman and mulled whether to ask Uncle Eli to drive him to Sunset at 4:30 a.m. Then again, the pain was easing and his Gmail inbox had 424 new messages. His ankle could wait.

"You're trending on Twitter!" shouted Perlman.

"What, where?"

"Everywhere, man. Nationwide, maybe global."

As Perlman blathered on, Sarono thought about the riot cop and what it portended.

He set his phone on the floor and hopped about the garage on one foot, searching for his missing shoe. Headlights flashed briefly through the side window; Sarono peeked outside and saw two cars parked in front of the house.

He hopped back to his phone, nearly falling over as he picked it up.

"Hey, gotta go," he told Perlman.

"Dude, did you just turn your blog private?"

Loud knocking outside—probably the front door.

"Hey … you there?"

Sarono snuck out the side door and hobbled toward the backyard. Holding his phone in one hand, he could hear Perlman's muffled voice:

"Down … reloading … shit! … 404 error …"

Sarono stuffed the phone in his pocket. Holding the side gate with both hands, he put light pressure on his bad ankle. Not too bad. A little weight was okay.

He heard his uncle talking loudly to someone—Eli's anxious tone.

Sarono unlatched the backyard gate, relieved that Eli had ignored his pestering to keep it locked. Crouching low, he hobbled along the back fence but feared he was too visible. He dropped to his hands and knees, crawling across the landscape rock to the propane grill, which backed against the rear fence.

Through the sliding glass door, he could see Eli at the front entrance, his uncle's oversized body blocking the visitors.

Should he go back in? Maybe. But as a fighter he wouldn't be of much use. He could barely walk.

Eli shut the door and immediately locked it, including the deadbolt, which he rarely used. He stayed there and appeared to be watching someone through the door viewer.

Sarono grabbed his phone and texted Eli.

thanks, im ok, no worries

Hoisting his body up and straddling the wooden fence, Sarono paused, remembering who lived next door: Dale, the cranky old fart with a concealed firearm permit.

Dale fantasized about shooting intruders—preferably dark-skinned—and wasn't shy about sharing his fantasies with Eli after a few beers.

Sarono would have to move fast.

He slid down the fence, landing in Dale's cactus garden, and limped clumsily toward the side gate. Iggy, Dale's miniature dachshund, was watching from inside the sliding glass door and started yapping as the intruder neared the house.

Sarono's phone pinged.

whatever u did, get ur ass back safe

A light flicked in the master bedroom as Sarono reached the side gate.

Dale, unlike Uncle Eli, locked his gate.

It took Sarono two tries to hoist his body over the top. He hobbled down the street, Iggy yapping the entire time.

He limped two blocks before hiding between a Winnebago and a Dodge Ram 2500. Catching his breath, he texted Perlman and asked for a lift.

Five minutes passed. Sarono was ready to call a cab when his phone pinged.

no wheels but can hack a car share, where u at?

Perlman promised to be there in ten minutes, tops.

Fifteen minutes passed, then twenty. No Perlman.

A few minutes later a purple Hyundai Accent with a dented front bumper cruised by. Sarono waved; the car stopped abruptly.

Sarono opened the passenger door and slowly lowered himself into the seat.

"Sorry, dude, hospital's gonna have to wait," said Perlman. "Doctors lie anyway, and if you can walk on it, it can't be that bad."

"Let's go."

Sarono checked for new messages from Eli.

Perlman extended his hand. "Gimme your phone," he said.

"What, why?"

"I'm a technical genius. Give it to me."

"It works fine."

"Trust me on this one. Hand it over."

Sarono hesitated, then gave his phone to Perlman, who rolled down his window and chucked the handset into a vacant lot.

"What the fuck!"

"You're broadcasting your location to the world, dipshit," Perlman said. "It's a beacon, you're a target."

"I need my phone. My life's in that phone!"

"Don't be naive," said Perlman. "Your blog's dead, which means that clip you posted is real. From here on out, the only phone you're using is a burner, like mine."

"I need web access."

"The web is for losers. What you need to do is kiss my ass for downloading your clip before it got snuffed. I'm torrenting that motherfucker everywhere."

"With what, your burner?"

"Is there anything I can't do? They'll have to

shut down the internet, I mean global, to keep folks from seeing it."

Perlman kept talking but Sarono wasn't listening. He was worried about Uncle Eli. Maybe he should have stayed and …

"Hey! You listening, pecker?"

"Huh? Yeah. Long night."

"Don't expect to sleep 'cause we got a lot to do. Did you happen to go downtown yesterday?"

"No, just the L'Auberge."

"Well, a bunch of cops were rounding up transients and losers near Container Park. Same deal—helmet heads, super tall, just like your video."

"You were there?"

"No, heard about it," said Perlman. "One cop climbed up the outer wall of the Westfield Inn, plucked a piss-bum off the fourth floor, and chucked him out the window. SPLAT, on the ground. Too bad you weren't there to shoot it, scoop."

"What about the face?"

"What?"

"I couldn't see the cop's face, it was covered."

"Doubt it has one," said Perlman. "This *Acceptos* shit is all mix and match. Who knows what's under that helmet."

"That woman, the kidnapped one, she came by my place and told me about—"

"What?" Perlman interrupted. "What woman?"

"From Henderson. She's on the news all the time."

"You mean Cheryl?"

"Yeah, her."

"Dude, you're losin' it. No way Cheryl—"

A loud pop silenced Perlman as the Hyundai began shaking. Pulling to the curb, they kept the engine running and looked out the window. The front left tire was shredded.

"Well, that's that," said Perlman.

"Maybe there's a spare."

"No way, I'm not getting out here. Could be an ambush. We're riding the rim to a safer spot."

Perlman edged the car back onto Rancho Drive. Checking the rearview, he spotted a pair of headlights gaining on them.

"Shit," he said. "When I stop, run."

The Hyundai swerved into a massive parking lot fronting the Rancho Discount Mall. At night the lot was a makeshift homeless camp filled with tents, trucks, and trailers. Scattered bonfires dotted the landscape.

Perlman tried to weave through the crowd. The Hyundai sideswiped two family-sized tents, narrowly missing a congregation of folks huddled around a trash-can fire. It crashed into a trio of containers, two of them burning.

The cans flew like projectiles, skipping across the lot.

An angry crowd swarmed the Hyundai; a gray-haired woman pounded Sarono's window with both fists.

"Come out, assholes!" she yelled.

"Now what?" Sarono asked Perlman.

"Just chill."

"What? They're gonna kill us."

"Better them than what's after us."

"Maybe."

"REALLY SORRY! BRAKES WENT OUT!" Perlman shouted over and over.

He kept smiling, waving, and shouting. Eventually the crowd cooled and dispersed, leaving the lone angry woman pounding on Sarono's window.

"Okay, let's go," said Sarono.

"Not in this rig," said Perlman, thumping the dashboard. "Besides, these folks seem pretty cool. We didn't kill anyone, just knocked over their cans."

"We could change cars."

"Not yet."

"So what then?"

"Your girlfriend," said Perlman.

"Huh?"

"The crazy wench mumbling outside your window. Ask her if she wants to party. Flirt with her."

Sarono rolled down the window an inch, just enough to let in fresh air. A pungent aroma filled the cabin.

The woman pressed her nose against the glass and stared blankly at Sarono. Long, grimy bangs covered half her face.

"Hey, babe," said Perlman. "Know what time it is?"

"No, I do not know what time it is," she replied slowly.

"It's 4:20 and we wanna party with you."

She stared at Perlman. "You're ugly," she said.

Sarono saw red lights flashing at the edge of the lot.

The woman pointed at Sarono. "I'll party with him, he's hot," she said.

"Well, I've got something pretty boy here doesn't have, a big-ass blunt," said Perlman. "Get ready to toke, hot pants. Party's at your place."

She said yes.

They weaved between the tents, Perlman cursing Sarono for hobbling behind and hampering their progress. The camp had grown in the short time they had been there; new tents and trash fires were springing up everywhere.

Perlman kept an eye out for trouble—hovering drones, squad cars, unmarked black vans—but no one appeared to be following them.

The woman led them to the rear of the strip mall, across an employee lot, and through a broken section of a brick wall that led to the outfield of a baseball diamond.

Sarono needed a rest. Wherever she was taking them, he hoped it wasn't much further.

They walked across the infield toward a tall dome tent pitched by the backstop.

"They sweep through here every night, so nobody camps here," the woman said. "But Pepe told me they're understaffed tonight and won't be patrolling the park, so here we are."

"Pepe?" asked Sarono.

"Oh, you'll meet him."

The woman unzipped the tent flap, tossing aside a sleeping pad, a plastic milk carton half-filled with yellow liquid, and a man's flannel shirt. She entered the tent on her hands and knees.

"Don't mind the mess," she said.

Sarono grabbed Perlman's arm. "What are we doing here?" he whispered.

"Hanging at the camp is suicide and, who knows, we might get lucky," said Perlman, pulling a cigarillo-sized joint from his shirt pocket.

"They're gonna search here too."

Perlman handed his phone to Sarono. "You know Cheryl's number?" he asked. "Give her a call. Have her come get us."

They entered the tent, which was spacious enough for four adults. A standard-sized hairless terrier sat in one corner. The animal did not move from its spot, despite having strangers in its den.

"Whoa, this Pepe?" asked Perlman, reaching toward the dog, which growled at him.

"Pepe, baby, how are you, my love!" the woman cooed, kissing the dog on the forehead and mouth.

"So what kind of breed is Pepe?" asked Sarono.

"Pure love, that's what."

Pepe's eyes moved from Sarono to Perlman, then back to Sarono.

Perlman pulled a lighter from his right sock and lit the joint. He took a hit and passed the joint to Sarono, who inhaled deeply.

Sarono rarely smoked pot, which usually made him paranoid. He wondered why he was partaking this time.

"I wasn't always living in a tent, in case you boys were wondering," said the woman, declining the joint. "Moved out from Michigan with this guy—okay, boyfriend—and his kid. Both are gone. Kid's somewhere in San Diego and the boyfriend, honestly, I don't care."

Sarono's THC paranoia was setting in. That fucking dog. Staring at him. Didn't it ever blink?

"Pepe found me a few months ago," the woman said. "Just wandered into my tent one morning. He's my BFF."

"You and the dog, how close are you?" asked Perlman.

"What do you mean?"

"Bet it gets pretty lonely out here sometimes."

The dog growled.

Sarono suddenly realized his ankle barely hurt at all, which calmed his nerves. He studied the dog's face. "That's strange," he said.

"Pepe is not strange," the woman said. "He's my companion. There should be more men like him."

"No, I mean it's almost like he understands what we're saying."

"And he's funny looking," said Perlman.

The dog's eyes locked on Perlman.

"Dude, text her now," Perlman whispered to Sarono. "That thing's gonna bite my pecker off."

Sarono opened his wallet and pulled out a crumpled paper scrap with Cheryl's number scribbled on it. He sent a brief text, asking her to meet them at the parking lot behind the outfield.

"I wouldn't be living here if things were better," the woman said.

Pepe placed its paw on the woman's wrist.

"Sure, baby," she said.

The dog rose and trotted out of the tent. It returned within a minute, carrying in its mouth a white plastic device shaped like a computer mouse.

"Time for my blood sample," the woman said, removing the device from its cellophane wrapper and positioning it on her upper left arm. "This draws my blood, which I do every day. Pepe takes it to the clinic."

"What's that?"

"Your dog does … what?"

Pepe stared at Perlman again. It wasn't blinking.

"Lady, your mutt's freaking me out."

"How dare you call him a mutt!"

Pepe bared its teeth, which looked unnaturally flat and smooth.

Perlman's phone pinged. "Cheryl, she'll meet us in ten," Sarono said.

"Hey, it's been great," said Perlman, nudging Sarono toward the exit. "Gotta run."

"Not until you apologize to Pepe," the woman said.

Perlman cleared his throat and looked directly at the animal. "I'm very sorry," he said.

Cheryl picked them up in a brand-new Chevy Cruze with dealer plates. Perlman demanded answers about everything. She had nothing to say.

"Please drive by my uncle's house," Sarono pleaded.

"No, dude, bad idea," said Perlman. "Probably staked out."

Cynthia agreed it wasn't a good idea, but said she'd try.

They saw black smoke from three blocks away. Then the fire trucks. The street was blocked when they tried to turn on it.

Uncle Eli's house was in flames.

Thirty-Seven

The note, handwritten on floral stationery, said to go to Angel Peak.

McCracken found the note, along with payment-past-due notices from Verizon and NV Energy, in Fuentes' mailbox the day after she vanished. The message instructed no one in particular to go to a dome-shaped structure at the peak as soon as possible.

"That's Cheryl's handwriting," said Buscado, examining the note. "The left slant, the small letters, the way she dots her *i*'s. I know it's her."

McCracken checked the letter again.

"This is bullshit," he said, crumpling up the pretty paper and tossing it on the ground. Buscado was no handwriting analyst. He saw signs of Cheryl everywhere.

"She implied Rosa is there too, you know. 'To get what you want, come here,'" said Buscado, quoting the note.

"Could mean anything."

"Do you want her back, I mean, really want her back?"

McCracken did, despite her treachery.

Driving there would be difficult. Freedom Checkpoints were now in operation across the Valley. Only authorized personnel could come and go freely.

Internet, cable, and satellite service was down. Official reports initially blamed sunspots, then global terrorism. Whatever the cause, digital devices were mostly useless.

Radio and TV news reports were limited to prerecorded tutorials explaining the benefits of Freedom Checkpoints and why they were necessary.

A digital billboard on I-15 near Tropicana showed a boomerang-shaped logo. All other billboards had gone dark.

Driving within Southern Nevada was permitted, but out-of-area routes were blocked. Self-driving semis and cargo jets continued to deliver food, medicine, and other essentials. Two-way communication with the outside world was suspended, with no word as to when it might resume.

"It's a bubble, we're living in a bubble," said Buscado over and over.

He and McCracken were sleeping in a Dodge Dart that belonged to Fuentes' neighbors—a part-time stripper named Private Browser and her boyfriend Heath. The Dart seemed safer than Fuentes' trailer.

The riots broke out soon after the first Freedom Checkpoint announcement. One started inside Caesar's Palace Race & Sports Book when game seven of the NBA Finals was blacked out. It spilled out onto Flamingo and resulted in two deaths—a protester and a bystander.

Another erupted for unknown reasons inside a recreational weed dispensary at a strip mall at Decatur and Twain. In both instances, helmeted riot officers were brought in to keep the peace, according to official reports.

McCracken spent much of his time in the Dart, listening to AM radio.

The only station broadcasting aired inspirational speeches, including one by Howser, who said the temporary information blackout was necessary to ease tensions during the "focused transition."

The payoff: higher-paying jobs and a better life for all.

"That's crazy AF—nothing's getting better, only nuttier," Private Browser told McCracken during a lap dance in the Dart. She liked the fact that he was tall and didn't talk much.

McCracken went to a public food drive in a Vons parking lot, a half-mile from Whispering Pines. Locals, lined up behind a fleet of big rigs, waited impatiently for five-gallon jugs of water and a shopping cart filled with organic canned and frozen foods. The supplies were free, but recipients were required to submit their driver's license or state I.D.

Waiting in line, McCracken wondered what Perlman was up to. Jail? Dead? Unlikely. The little shit was like a cockroach. Even nuclear war couldn't wipe him out.

The thought made McCracken smile.

When he reached the front of the line, McCracken inserted Buscado's driver's license into the chip reader. He didn't have his own I.D.—not that he would have used it anyway.

A few seconds later, a water jug and a

suitcase-sized container of food slid down a chute from the back of the truck.

On the walk back to Whispering Pines, McCracken spotted several kids huddled in a large, vacant lot between a medical supplies store and an abandoned car wash. From a hundred yards out, the kids appeared to be throwing rocks at something—maybe a small animal—cowering against a brick wall.

McCracken was angry. Leaving his supplies on the sidewalk, he sprinted towards the kids.

The children were younger than he had thought—middle-schoolers, three boys and a girl. They looked terrified as McCracken neared.

The two tallest boys dropped the rocks they were holding. The girl did not, but shielded herself behind the boys.

"What's going on here!" McCracken shouted.

"Nothing, sir," said the tallest boy. "It's that ... *thing.*"

He pointed at the back of the lot.

A man in tattered jeans was lying on the ground. McCracken saw what looked like a fair-skinned woman wearing green hospital scrubs kneeling by the man's side. She appeared to be resuscitating the man. Maybe she was a paramedic on an emergency call, McCracken thought.

He walked over for a closer look. When he was ten feet away, the woman turned.

Her smooth, metallic face glistened in the sun. There was no nose or mouth. Her eyes, bright and built from animal tissue, were almond shaped and distinctly unhuman. They darkened as McCracken approached.

The girl threw a rock at the creature, missing by a yard.

The thing leaped ten feet and landed beside the girl, grabbing her by the waist. The other kids screamed and scattered.

McCracken didn't move.

Clutching the girl, the thing jumped again, returning to its spot beside the man on the ground.

McCracken grabbed a fist-sized rock near his feet. He flung it hard, smacking the creature between the eyes.

The thing fell back and released the girl. It crouched low, grabbed something off the man's chest, and leaped away, landing on the rooftop of a nearby apartment building.

It jumped from roof to roof until it vanished from sight.

"What was that?" asked the girl, shaking and crying. She ran back to the other kids.

"Go home," McCracken told them.

They stood there in shock.

"Go!"

The kids ran off.

McCracken walked over to the man and checked his pulse. Dead. The eyes had been removed, and a small plastic device resembling a computer mouse was attached to the man's arm.

When McCracken picked up the device, blood dripped out of one end and coated his fingers.

Sirens in the distance. Growing louder.

McCracken hurried to his groceries and jogged back to Whispering Pines.

When he arrived, an agitated Buscado was pacing beside the Dart. "Hear the news? More checkpoints tonight," he said.

McCracken pointed at two envelopes in Buscado's hand. "What are those?" he asked.

"Posted on Rosa's door, saw 'em an hour ago."

"You read them?"

"This one's addressed to both of us," said Buscado, waving the open envelope. "Told us to go to Angel Peak, same as before."

"Cheryl's handwriting?"

"No, printer."

"What's the other one?"

Buscado handed the sealed envelope to

McCracken, who tore off one end and pulled out the letter. All caps:

ACCEPTOS WORKING AGAIN — NEW PRIMARY SOURCE IN PLACE AND OPERATIONAL

McCracken crumpled up the letter and kicked the Dart's passenger door several times. Calming a bit, he uncrumpled the note and read it again. He leaned against the Dart and took a long, deep breath.

He handed the note to Buscado, who read it.

"So … what now?" asked Buscado.

"Let's go."

Thirty-Eight

Buscado was behind the wheel as they headed northwest on US-95. He had been to Angel Peak several times, most recently to drop off his kids at a summer sports camp near there.

"Great place to cool off in the summer," he told McCracken, who wasn't listening. "Only an hour away but a zillion degrees cooler."

The scorched-earth landscape of the Las Vegas Valley was starting to get on McCracken's nerves. He yearned for the greenery of Georgia and made a mental note to return there when—or if—he got the chance.

They slowed for a Freedom Checkpoint near the Durango Drive exit.

"What should we say?" asked Buscado.

McCracken grunted, meaning he didn't know. He saw a school bus creeping forward in the right lane. Turning his head for a better look, he noticed the bottom half of each passenger window was blacked out. The bus was full, but McCracken could see only the top of the kids' heads.

The autonomous truck in front of them moved slowly through the checkpoint. A police officer—white, short, pudgy, sunglasses—waved the Dart forward.

Some fifty feet ahead, a row of black-helmeted officers stood at attention near the side of the road.

The Dart came to a stop and Buscado rolled down his window. "Afternoon, Officer," he said pleasantly.

"License and registration," the cop replied.

Buscado opened his wallet and handed over his license. McCracken searched the glove compartment and found what looked like a vehicle registration slip, which he passed to Buscado.

The cop examined the documents closely. "Who's … Gail Boechner?" he asked.

"Excuse me?" Buscado asked.

"The car's registered to a Gail Boechner. Is that you?"

"Private Browser," McCracken mumbled.

"Oh, she owns the car," Buscado said. "We're just borrowing it."

"Where you headed?"

"Just camping."

McCracken glanced at the school bus again, hoping for a better look. No luck. The kids appeared to be well-behaved—all sitting quietly, not jumping around.

"Camping? Doesn't look like you brought much gear."

"Our friends have it," said Buscado. "We're meeting them up at Angel Peak."

McCracken bit his lip. Dumbass Buscado could have named any Southern Nevada campsite, but just had to give their actual destination.

The bus inched forward. The kids weren't moving about. In fact, they didn't seem to be moving at all.

"Any gear in the trunk?"

"A few things."

"Pop open the trunk, sir," the officer ordered.

"Well, I don't see why—"

"Pop the trunk."

"Excuse me, Officer," said McCracken, leaning toward the driver's window. "Why is this called a Freedom Checkpoint?"

The cop bent down, removed his sunglasses,

and looked McCracken square in the eye. "Is there a problem here?" he asked.

"Nope, no problem," said Buscado.

"Then open the trunk."

"I'm just not clear where the 'freedom' part comes into it," said McCracken, glancing at the school bus again.

"What are you, a troublemaker?"

"No, Officer, not at all," Buscado answered.

The cop pointed at McCracken. "Got a problem with freedom, buddy?"

"Doesn't feel too free to me, that's all."

The officer stood upright and nodded in the direction of the riot police. He took a step away from the Dart. "Out of the car, both of you," he said.

Buscado looked at McCracken, who nodded and opened the passenger door. Stepping onto the pavement, McCracken watched the bus inch forward through the checkpoint.

He was right. The kids weren't moving at all.

"Hey, you, over here!" the cop shouted at McCracken, who stood staring at the bus.

It was him. He was sure of it. Last kid, back of the bus. The head, the hair, same as before. Just like Thryce's age-progression photo.

"Stop!" McCracken shouted.

The bus accelerated and pulled away.

McCracken ran after it but stopped when four helmeted officers blocked his path. He turned and ran back to the Dodge.

The checkpoint cop unholstered his gun. "On the ground!" he shouted, aiming his weapon at McCracken's chest.

McCracken mulled his options. He sensed the cop was frightened, maybe even terrified, and didn't want a confrontation. He simply wanted McCracken to comply.

But he was either inexperienced or poorly trained.

For starters, he was standing too close to his target.

McCracken lunged forward, grabbed the gun barrel and twisted it down. The trigger went off; a bullet hit the pavement and ricocheted away.

McCracken wrestled the gun away and kicked the cop in the groin.

"Look out!" shouted Buscado.

A riot cop leaped fifty feet and landed on the hood of the Dart. McCracken fired three shots into the cop's torso, knocking the creature to the pavement.

"Let's go!" shouted McCracken, jumping in the passenger seat. Buscado got behind the wheel and gunned the engine as another riot cop landed on the roof.

McCracken reached out the window and fired two shots at the cop, who tumbled off the roof.

Using the shoulder, Buscado pushed the Dart up to 85 mph.

"Nobody's following us, go figure," he said, glancing in the rearview mirror.

They stayed on US-95 for several miles before turning left onto Kyle Canyon, the road to Angel Peak.

"Crank it," said McCracken.

"I'm doing a hundred."

"Faster."

Buscado floored the pedal; the four-cylinder engine whined and rumbled.

The incline was gradual with few curves, allowing Buscado to relax a bit. At this speed, any unexpected turn could be deadly.

A metallic object was gaining on them.

"Shit, I'm doing one-twenty."

McCracken looked out the rear window. "Faster!" he shouted.

"Won't help," said Buscado. "Turn-off's coming up."

"What?"

"I'm taking the fire road."

"In this thing?"

Buscado slowed to ninety, then sixty. Their tail was less than a half-mile behind and gaining fast.

He spotted the guardrails, the sign that Powerline Road, the trail up to Angel Peak, wasn't far off.

The Dart swerved onto the shoulder and made a hard right up a steep dirt path. Buscado countersteered to keep the car from fishtailing.

"A Dart can off-road?"

"Depends on the road condition, but you'd be surprised," said Buscado, finding the trail wider and easier to navigate than he had anticipated.

A large black vehicle, possibly a van or truck, was gaining on them. The dust made it difficult to gauge the distance.

The trail narrowed with barely enough room for one vehicle. Beyond the ledge to the left was a 300-foot drop into a box canyon.

The Dart slammed against a small boulder. Buscado downshifted and edged the front tires over the rock, which wedged against the undercarriage.

The wheels spun uselessly.

"Hold on," said McCracken, opening his door. He ran behind the Dart and began rocking it up and down.

Buscado checked the rearview; the black vehicle was bumping up the hill, getting closer.

McCracken's rocking caused the boulder to shift, creating a small gap between it and the undercarriage. "Go!" he yelled.

Buscado floored it, spraying gravel and dust in McCracken's face. The Dart lurched forward.

McCracken ran to the passenger side and tried to open the door. It was locked. He slapped the window.

"Open it!"

"Got an idea!" shouted Buscado, who drove forward five feet and turned right onto a hiking trail obscured by tall sagebrush.

McCracken ran over and pounded on the driver window.

"Just shut up and watch!" yelled Buscado.

As the dust cleared, McCracken got a clearer view of the approaching vehicle: an elevated passenger van with off-road tires. It slowed as the trail narrowed.

Buscado put the Dart in reverse and gunned the motor, ramming the car into the side of the van, which fishtailed over the ledge.

"Booyah!" he shouted.

The van tumbled down the hill, hitting a large boulder before crashing on the canyon floor.

The Dart, just inches from the ledge, was slipping too.

Buscado opened his door and crawled onto the hillside, grabbing a clump of weeds and holding on as the car slid down the hill and smashed onto a ledge below.

McCracken pulled Buscado back up onto the fire road.

"Nice," he said. "Very nice."

Buscado stayed on his hands and knees for a minute. "I almost crapped my pants," he said, catching his breath.

He rose to his feet. "Okay, what now?" he asked.

"We walk."

"It's really hot."

"Got a better idea?"

It took an hour to hike up to Angel Peak.

Buscado pointed at the white bubble dome. "Note said to meet there," he said, his shirt soaked with sweat. "Man, I need water bad."

A paved road led to the dome, which sat atop a two-story octagonal building. A thin man was leaning against the structure. He looked up when they approached.

McCracken recognized the face immediately—the reporter.

"So, you got her messages," said Sarono.

"See, it was Cheryl!" said Buscado, his voice hoarse. "Where is she?"

Sarono walked up the steps and knocked on the front door. Perlman's face peeked through the window.

The door swung open. Perlman walked onto the landing and frowned when he saw Buscado.

"What the fuck is he doing here?"

"Easy," said McCracken. "It's settled."

"No, it's not," Perlman snapped. "That fungus ratted us out, I know he did."

"It's not like that," said Buscado.

"McCracken, we can't trust this guy."

"Let it go," said McCracken. "Like I said, you'll both get your money."

Perlman pointed at Buscado. "This isn't over between us."

Cheryl appeared at the door, holding two plastic water bottles. Buscado ran up the steps and wrapped his arms around her. She smiled and, extricating herself from his sweaty embrace, handed him a bottle. She walked down the steps and handed the second bottle to McCracken.

"There's a bathroom inside, to the right," she said. "Get washed up, there's plenty to talk about."

"Where'd you go, baby? Who took you?" asked Buscado, wiping his mouth on his shirt. "I've been worried sick."

"Later," she said. "Inside, now."

She walked up the steps and entered the building, followed by Sarono.

McCracken glanced at Perlman.

"She knows stuff, dude," said Perlman. "Important stuff."

"Not sure I like this," said McCracken.

"Got a Plan B?"

McCracken did not.

After washing up, McCracken and Buscado joined the others in a large, circular room with an old sofa, an antique roll-top desk, and three folding chairs. A spiral staircase descended from an upper level, and a sliding glass door opened onto a deck that overlooked the mountains and desert valley.

"Babe, could you fill us in here?" Buscado asked Cheryl.

Sarono slouched on the sofa and stared at the floor.

"What's wrong?" Buscado asked.

Sarono shook his head.

"Bad scene at Uncle Eli's," Perlman whispered.

Cheryl walked over to McCracken. "We have an important guest," she told him. "Someone you really should see."

McCracken rose to his feet. "Where?" he asked.

"Come, I'll show you," said Cheryl, opening the sliding glass door.

McCracken and Buscado followed her. She allowed McCracken onto the deck, but put her hand out to block Buscado.

"Just him, I'm sorry," she said firmly.

Buscado frowned and stepped back inside.

"In the distance, toward the valley," she told McCracken, who walked to the edge of the deck and looked out.

Cheryl closed and locked the sliding door. McCracken ran over and pounded on the glass.

"Open it!" he shouted.

Cheryl pressed a button on a wall-mounted intercom. A floor speaker on the patio crackled.

"I'm sorry," she said. "Just be patient and listen."

McCracken stared into the room. Someone was descending the spiral staircase.

Baldwin.

Thirty-Nine

Baldwin quickly calculated how thick the glass was, and what effort McCracken would need to break it. He stood on the lowest step of the staircase, debating whether to stand his ground or flee upstairs through the fire escape.

After a few seconds, he walked with a slight limp to the intercom and pressed the "talk" button.

"I apologize for our last encounter," he said in a rehearsed tone. "It was never my intention to harm anyone."

McCracken glared at him through the glass.

Baldwin stepped away from the intercom, his hands trembling. "I'm not sure I can continue with this," he told Cheryl. "That man wants to kill me."

"He should," said Buscado.

"Unnecessary human suffering was never my goal," said Baldwin defensively. "*Acceptos* was—and still can be—a noble effort."

Perlman snickered.

"My intention was to correct the chaos we see around us," Baldwin continued. "But it's been taken from me."

"We've seen your handiwork, dude," said Perlman. "Gross."

"*Acceptos* is only as good as its donor stock," said Baldwin, nodding toward the deck.

McCracken kicked the glass door.

"I swear, if that man harms me …"

Cheryl pressed the intercom. "Calm down," she told McCracken. "We—you—need his help."

McCracken, eyes locked on Baldwin, pressed his face against the glass.

"I say we let wild man loose and enjoy the carnage," said Perlman. "Who's with me?"

"Count me in," said Buscado.

"Ask yourself what you really want," Cheryl told McCracken.

Baldwin took a tentative step toward the glass door. "They wouldn't have invited me here if you didn't need my input!" he shouted.

"I say let him in," said Sarono.

Baldwin returned to the intercom, pounding

the "talk" button with his fist. "I'll repeat her question," he said. "Ask yourself, 'What do I want?' Because I'm the only person here who can help you."

McCracken stepped back from the glass and took a deep breath.

"Yes, think hard, sir," said Baldwin.

McCracken kicked the door handle, causing the glass to wobble violently. A crack appeared. He kicked it again.

A second later, the glass sheet splintered into tiny fragments. With another swift kick, McCracken sent shards flying across the floor.

Baldwin tried to flee up the stairs. Buscado grabbed his arm.

McCracken reached inside and unlatched the glass door, sliding it roughly across a pile of shards. He took two steps toward Baldwin.

Cheryl blocked his path.

"Babe, no!" shouted Buscado.

McCracken towered a foot over Cheryl. "Out of my way," he snarled.

"Don't do this, please," she asked.

McCracken lunged at Baldwin but felt himself falling instead. His right shoulder thumped the hardwood hard, then his cheek.

His legs were pinned. Someone pulled his right

arm behind his back, then his left. A tremendous force was anchoring him to the ground.

He twisted his neck and looked behind him.

"Holy shit," whispered Sarono.

Buscado stared in disbelief.

Perlman clapped his hands.

Cheryl straddled McCracken, holding his wrists and preventing him from rising. "Relax and listen," she told him.

McCracken took a deep breath and rested his head on the floor.

"So, you're one of them," he said.

Buscado turned and walked out, slamming the front door behind him.

"My arms hurt," said McCracken. "Ease up a little."

"Can I trust you?" she asked.

"Sure."

"That's not very reassuring."

"If I kill him, you'll kill me."

"No, I won't."

"Don't let him up!" shouted Baldwin.

"I won't kill anyone," said McCracken, looking at Baldwin. "You know what I want. Just tell me where he is."

Baldwin sat on the stairs. "Howser has that information, not me."

"Then what good are you?"

"I know where he is."

"That's where we're going," Cheryl said. "Right away, with your help."

"Why should I trust you?"

"What are your options?"

McCracken's eyes moistened. He looked at the floor.

"Is he crying?" asked Perlman.

"I'm turning him loose," said Cheryl, releasing McCracken's wrists and rising slowly off his back. She stepped away, giving McCracken plenty of room to rise.

"To Howser's house," she said.

"Yes," he replied.

Forty

Perlman crouched under a cluster of tall pines a half-mile from the gated entrance to Howser's estate. The night was chilly and his knees ached. He was in a foul mood.

He missed the old McCracken.

The new version was still pensive and quiet, but not in an angry, neck-snapping way. He was taking orders from Cheryl. When did she become the boss?

Perlman also feared his Mauritius fantasy was gone. Maybe everything was gone. He had no idea what was happening beyond Vegas.

Using the moon as a backlight, he browsed an issue of *Vegas Beau Monde* magazine, which he had gotten from Cheryl. The issue had a six-page spread on Howser's estate.

Very impressive: six bedrooms, nine baths, lofty ceilings, wide expanses of wood and glass, and a commanding view of the valley below. Perched atop a mountain two miles west of Angel Peak, the double-gated contemporary was an architectural tour de force, the article gushed.

What a load.

Perlman wondered how Howser managed to afford such palatial digs on a professor's salary. The lecture circuit? Doubtful.

A few feet away sat Buscado and that reporter guy, who was scribbling on a notepad. Cheryl was crouched beside McCracken, planning their attack.

Baldwin stood at least five feet from McCracken, trying to listen in while keeping a safe distance.

"This may or may not work," Baldwin told Cheryl. "He'll wonder why I showed up unannounced."

McCracken was anxious. Too many thoughts—bad thoughts—were swirling through his head. He feared the worst.

"Are you listening?" Cheryl asked him.

McCracken nodded. He cleared his mind of doubt and fear.

It was time to move in.

Baldwin left first, walking several hundred yards along Lucky Strike Road toward Howser's front gate. A miniature air horn, one he always carried on nature walks, was attached to his belt.

The others hiked down the hill a few yards and walked parallel to the road, moving between the pines.

When Baldwin reached the wrought-iron front gate, he pressed the intercom and had a minute-long conversation with a staticky voice. The others were too far away to listen in.

A loud buzz followed. Baldwin pushed the gate open and signaled the others, who raced across the road and inside the compound.

A lighted stone pathway curved and climbed around meticulously landscaped gardens and trees.

They ran up to the front door, which was ajar. Cheryl entered first, followed by McCracken and the others.

The cavernous living area resembled the lobby of a ski lodge, with stone walls, skylights, and a lofty ceiling supported by massive wooden beams.

Howser sat alone on a mission-style sofa, sipping a glass of white wine. He looked up at Baldwin and grinned. "You've brought along your new friends," he said.

His hands shook as he refilled his wine glass from a bottle of Riesling.

"Where is he?" McCracken demanded.

"Wouldn't you rather save your girlfriend? The two of you could be quite happy together."

McCracken lunged at Howser; Cheryl pulled him back.

"It's happening, you can't stop it now," said Howser, looking up at the skylights. "Even if I tell you what you want to know, you can't stop it."

"That's not true," said Baldwin.

"You, my old friend, know exactly what we're dealing with. I understand your frustration but—really—were these theatrics necessary? The world we knew is gone."

McCracken struggled to break free from Cheryl's grasp.

Howser smiled. "How does it feel to be vulnerable for a change?" he asked McCracken. "Know why she's so strong? Because she's the future, you're not."

Buscado took a step toward Howser.

"Stand back," Cheryl warned him.

Howser looked at Cheryl and grinned. "Do they know who you are? What you are?"

She didn't answer.

"Exactly as I suspected," said Howser, rising to his feet.

A mechanized hum filled the room.

"I want each of you to understand something,"

Howser continued. "These changes will help us all, even if it doesn't seem that way initially. And, Mr. McCracken, don't obsess so much over a single life. We're all expendable."

The hum grew louder. Searchlights shone through the trees into the living room.

Howser bolted toward the kitchen.

Two bullets shattered the ceiling-to-floor window. Several more followed.

Cheryl was hit in the chest and fell backward. Buscado dragged her to a bathroom off the living room and locked the door behind them.

He bent over her, grabbed a towel, and tried to stop the blood gushing from her chest wound.

Cheryl mumbled something he couldn't understand.

"Hang on, babe, we'll call an ambulance."

"No ambulances," she whispered, coughing up blood. He wiped it away with his hand.

"You might as well see for yourself."

"You'll be fine, I swear," he said, frantically searching his pockets for a phone he didn't have.

"Remove my pants."

"What?"

Cheryl coughed up more blood and spat it out. "Please, I want you to."

"No."

"Please."

He was crying, pressing his hands against her chest. Her blood was thick and warm.

"Do it."

He unzipped the fly, stopped, and pulled her jeans down. He took a quick look, then turned away.

"It's okay."

He looked again.

She was metallic in places, furry in others. Almost insect-like, but elegantly mechanical as well.

"Don't go."

Her eyes rolled back in her head. Buscado bent down and gently kissed her lips.

Cheryl was gone.

Perlman and Sarono raced out the front door and stopped abruptly. Searchlights were combing the main road.

They spotted Baldwin hobbling down a narrow path that curved around the back of the house. They tried to catch him, but he seemed to vanish.

Reaching the perimeter, they scaled a wall and fled into the woods.

McCracken followed Howser into the kitchen and tackled him on the tile floor. Bullets bounced off the Viking range.

McCracken dragged Howser to a locked rear door.

"Open it."

Howser's shaky fingers took three tries to get the code right.

Opening the door, McCracken pushed Howser outside and down a hill, staying under the pines to avoid the hovering craft.

"Can we make a deal?" Howser asked.

They exited through a back gate leading to a wilderness area, where McCracken stopped to look for the others.

"Where is he?" he asked.

The craft were closing in.

"Are you familiar with the many-worlds interpretation, Mr. McCracken?"

McCracken glanced up at the searchlights.

"It's an interpretation of quantum mechanics, suggesting that all possible alternate histories and futures are real, and that each represents an actual universe ..."

"Where is he?"

"Every event is a branch point ..."

"Where's Finn?"

"Schrödinger's cat. You know Schrödinger's cat?"

"Where is he?"

Howser was crying now.

"The cat is both alive and dead but in different worlds, both of which are equally real ..."

"Tell me!"

A light bounced off McCracken's shoulder.

Howser sighed. "There's a bus in two days traveling from Las Vegas to a compound near Pahrump."

"Okay."

"You'll want to stop that bus, Mr. McCracken."

The searchlight reached the trees above them. McCracken pulled Howser deeper into the woods.

"You think I'm one of them, but I'm not. They really don't care about me either."

McCracken knew it was time.

"A deal?"

"No."

"Angel Peak, there's a weapons cache there. You might need it. Do we have a deal now?"

McCracken didn't answer.

Howser grinned. "This isn't over," he said. "Not in the least."

McCracken turned his captive toward the searchlight. He waited until the light blinded their eyes before snapping Howser's neck.

Forty-One

McCracken wandered under the pines for several hours, avoiding the drones buzzing just above the treetops. As dawn approached he hiked parallel to the road, slowly making his way back to Angel Peak.

Stopping fifty yards from the bubble dome, he spotted three human shapes near a storage shed. One of them repeatedly slammed the shed's door handle with a large rock.

"Let me try, dumbass!" a voice shouted.

McCracken walked over and told them to shut the fuck up.

"We're really hungry," Perlman told McCracken.

Sarono agreed.

Buscado walked off and sat by himself.

McCracken examined the door: exterior design, solid core, swing-in. A swift kick just about the deadbolt would do the trick.

"Watch for splinters," he warned, facing the door and kicking twice with his right foot.

The crackle of fracturing wood was a good sign. On the third try, the door flew inward.

Two drones flew past, hovering briefly over the bubble dome but not the outbuildings. When they were gone, McCracken entered the shed, followed by the others.

They found plastic pails of vacuum-sealed food pouches.

"Creamy stroganoff and fettuccine alfredo, guaranteed for twenty years," said Sarono, reading the label.

Everyone grabbed a few pouches and took them outside. They stopped at a clearing near an east-facing ledge, and squeezed the contents directly into their mouths.

McCracken reconnoitered the area while the others rested for an hour. Sarono got a little queasy from the stroganoff, but everyone else was fine.

When McCracken returned, the others were restless. "Rome's burning and we're up here holding our dicks," said Perlman.

"There's supposed to be another shed up here," said McCracken. "Anyone see it?"

Buscado stared at his feet. He hadn't spoken in hours.

"What's wrong?" McCracken asked.

"Cheryl," whispered Perlman. "She … uh …"

"They got her," said Buscado. "They had no right, what they did to her."

A quadcopter swooped in from the north and hovered 20 feet above the hillside, focusing a camera on them. They watched it for a few seconds before McCracken threw a rock at it.

He missed and the drone flew off.

"Four domestic terrorists, digitized for posterity," cracked Perlman.

An air horn blared in the distance. Three seconds later, it sounded again.

"Let's go," said McCracken.

They took a circuitous route toward the noise, moving under heavy tree cover. Passing the bubble dome, they continued west.

The horn blared again.

McCracken spotted a corrugated metal building, much larger than the food supply shed, in a small clearing. A white cargo van was parked on a fire trail nearby, and a dark-skinned man was standing outside the vehicle.

"Mr. McCracken!"

Baldwin approached, holding a quadcopter. His awkward gait was much more pronounced.

"You alone?" asked McCracken.

"Are you?"

Buscado ran up to Baldwin and pushed him roughly. "You did that to her!" he shouted.

McCracken grabbed Buscado and pulled him back.

"I did not," said Baldwin.

"Tell me about her."

"Well, she was special, yes."

"Last night … she …" Buscado couldn't finish his sentence.

"I saw her fall, unfortunately, and I assume from her absence here that the outcome wasn't, well, good."

"Where'd you run off to last night?" Perlman asked Baldwin.

"When bullets are flying, it's no crime to flee."

"Who was shooting at us?" asked Sarono.

Baldwin took a step back. "Look, we're wasting time here," he said. "You've found the shed, so let's go inside."

He turned toward the building, then tripped and fell on his right side. The quadcopter fell to the dirt but was undamaged.

"That a CGX7 Phantom you got there?" Perlman asked. "They're badass."

McCracken offered his hand. Baldwin ignored it.

"I fear I'm losing my ability to walk," said Baldwin, rising to his feet and teetering briefly before finding his balance.

"Let's see the shed," said McCracken.

"Take what you want and load the van quickly," said Baldwin. "I'll show you where you need to go."

"Leave the drone with me," said Perlman.

As they walked to the shed, Baldwin tugged on McCracken's arm. "Where's Howser?" he asked.

McCracken shook his head.

"I have a little surprise for you," said Baldwin, his eyes widening. "Just like old times."

"What's that supposed to mean?"

Baldwin fell and vomited. A minute later, he vomited again. McCracken helped him to the white van and didn't press for an answer.

Forty-Two

The shed met McCracken's expectations. AK-47s, various handguns, even a shoulder-launched anti-tank weapon, which McCracken guessed was an Argentine MARA.

Baldwin drove them to the ambush site and left immediately, saying he had an errand to run. He was sweating and mumbling, and everyone except McCracken was glad to see him go.

The bus was scheduled to arrive at 1900 hours, giving them an hour to prepare.

Perlman was keyed up. Were his balls big enough for this challenge? Stopping a self-driving vehicle moving at highway speeds without a laptop, mobile phone, or Internet access was the ultimate hack.

"Soiled my shorts just thinking about it," he told Buscado and Sarono as they lugged the AK-47s and MARA out of the van.

"The key is to jam the cellular or GPS link, forcing it into hibernation," Perlman continued. "The CGX7 Phantom is my secret sauce. Military grade, operates via cellular and GPS, and—this is the classified part, peckers—can easily be rejiggered via internal DIP-switch reconfiguration into a long-distance jammer to disrupt UAV signals."

"Whatever," said Buscado.

"You don't get it," said Perlman. "This is seriously top-secret shit, which I alone know. I'll use the drone to scramble the bus's navigation. Hell, I'll scramble all GPS in the area."

They were thirty miles southwest of Pahrump, a quarter mile east of Sainte Clotilde Mission—a religious compound on the California side of the border. The Mission's main building was surrounded by a tall masonry wall topped with barbed wire.

Sarono was agitated. Perlman was getting on his nerves, McCracken wouldn't answer any of his questions, and he had no way to contact Uncle Eli.

"Remind me again why we're here?" he asked Perlman.

"The bus," replied Perlman. "We're hijacking it."

"And why are you here?"

"Money, lots of it. McCracken knows where it's buried. We help him, he helps us. Simple."

Sarono wiped his forehead. "Why am I here?" he mumbled.

Perlman overheard him.

"Look, you're a journalist," he said. "Expose this whole *Acceptos* thing and *bam!* There's your Pulitzer."

"So, who's behind all this?"

Perlman walked away.

"Hey, you didn't answer my question."

McCracken called them over. They were falling behind schedule and he wanted to review their plan one more time.

Sarono picked up an AK-47. "I've never fired one of these things before," he said.

McCracken gave a quick tutorial and walked off to be alone.

"Something wrong?" Sarono asked Perlman.

"He's the sensitive type."

"Buscado, Perlman, come over here!" shouted McCracken, sitting on the ground, drawing in the dirt with a stick.

He pointed at a large *X* on his dirt diagram. "The treasure is buried under a spray-painted green rock across the road from the mission," he said. "You guys can split it, no matter what happens today."

He stood and walked fifty yards to the top of a short hill. Sainte Clotilde was visible to the west. He looked back: Perlman and Buscado were huddled, talking quietly.

A caravan of vehicles approached from the east.

"Rev that thing up, Perlman!" McCracken shouted. "We're on!"

Perlman ran to his handheld base station and launched the drone, which rose slowly, teetering to the left and right before stabilizing.

A Humvee was leading the three-vehicle convoy, followed by a yellow school bus and a trailing Humvee.

McCracken could hear, but not see, a helicopter in the distance. "Now!" he yelled.

Perlman activated the drone's GPS jammer.

"It's a shit-disturber now," he gushed. "Radio control frequency disruptor, out to jam every satellite link it finds."

"As long as it works," said Buscado.

It did work.

The Humvees slowed to a stop in the middle of the road. The bus rammed the bumper of the lead Humvee, and then stalled.

"Woo hoo!" shouted Perlman.

A minute passed. Then two. No movement in or around the vehicles, only the distant sound of a helicopter in flight.

Perlman, Buscado, and Sarono—the latter two armed with AK-47s—walked up the rise to where McCracken was standing.

"What now, boss?" asked Buscado.

McCracken stared at the bus.

"We moving in or what?"

A tall figure emerged from the leading Humvee.

"Cop!" shouted Sarono.

McCracken grabbed an AK-47 and opened fire, hitting the cop twice. The creature fell to the ground, but immediately jumped back on its feet.

A second cop exited the trailing Humvee. McCracken fired at it but missed. The creature leaped high into the air, landing fifty yards from McCracken.

Buscado and Sarono fired at the cop, which jumped again, dodging the spray of bullets and landing a foot from McCracken, kicking him to the ground.

The cop grabbed McCracken's rifle and snapped it in half.

Buscado and Sarono fired again, striking the cop in the head and torso. The creature collapsed on top of McCracken, pinning him down.

"Get it off me!"

The others lifted the rigid body, allowing McCracken to slither free.

"A dozen bullet holes and not a drop of blood," said Perlman, examining the cop. "Look how the helmet blends right into the neck. There's no head under this thing, I'm sure of it."

McCracken rose to his feet and dusted himself off. "Cover me," he said, slinging the rocket launcher over his shoulder and grabbing an AK-47.

"We're staying here?" asked Sarono.

McCracken nodded.

"No, we should go in together."

"Hey, if that's what he wants, do it," said Perlman.

McCracken glanced at Perlman, then Buscado. Neither made eye contact with him.

"Cover me," repeated McCracken, crouching low and moving in. He paused at the road for a quick visual scan of the perimeter.

The school bus, aside from a dented front bumper, was undamaged. Black curtains covered every window except for the driver's compartment, which was sealed off from the rest of the cabin.

McCracken walked up to the driver's-side window and looked in. An interior ceiling camera was pointed directly at him, a red light glowing above its lens.

The MARA was heavy, so McCracken set it on the ground near the front bumper. He looked back at his team. One of them waved. Sarono, maybe.

A horn blared in the distance.

Facing Sainte Clotilde, McCracken spotted a white van moving erratically toward him. The vehicle swerved into the oncoming lane, then veered back.

Baldwin's van.

McCracken raised his AK-47 and aimed at the windshield. The van slowed; a waving arm emerged from the driver's side.

A hundred yards, fifty, twenty-five. It stopped ten yards from McCracken.

"Don't shoot!" shouted Baldwin, exiting the van, hands in the air.

The background din grew louder. A black helicopter flew in from the north and hovered a few hundred yards east of the stalled caravan.

Baldwin stumbled toward McCracken, his nose bleeding. His eyes were orange, his skin bruised and sagging.

He turned abruptly and began walking back toward the van.

The helicopter noise was deafening now. McCracken looked for his team but couldn't spot them anywhere.

Baldwin reached the rear of the van and motioned for McCracken to join him.

McCracken hesitated, unsure of his next move, until a bullet ricocheted off the pavement near his feet. He sprinted toward the van for cover.

Baldwin was opening the van's cargo door.

McCracken glanced inside the cargo hold and saw Fuentes, muzzled, her feet and hands bound loosely with rope. She squirmed to free herself, her eyes pleading with McCracken for help.

"Ready to play?" asked Baldwin.

The helicopter rose and moved toward them.

Baldwin pulled a handgun from his waistband and pointed it at Fuentes, who shook her head frantically.

"Ready?"

"What's on the bus?" McCracken asked.

"If you're wondering about my physical decline, I injected myself with Acceptos serum not long ago, seeking certain characteristics. The deterioration is accelerating."

"What's on the bus!"

"You've failed me on multiple levels, Mr. McCracken."

The helicopter veered off toward Sainte Clotilde. McCracken heard distant gunfire.

"Let's play a game first," said Baldwin. "Your

choice: enter the bus and your girlfriend dies. Or save her and forget about the bus."

"I don't want to play."

"Choose!"

McCracken mulled his options, all of which were poor.

Baldwin was growing irritated. "Are you going to play or not?"

"What's on the bus?"

"Only if you play."

A cloud of dust swirled across the road, obscuring McCracken's view of the hills where his team was supposed to be.

"Stop this," he said. "Let's go."

"Choose!"

The helicopter was returning. He was out of time.

"I choose the bus."

Fuentes' muffled cries were drowned out by gunshots. Baldwin screamed as a bullet pierced his right thigh. He fell to the pavement.

The van's front right tire exploded.

McCracken pushed Fuentes inside the hold and slammed the door shut. He raced back to the bus, kicking in the folding front door as two bullets struck the roof.

He caught his breath.

A black door separated the driver's compartment from the passenger section. McCracken placed his hand on the doorknob and paused, hoping to hear something normal—voices, maybe crying—on the other side.

Silence.

He raised his weapon and entered.

Sunlight streamed through a row of skylights along the ceiling. One boy, maybe nine or ten years old, sat alone ten rows down. Wearing black slacks and a white collared shirt, he sat still and silent, staring straight ahead.

Eyes, facial structure, hair—all similar to the boy he had seen on the back of the bus. Similar to Thryce's age progressions. Similar to the photo Howser and Baldwin had shown him long ago, the one that had made him cry.

Staring straight ahead, not moving or speaking. Free to move, but not moving.

McCracken was shaking as he approached the child. He knelt beside him. A loud explosion made him jump.

The boy didn't move or blink.

"Hello?"

No response.

"Finn?"

The child slowly turned his eyes toward

McCracken, who felt a burst of fear and love and revulsion.

A bullet shattered a window, missing them by inches.

"Get down!" shouted McCracken, hugging the boy and pulling him gently to the floor.

He studied the boy's healthy, normal face, which terrified him. Was this Finn? An *Acceptos* creation?

It didn't matter.

"Stay here!" he ordered.

McCracken raced off the bus, hitting the ground and rolling 10 yards to the rocket launcher. Two more bullets whizzed past his head.

He snatched the MARA and scooted under the bus for cover.

"Hey!"

Four legs outside the bus.

"McCracken!"

Buscado dropped to his knees and looked under the vehicle.

"Come on!" he shouted.

"Can you drive this thing?" McCracken asked.

"What?"

"The bus—CAN YOU DRIVE IT!"

Sarono, AK-47 in hand, crouched to his knees and looked under the bus.

"Yeah, maybe," said Buscado. "We'll need cover."

"Get in there, both of you!"

Buscado and Sarono boarded the bus.

McCracken did a quick visual inspection of the MARA: projectile, check; launcher tube, check. Everything in order. McCracken calculated a range of approximately two hundred meters.

The helicopter flew off toward Sainte Clotilde, then circled back. McCracken slid out from under the bus, mounted the launcher on his shoulder, and waited.

Five hundred meters. Two hundred.

He fired.

The projectile clipped the rotor mast before spinning off. The helicopter wobbled but stabilized quickly, black smoke rising from its mast.

McCracken studied the perimeter. Fuentes, rope trailing from one ankle, was crying hysterically and sprinting toward the west hills.

He started after her but stopped. He looked at the bus. Then Rosa. Then the bus again.

Buscado started the engine. McCracken jumped aboard.

"Where to?" asked Buscado.

"Just head west," replied McCracken.

"Where west?"

"Anywhere that's not here."

McCracken glanced at the hills. "Where's Perlman?" he asked.

Sarono shrugged. "He was with us when we moved in, then he just vanished."

"I'm staying behind," said McCracken.

"What, why?"

"Just go!"

McCracken looked back at the child, who was still on the floor.

"Finn, don't move!"

"Is that …?" asked Sarono.

"Go back there, stay with him," replied McCracken. "Make sure he stays down."

McCracken jumped off the bus and sprinted to the van. Baldwin was lying on the pavement, bleeding but conscious.

The bus bumped the rear Hummer, then pulled forward and headed west toward California.

The helicopter was spinning out of control.

McCracken knelt beside Baldwin.

"On the bus—is that him?"

Baldwin grinned. "Couldn't you tell?"

McCracken grabbed Baldwin's neck.

"Tell me!"

Baldwin spat blood. "Your violence won't save you now, sir."

"Just tell me … please!"

"Tell *me* something, Mr. McCracken. Am I a good human?"

"Please, please, tell me."

"A decent, moral person?"

McCracken looked up. Black smoke filled the sky as the helicopter turned upside down.

"They're blood-testing everyone now, trying to find donors—women too," said Baldwin, coughing. "Not sure how that will work."

The helicopter was spinning toward them.

"Please, just … I'm begging you," said McCracken, crying. "Tell me!"

"Do you think I'm good?"

The helicopter righted itself, swooping to within 20 feet of the van and wobbling to the east.

McCracken ran off the road and dove in a ditch.

The helicopter hit the ground right outside Sainte Clotilde, blowing a massive hole in the compound's exterior wall. The impact sent the rotor blade spinning into the courtyard.

Dark smoke obscured McCracken's view of the compound. To the west, he saw Fuentes running up a hill.

A cacophony of animal and human screams filled the air. Through the smoke, unidentifiable creatures fled Sainte Clotilde, scurrying in all directions.

More vehicles and drones were moving in from the east. McCracken sprinted toward where he had last seen Fuentes.

She was easy enough to track. He caught up with her over the next hill, where she had stopped to catch her breath.

"Rosa!"

She saw him approaching and began to run, but tripped over a rock.

He tried to help her up. She slapped his hand away.

"You wanted me to die, so let me!" she screamed, rising to her feet and running.

McCracken let her go.

He ran up the hill and looked to the west. There, beyond Sainte Clotilde, the bus was stalled, its engine on fire.

Three drones hovered above the vehicle.

Heavy, black smoke blocked his view of the bus. He thought he saw shadows, human figures, running away from the vehicle, but wasn't sure.

"Finn!" he yelled.

The bus exploded.

Forty-Three

McCracken woke from a dreamless sleep. He spent a minute or so determining his location and how he had gotten there. Sitting up, he pressed his back against a large boulder and watched the sunrise.

McCracken scanned the horizon for signs of danger. The sky was clear and blue, smoke billowing from the direction of the helicopter crash. How far was he from the bus carnage? Maybe two miles, he guessed, but it didn't matter. He couldn't return now, not with drones and helicopters hovering nearby.

He was thirsty but had no water. Hours before, he had hiked through a dense patch of prickly pear cacti, some packed with fruit. He returned to the patch and, using a flat rock in each hand, twisted a dozen spiny fruits off the cacti, carefully avoiding the sharp, needle-like thorns.

He then went rock-hunting, knocking large stones together until he found a pair that sounded like glass clacking. Wielding a hammer stone, he chipped several blades off the smaller rocks, and used the sharpest blade as a makeshift knife to slice open the cactus fruit.

McCracken cut the fruit into tiny chunks. He ate six prickly pears, including the hard, tiny seeds.

Finding shade under a tall mesquite tree, he sat and rested, wondering what had become of his crew. He hoped they were safe and far away by now.

The bus. He didn't want to think about it.

Finn.

He thought of Fuentes instead.

She was nearby, he guessed. Or maybe she had hiked back to the Old Spanish Trail and thumbed a ride into town.

Or she was dead.

He wanted to die.

It was around eight a.m. judging by the sun's position. The desert was already hot.

McCracken hiked to a nearby hill for a 360-degree view. The smoke was gone, as were the helicopters. A small object was hovering above the crash site, maybe a solitary drone, but he was too far away to know for sure.

A few hundred yards to the east, someone was walking alone on a trail.

He followed her from a safe distance, making a mental note of the gully where she had stopped briefly to find shade. He then returned to the cacti patch and picked a half-dozen prickly pears.

When he returned to the gully, she wasn't there but her shoes and socks were.

McCracken sat in the dirt, pulled his new stone knife from his pocket, and peeled the prickly pears. He left the prepared fruit in a neat pile on a large rock, and returned to his shade spot.

Morning turned to afternoon.

He wondered who would find his body. He hoped a human would before animals tore his carcass to shreds, consuming his entrails and shitting out the rest of him.

He wondered what his life might have been like had things turned out differently.

He swept the most painful thoughts from his mind.

Soon it was dusk and he had barely moved since morning. He wasn't hungry but figured Fuentes was.

He spotted rabbit tracks and scat near a boulder.

He pulled a thick branch from a California juniper, and used his stone knife to reshape one end of the branch as a crude club.

He ambushed a colony of feeding rabbits, swinging his club wildly until he hit one. He quickly snapped the animal's neck to end its misery.

McCracken skinned the rabbit and drank its blood.

He would need a fire.

Walking along the riverbed, he found a muddy Corona bottle and a cardboard Cocoa Krispies box. Using the bottle as a magnifying glass, he heated the weathered cardboard until it began smoking. Dry grass and juniper bark provided the tinder.

He cooked the rabbit and carried it on a stick to Fuentes' hideaway. She wasn't there. The prickly pears were gone too.

McCracken returned to his dying fire, adding timber to get it roaring again.

He sat there clutching the rabbit meat, unsure of his next move. He had no intention of eating the rabbit and was only holding it for Fuentes, who was sure to be hungry.

"Hey," a scratchy voice said behind him.

He turned and saw her. Her eyes were sunken, her hair matted with dirt. She had a chipped tooth.

Fuentes was cradling several prickly pears in

her shirt. "Wrecked my hands picking these," she mumbled.

She sat beside him, eating the rabbit while he skinned the fruit. She insisted he eat too. He declined at first, then took a few bites.

She looked pretty, he thought.

He added more twigs to the fire. She reached over and held his hand.

They watched the fire in silence for several minutes.

"The bus, what did you find?"

He told her.

She inched closer.

"I'm sorry," he said.

She placed her hand on his thigh.

"So ... he's alive?" she asked.

McCracken ignored her question. "Where did they take you?" he asked.

"I was blindfolded."

"What did they ...?"

She didn't answer.

No one spoke for several minutes.

"So, what now?" she asked.

"Nothing."

"Nothing? We stay here?"

McCracken added leaves to the fire. When he sat down, he put his arm around her.

"Let me help you," she said.

"Why?"

"Have a better plan?"

McCracken did not.

He felt good—a strange sensation he hadn't felt in a long time.

He didn't want to die.

"What do you think's going on out there?" he asked.

"Where?"

"Everywhere."

"I have no idea."

He took a deep breath and exhaled slowly. He kissed her.

"Let's go find him," she said.

McCracken mulled his options.

"Yes," he said.

Shadows lurked in the distance, watching them.

CPSIA information can be obtained
at www.ICGtesting.com
Printed in the USA
BVHW070703090720
583241BV00003B/569